Friends & Foes

OTHER BOOKS AND AUDIO BOOKS

BY SARAH M. EDEN:

Courting Miss Lancaster

The Kiss of a Stranger

Seeking Persephone

Friends & Foes

Sarah M. Eden

Covenant Communications, Inc.

Covenant

Cover image: *Victorian romantic couple whirls while dancing together* © Studioxil. Courtesy Istockphoto.com

Published by Covenant Communications, Inc.
American Fork, Utah

Printed in the United States of America
First Printing: January 2012

18 17 16 15 14 13   10 9 8 7 6 5 4

ISBN 978-1-60861-376-2

To F.E.G., who cheered for Philip from page one,
and to M.O.M., who cheered for me from day one

One

England, December 1814

Philip Jonquil walked with deceptively lazy strides down one of Maidstone's back streets. He'd traded his signature attire of bright colors and expensive tailoring for something far more subdued. Knowing he'd be walking about in an area of town known for thieves and cutthroats, Philip judged it best not to appear prime for the plucking.

The ruse hadn't proved entirely successful. Two nip-purses had been doing a ridiculously bad job of tailing him for several streets. They made quite an effort at not being seen, but he'd spotted them easily. Philip had less than a half-mile to cover before meeting up with Hanover Garner, a man known to the Foreign Office as something of a genius at tracking spies, a title Philip had earned as well over the past half-decade.

Not so ingenious this time, though, were you? They'd come to that particular corner of Kent on a solid bit of information and still managed to miss their man. Le Fontaine, a particularly notorious spy for France, was supposed to have been there. Someone must have warned Le Fontaine. By the time Philip and Garner arrived, the French spy was gone.

Finding himself the target of would-be thieves proved a fittingly annoying addition to an already bothersome day. Society, no doubt, would expect such a confirmed dandy to swoon or

flutter about in terrified agitation at being accosted by footpads. But society was far too easily duped. Philip had simpered and minced amongst the upper crust for five years, but underneath the carefully constructed persona, he was anything but a fribble. He encountered with shocking regularity criminals who would make the seediest of London neighborhoods seem like nurseries at nap time and, thus far, had always emerged relatively unscathed.

Philip could hear the knucklers drawing closer. He sighed in annoyance. He'd simply have to take care of the bothersome duo.

As their footsteps grew louder, he spun around without warning, catching them entirely off guard. "Let me guess. This is to be a bulk-and-file operation. Which one of you means to knock me down and which plans to go for my billfold?"

Obviously the pickpockets hadn't expected that response. They stood frozen a moment, eyes darting between him and one another.

"A gentleman?" the shorter of the thieves sputtered. He looked to his partner. "'E's a thumpin' nib!"

Philip supposed he ought to have affected a lower-class accent, but, quite frankly, he hadn't the patience for it at the moment. "My apologies for not dressing the part of a well-twigged gentry cove—I wasn't expecting company."

They only looked further shocked at his knowledge of cant expressions.

"Now, if the two of you intend to relieve me of my burdensome coins, I suggest you get on with it. I've an appointment to keep."

The thieves looked briefly at each other before advancing on him. Had he not personally stood down a vast collection of hardened criminals and murderous spies in his time, Philip might have found their approach menacing.

"Hand it over, and we'll not give ye trouble."

Philip affected an expression of ultimate gratitude. "Very considerate of you."

"Come on. We 'aven't got all night." Apparently only one of the thieves meant to talk to him.

He reached inside his jacket and pulled out the small coin purse he carried there.

"Toss it over."

Philip clicked his tongue and shook his head in disapproval. "That would get the coins dusty. Surely you've no desire to deal in dirty money."

"Wha'?"

"Obviously we're not destined to share any witty banter." Philip shrugged and held out his coin purse. "There's not much more than a few quid in here, but if you want it so badly . . ."

The more talkative of the few inched closer. As he came near enough to almost take the purse, Philip dropped it on the ground.

"Oh, dear. I'm afraid I always have been a bit of a clumsy fellow."

The pickpocket bent to retrieve his loot. The moment his head came low enough, Philip slammed his knee into the man's forehead, sending him reeling backward.

His partner came rushing forward, fists raised. After the day he'd had, Philip sorely needed to hit someone. Very thoughtful of the haggard partners in crime to oblige him as they were. He stepped into the punch. His knuckles burned at the force of the impact. The sting proved exceptionally cathartic.

"Ye broke m'nose, ye blackguard."

Philip rolled his eyes. "Pot. Kettle."

The first thief had recovered enough to take a swing of his own, which Philip deftly avoided. "I'd be much obliged if you'd avoid the face—black eyes are deucedly hard to cover up."

Just as he knew they would, his assailants took that as their cue to aim high, leaving their midsections conveniently unguarded. Philip delivered a swift kick to the shorter man's gut, dropping him to the ground gasping for air.

Philip turned immediately to the only pickpocket still on his feet. "That leaves the two of us, I suppose."

With a grin of triumph, the thief brandished a decidedly unclean knife.

"Interesting choice. I would have guessed pistol, but this will do."

The thief lunged. Philip dodged the blade. While Philip hadn't the infamous Duke of Kielder's penchant for being armed at all times, he made a point of not wandering about in questionable areas of town without some means of defending himself.

"This has been tremendously enjoyable," Philip said, "but I truly am in something of a rush." He pulled forth the menacing pistol he brought on every mission he ever undertook and made quite a show of brandishing it.

The thief backed up immediately. He lowered his knife, eyes darting between Philip's face and his weapon. "No harm done, then, gent?"

Philip shook his head good-naturedly. "If you'll just scrape your friend, there, off the ground and be on your way. No point parting enemies over a few paltry guineas."

"Right, guv'nuh." He kicked at his moaning partner, still prostrate on the ground. They stumbled their way back into the dark recesses of the alley.

In the very next moment, a rustling from behind spun Philip around. Hanover Garner rushed into the street, eyes wide and alarmed.

"Good afternoon, Garner," Philip said, putting away his pistol.

"You were late," Garner said.

"*I* was late?" Philip gave him a look of reprimand. "If you'd shown up five minutes ago, you might have saved me a great deal of bother."

He retrieved his coin purse from the dirt where it had sat throughout the altercation.

Garner looked understandably confused. "What the devil?"

"I doubt the devil himself was attempting to rob me. *He* might actually have succeeded."

"You were set upon by footpads?" Garner sounded alarmed, quite as if they hadn't both faced such things on multiple occasions.

Philip's mother would suffer endless heart palpitations if she knew just how often he'd found himself held at knifepoint. It was an occupational hazard when one spent one's days tracking murderous spies. His mother was also unaware of the fact that he had an occupation, dangerous or not.

"I am getting too old for this," Garner moaned.

"You are my age, Garner, and I am certainly not old." Philip straightened his cuffs with exaggerated flamboyance. Laughable levels of flare had become a habit of his—part of his disguise in society. He hardly needed the airs in his current attire and company, but he'd grown so accustomed to the role that he rarely slipped from it regardless of his situation.

At the moment, Philip's companion was continuing to catalog complaints. "Thirty is far too old to have a bullet lodged in one's—"

"Twenty-eight," Philip corrected, recalling the very incident to which Garner referred. "And that shot went wide."

"Barely." Garner pushed out a tense breath.

Philip took up his lazy meandering once more. They had an inn to reach before nightfall. They arrived at their original meeting spot a few minutes later, a nondescript, abandoned building where Grimes, a Bow Street runner Philip had worked with on a number of occasions, kept watch over Philip's carriage and team.

With a swiftness borne of familiarity, they all took their usual positions: Philip and Garner tucked inside, Grimes up top with the driver, armed and ready should trouble arise.

"Why is it that every time we fail to find one criminal, you manage to find another?"

"I appreciate your concern," Philip said, his tone more than a touch theatrical, "but I assure you the cutthroats were laughably incompetent. Only one knife between them."

Garner sighed. "I *am* too old for this."

"Tell it to the Foreign Office."

"They'll never let us off this one." Garner rubbed his eyebrows. Philip knew that gesture. From the time the Foreign Office had paired them up for their first mission, Garner's eyebrow-rubbing meant he'd nearly reached his endurance for the day. "If it is important enough to risk the life of the Earl of Lampton"—Garner motioned toward Philip—"then they will think nothing of placing the life of a mere 'mister' on the line. Besides, we're—"

"—too amazing to be replaced?" Philip answered with abundant confidence. He'd learned early on that an increase in foppishness on his part kept Garner from falling completely into the doldrums. If the man weren't a genius at tracking the movements of even the most elusive spies, Philip might have wondered why the Foreign Office kept him on. Philip continued his exaggerated recounting of their mutual assets. "It's a curse being wonderful, isn't it? Not to mention good looking and well dressed."

"Of what worth can such assets, real or imagined, be," Garner asked, "if we only ever spend time in one another's company?"

Philip grinned. "Pining after the ladies?" he asked.

"You never wish you could be searching out some sweet young lady instead of being a spy?"

"*Sweet*?" Philip scoffed at the thought. He'd far prefer a lady with a little fire. Garner was correct on one point, though. Their chances of meeting any young ladies, fiery or sweet, were decidedly slim of late.

After several moments silence, Garner spoke again. "Le Fontaine is proving very elusive."

Philip shrugged. "True."

"The entire reason we are in Kent has slipped from our grasp, *again,* and all you can say is 'true'? The Foreign Office is getting anxious, Lampton."

"I'm getting a little anxious myself," Philip admitted, his gaze shifting to the growing darkness outside the windows. He and Garner had attempted to track down the dangerous French spy for longer than he cared to admit, even to himself. The peace on the Continent was precarious even with the Corsican in exile. If, as their sources hinted, Napoleon planned to escape . . . No. They must capture Le Fontaine. The damage the spy could do didn't bear thinking of.

"Le Fontaine wasn't in Kent, after all—"

"Any longer," Philip corrected. They had reached their designated meeting place only to discover the British agent they were to have met with had disappeared, leaving behind significant signs of foul play. Yes. Le Fontaine had been in Kent—they'd simply arrived too late.

Garner let out a deep, worried breath. Philip knew precisely how the man felt. Every person working for the Foreign Office would be in danger until they captured Le Fontaine.

"I, for one, will be quite relieved to reach the inn." Philip painstakingly smoothed the hairs in his eyebrows. Garner allowed the slightest smile at the ridiculous mannerism. "I need to change out of these horrid clothes," Philip added for good measure.

"Clothes? Hah! What I need is brandy!"

Philip clucked his tongue in feigned disapproval. "You, sir, will never be a hero."

"Fabulous. Perhaps the Foreign Office will release me from duty." Garner looked quite hopeful. "You could tell them I am a coward. Or a drunkard."

Philip yawned, mostly for effect. "And be assigned a partner who suffers carriage sickness?" He shook his head, his eyes wide in feigned horror. "I would never subject my high-sprung equipage to such abuse. No. A cowardly drunkard suits me fine."

"I feared you would say that," Garner grumbled, slouching ever lower.

Nearly two hours later, they stopped at a small but relatively clean inn lit by the barest number of lanterns. It would do for one night, Philip supposed. After Philip changed into his brightly colored, fashionably tailored society togs, he met up with Garner in the private parlor for dinner. The moment the serving girl bowed out, they resumed their earlier conversation in low tones.

"So what comes next?" Garner dropped his head into his hand, looking beaten down and weary.

"The only other place Le Fontaine has been known to make port is Ipswich."

"Suffolk?"

Philip nodded. "That is our next destination, I daresay."

"Do you have property in Suffolk?"

"Sadly, no," Philip answered, taking a generous forkful of roast beef.

"Then how do you plan to explain your presence? Wouldn't want Le Fontaine to be suspicious."

"That is where being unfathomably popular has its benefits, Garner." Philip smiled. "I have been invited to a Christmas house party. 'Where is this gathering of the elite?' you may ask."

Garner nodded, obviously guessing the answer. "Suffolk," he said.

"Not twenty miles from Ipswich." Philip raised his eyebrows repeatedly to communicate his satisfaction with his own ingenuity. "Lord Cavratt and his lovely wife have invited me and my horde of siblings to Kinnley, along with a few other choice individuals."

"Then I shall leave you to sort out Le Fontaine." Garner smiled with obvious relief.

"Nonsense." Philip dabbed at the corner of his mouth with a clean but hopelessly stained napkin. The inn appeared a little less respectable than he had originally hoped. "Your cousin and his wife, Lord and Lady Henley, will also be in attendance. I believe Lizzie is the mastermind behind the gathering, as a matter of fact. You shall simply have to come by."

"Uninvited?" Garner clearly didn't like the suggestion.

"I daresay you hardly need an invitation to spend the holiday with family."

"You will smooth it over for me, then?"

"Not a chance, man. You and I are not supposed to be acquainted. Or have you forgotten already?"

Garner let out a long-suffering sigh. "I shall have to impose?"

"Like any relative worth his salt."

"I shall return to London, then, to make our report." A healthy dose of resignation tinged Garner's words. "I will make my way to Kinnley shortly thereafter."

"Remarkable plan, Garner. How do you come by such ingenious stratagems?"

"You know very well that you laid out that strategy at least ten missions ago."

"Ah, so I am the source of your genius." Philip offered a succession of exaggerated nods. "Very good. Very good."

"No. Not very good. I shall have to return to Town on horseback while you proceed to your destination in the best-sprung coach I have ever had the opportunity to ride in."

Garner grumbled something about drunkenness and carriage sickness. Philip sauntered to an armchair near the fire and sat back lazily, absentmindedly playing with his ivory-tipped walking stick.

"When do you expect to arrive at Kinnley?" Garner asked, leaning against the mantelpiece after another glass of amber-colored numbness.

"Thursday. Perhaps Friday."

Garner's gaze froze abruptly on the doorway.

"Forgive me," a voice said. "I did not realize the room was occupied."

Philip looked up from the crackling fire across the room to the doorway and into the face of a stunningly pretty young lady, dressed well if not in the first waters of fashion. The pale green shawl wrapped around her thin shoulders looked Parisian. She was *Quality*, then, as the servants were wont to say.

Her nearly black eyes took in the entire room quickly but, no doubt, accurately. She had an air of observation about her that made Philip uneasy. How long had she been standing there? How much of their conversation had she overheard?

"Might we be of assistance?" Philip asked as he rose, tugging at his deep green waistcoat and leaning quite dapperly on his walking stick.

"I dined in this parlor earlier this evening and left behind a personal item. I have come to retrieve it."

She was direct, Philip would give her that: no blushes nor demure posturing. Her frankness in the current situation, however, did not appeal. If she had arrived in the parlor in time to overhear their conversation, this black-eyed beauty would not have missed nor misunderstood a word of what they'd said.

"We would, of course, be happy to help you search out whatever you have misplaced." Garner offered a bow along with his services.

Now the man wished to play detective? He had practically begged to be tossed off the list of national agents not five minutes earlier.

"No need to search, sir," the young lady replied. "Your friend, there, seems to have located the very thing for which I am looking."

Both Garner's and the mysterious stranger's eyes focused on Philip. She hadn't taken a single step inside the room but stood leaning against the doorframe, her calculating gaze uncomfortably unflinching.

"And what precisely are you looking for?" Philip smiled a little, the selfsame smile that more than one impressionable miss had all but swooned over.

She appeared entirely unimpressed—annoyed, almost. "My walking stick," she said sans emotion, flicking her hand toward the stick in Philip's hand.

Philip laughed. A walking stick? *His* walking stick? "I do not believe I know a single lady who carries a walking stick."

"Congratulations," she said dryly. "You now know one. Will you return my property to me or not?"

She had backbone. But duty called. She might have overheard too much—dampening any suspicions was quite necessary. "My dear woman"—he minced his way across the room to where she stood in the doorway—"I realize Lord Byron has made limps quite couture, but I do believe you would be carrying the affectation a bit far with a walking stick."

"You are an expert on fashion, then?" She raised an eyebrow in disapproval. *Disapproval.* How often had he received just such a look from society ladies for his simpering ways? It shouldn't still rankle after so many years.

"Beau Brummel has been known to consult me." True enough, though hardly the sort of thing Philip felt gratified by. He gave no outward indication that he felt anything but pride at Brummel's singling him out. Pretending to be a mindless dandy had protected him on more than once occasion.

"He consults you on how to insult and contradict a lady?"

"I understood we were speaking of fashion." Philip stepped closer to the open door and his inquisitor.

"Fashion being the all-important focus of your mental faculties?"

"You disregard fashion?" He cloaked himself in an air of shock as he stepped closer still, the ivory-tipped stick still in his hand. "That is rather single-minded."

"As is your view of a lady who possesses a walking stick."

"And now our conversation has come full circle." Philip bowed his head in acknowledgment of her wit.

"Hardly. You still have my stick, and I am still without it."

"But I profess this is *my* stick, and I have no intention of handing it over to you." Especially considering the very sensitive documents hidden in its hollowed-out center.

"You believe I am a liar, then? And a thief besides?"

"I believe you are mistaken."

"You believe I meant to come searching for my sewing but found myself overcome by the splendor of your walking stick, rendering my poor addled brain unable to focus on anything other than your appearance?" The baffling young woman fixed him with a look of utter disdain. "On the contrary. There is nothing in this room so devastatingly overpowering as to leave me unable to think clearly. I find the entire scene quite unimpressive, as a matter of fact."

Philip pulled his quizzing glass to his eye and inspected the daring young lady. She found nothing devastating about him? She was unimpressed? Odd, that. A man couldn't wear such dangerously high shirt points as his and not make an impression of some kind.

"That, sirrah"—her disconcertingly pointed gaze narrowed on his quizzing glass—"is taking an affectation too far. One wonders if you are simply in need of spectacles but your vanity will not permit you to wear them."

"There is nothing wrong with my eyesight." Philip let the glass drop on its string as he closed the distance between them. He stood directly across from the maddening woman still leaning against the doorframe but glaring at him as if she were royalty.

"Then it is your hearing that is wanting. I have requested the return of my walking stick."

"But this is not *your* walking stick." Philip twirled it with the familiarity of a longtime owner.

"Because I am a female?" The militant glint in her eye caught Philip completely off guard.

"Because it is *mine*." He gave her a winning smile.

She let out a sigh of condescension. "If you will kindly glimpse at the wood directly beneath the ivory-tipped handle, I believe you will stumble upon a set of initials."

"There have never been—"

"Indulge me," she drawled.

Philip bowed absurdly deep to hide his smug expression. Returning to his full height once more, he made quite a show of lifting the cane handle to his line of sight. "As I suspected, there are no—" He stopped short. Initials. *SK.* Those had never been there before. He also spied a swirl in the grain he'd never noticed in his walking stick. "Oh."

"If you would be so kind as to return it to me." The woman sounded and looked thoroughly disgusted with him.

"My apologies," Philip replied with a slight bow. "*Your* stick." He couldn't help the doubtful sound of his words. Ladies simply did not carry walking sticks. "It is quite nearly identical to my own."

"Then surely Beau Brummel owns a matching one, as well." She smiled insincerely and held out her hand for her cane.

"Um, Philip." Garner's voice came from behind. He had all but forgotten about the man.

Needing a respite from the shrew's piercing look, Philip glanced over his shoulder at his cowardly partner, who, at that moment, held a walking stick that was the very copy of the one he had only just handed over to their visitor. "I found it beside the chair you were sitting in."

"Thank you," Philip answered dryly. "I suppose you could not possibly have mentioned your find sooner?"

"The two of you never paused long enough for me to get a word in edgewise," Garner said. "Besides, the way you were going at one another, daggers drawn and what, I didn't dare jump in."

"You really are a coward."

"As I have told you hundreds of times."

He owed the blasted fishwife an apology for unknowingly claiming her walking stick as his own, for being fashionable when she so obviously disapproved—most likely she'd expect him to apologize for breathing. He turned back toward the doorway—the *empty* doorway.

"She leaves without a word. Fitting." He turned back to Garner and claimed his walking stick. "I don't suppose you saw her go?"

"Perhaps she disappeared. A witch, or something."

"Witch? Probably, old man. Probably."

"Black eyes." Garner shook his head. "I tell you, I found the young lady unsettling. Skin so pale she must never venture out into the sun, hair and eyes both black as tar."

Obsidian, Philip silently corrected. Her hair reminded him of obsidian. Hues ranging from green to violet infused the black, though Philip couldn't say how that was even possible. Garner had described her eyes correctly, however. They were very much like tar, so black the pupils simply disappeared, and bubbling with fire. Despite himself, Philip found the anonymous young lady unnerving and intriguing. Warning bells rang in Philip's brain. This Miss SK was trouble.

"This is where we part ways, then?" Garner held a hand out to Philip.

"Send along any instructions you receive from the Office," Philip instructed, shaking Garner's hand. "To Kinnley."

Garner nodded his understanding and stepped from the parlor. Philip tossed an extra coin to the servant girl who entered to clear the table, thus assuring himself of his privacy. The moment she left, Philip ran his hand through his perfectly coiffed hair and slumped over the empty table. The only person in whose company he did not automatically revert to the role of care-for-nothing fop was himself.

Le Fontaine, or "The Fountain," as the elusive French spy had fashioned himself, had provided a ceaseless flow of information for the wrong side of the Continental dispute. For more than a year, Philip had tracked and trailed the man. Hot on the heels of such a prized catch, Philip ought to have been shaking with anticipation, anxiously planning the hunt. He'd certainly found vast satisfaction in his assignments before. Instead, he felt restless, discontented. To own the truth, he'd felt rather dissatisfied with his life for nearly a year. Playing the idiot to the *ton* had lost what little amusement it had once held. His dissatisfaction, however, stemmed from more than his social mask. Philip simply couldn't pinpoint what precisely was eating at him.

His uneasy thoughts settled on the odd young lady who had invaded the parlor only moments earlier. She was not a witch—Philip certainly didn't believe in such superstitious nonsense. Something about her, though, weighed on him.

Years of evaluating people had developed into an almost sixth sense. Philip knew he wouldn't likely run into the unsettling female again. Only chance had crossed their paths, after all. Chance seldom proved so unkind twice.

He rose to his feet and strode purposefully to the door before adopting his trademark mincing stroll to climb the stairs to his rented chamber. The next morning would see him in his carriage once more: warm brick at his feet, accommodating lap blanket offering respite from the cold mid-December air, the smooth carriage ride protecting him from the wear and tear of road travel.

And he would hate every minute of it.

Two

Sorrel Kendrick spent yet another morning enduring the all-too-familiar histrionics of her mother. "If I cannot wear the green dress, I shall simply refuse to continue!"

"Wonderful," Sorrel replied. "I will tell George Coachman to return home." If she had even remotely believed her mother's declaration, she'd have driven the coach personally. She had come to realize as a child that her mother lived in a constant state of hysterics, especially in matters pertaining to her wardrobe.

"How can you be so cruel? To your own mother, even!" Tears began trickling precisely on cue.

Mother could have made a career as an actress. Sorrel, of course, would never have uttered that conclusion out loud. Mother would swoon or, worse yet, seriously consider the idea.

"I am not attempting to be cruel, Mother." Sorrel leaned back in the straight-backed chair beside the sparse chamber's fireplace, head propped up by her hand. "If you want to wear a dress hardly warm enough for springtime, let alone winter, by all means, do so. Only please do so quickly. And do not expect to appropriate all the lap robes when the chill becomes too much for you."

"But an earl, Sorrel! An earl will be there! And a baron. And—"

"And you couldn't possibly be seen by a Peer in anything but your green dress."

Mother smiled. "I knew you would understand."

Sorrel resisted the urge to roll her eyes heavenward and bit back a long-suffering sigh. Marjie, Sorrel's fair-haired, fair-skinned, blue-eyed china doll of a sister, entered the bedchamber with her customary sunny smile. Sorrel brushed back her own straight-as-a-pin, absolutely black hair and reminded herself that she was not jealous of her sister.

"Of course you should wear the green gown, Mother," Marjie said. She always guided and persuaded and steered their mother with the capability of a woman twice her seventeen years.

"Sorrel seems to think I should arrive at Kinnley in a hideously serviceable shawl and equally ugly dress."

The sniffles are a bit much, Sorrel thought.

"I am certain Sorrel will not begrudge you your wardrobe," Marjie reassured their overly emotional mother. "She is simply anxious to be leaving. This journey has not been easy on her, you know. Her leg must pain her so badly, what with—"

"And I refuse to wear short boots." Mother began dressing in earnest. "The matching slippers will be perfect."

Marjie gave Sorrel a conspiratorial glance. Talking of Sorrel's nearly crippled physical state always brought out Mother's more efficient side. She would avoid by all means possible discussing the event that had changed Sorrel's entire life two years earlier, even if sidestepping that conversational topic meant not arguing over clothing and beginning the final leg of their already delayed journey.

Sorrel gripped the top of her walking stick, her mind flashing momentarily to a pair of laughing blue eyes and a ridiculously colorful waistcoat in an inn's private parlor. She shook her head at her own wayward thoughts. She did not wish to think of the encounter only two nights earlier. That arrogant popinjay had been bother enough when present without invading her thoughts now that he was, with any luck, many, many miles away.

With the grace of an arthritic octogenarian, she raised herself to her feet. After a moment's painful rebalancing with a white-knuckle grip on her walking stick, Sorrel began her less-than-dainty walk across the chamber.

"Ten minutes, Sorrel." Marjie smiled at her as she limped past.

Sorrel nodded. "I will be waiting in the carriage."

Fifteen minutes later, Mother and Marjie joined her. Mother inquired twice after the state of her luggage before they pulled away from yet another inn of questionable sanitation. They had been traveling for four days. Four days of jarring and jerking on uneven roads. Four days of rented lodgings. Four days of pain. Pain in her back. Pain in her hip. Pain in her leg. And that arrogant fop who'd been a pain in the—

No. She would not finish that thought. Despite what *he* might think of a female with a walking stick, she was a lady—a lady who already felt uncomfortable only one-half hour into their resumed journey.

Why have I agreed to this madcap scheme? Sorrel demanded of herself for the hundredth time since the invitation to Kinnley had arrived. The answer came easily. Because of Lizzie.

Lizzie Handle. Had it really been nearly three years since that Season in London? It felt more like thirty. Balls. Gowns. Rides in Hyde Park. Bowing to the Queen. And Lizzie. They had both enjoyed, endured at times, their first Season. They had become fast friends despite their remarkably disparate personalities. Lizzie oozed drama, cheer, and optimism. Sorrel tended to err on the side of caution, quiet observation, and realism. They had been opposites and complements.

Lizzie brought out Sorrel's smile. Sorrel kept Lizzie in check, much to the relief of Lizzie's older brother and guardian. Lord Cavratt's dissatisfaction with society had been obvious, and his frustration with his sister had, at times, been almost humorous. Lizzie had despaired of her brother ever marrying. Lord Cavratt had despaired of his sister ever behaving. Sorrel's sobering influence on Lizzie had met with Lord Cavratt's instant approval.

Since those short few months three years earlier, Lizzie had married a baron. Based on her cheery correspondence, Lizzie was happy. Sorrel had to admit she envied her friend. She did not covet the title Lizzie had acquired, for Sorrel cared little for such distinctions. Nor did she envy Lizzie's wealth, for Sorrel's needs were met through her late father's estate, thanks to the youth of her brother, the heir, and the fair-minded nature of the family's man of business. No. She envied the happiness. Sorrel had never had Lizzie's disposition and therefore doubted she would ever have Lizzie's full measure of joy. But she would have settled for contentment.

The carriage hit another rut in the road that Sorrel felt through every inch of her aching leg. She bit back a grimace and closed her eyes to the all-too-familiar pain. There were moments, like that one, when she wondered how she would ever endure a lifetime of such agony.

"Do we need to stop at the next inn?" Marjie asked.

Sorrel opened her eyes. Marjie watched her with almost maternal concern despite Sorrel's being the *older* sister.

"No," Sorrel replied. The sooner they reached Suffolk, the better. Stopping to stretch her travel-battered limb would only lengthen the journey.

"You appear to be in pain," Marjie pressed.

"I am always in pain. And no tears over this, Marjie," she hastily added, seeing the well-known look on her sister's face. "If I can endure this journey without crying, you can certainly do so."

"But it is so unfair!" Marjie's eyes sparkled with moisture. "If it weren't for your unfortunate incident—"

"We shall never know what life would have held if not for that 'incident,' so there is little point hypothesizing."

"But you could have married. Had a family of your own."

"With my argumentative nature?" Sorrel managed a smile for her chin-quivering sister. "I doubt I had much of a chance for matrimony even before *this*." Sorrel waved her hand over her twisted, painful leg and tapped the tip of her walking stick.

"Nonsense," Marjie retorted with conviction. "You are wonderful. Intelligent. Kind. Beautiful."

"Bless your lying tongue, Marjie." Sorrel laughed. Her unchecked volume woke their sleeping mother and ended all discussion of Sorrel's assets and, especially, her liabilities. Mother never wanted to hear about either.

"Did I tell you the *entire* Jonquil family will be there?" Mother asked eagerly.

"Yes, Mother. Several times."

"The Earl. The Countess. The heir to a barony."

If Mother rattled off one more rank in the Peerage, Sorrel would throw herself from the carriage. Perhaps she should have stayed home, after all.

"The young captain has been invited, as well."

So the army would be accounted for.

"Also the brother who is a barrister."

And the law. Just how large was this family?

"And is theirs the only family attending?" Marjie asked like a dutiful daughter.

Sorrel, however, let her mind wander again. They would pass their holiday with an earl and his countess, a future baron, a captain, and a barrister. Of course, she couldn't leave herself off the guest list: the cripple.

"Do look, girls!" Mother cried out some eight hours later—Mother's continued need for a few moments before a warm fire, combined with Sorrel's growing discomfort, had lengthened their journey. "We have reached Kinnley, I am sure of it!"

Despite her usual determination not to appear like a green girl, Sorrel pressed her face to the carriage window to get her first glimpse of Lizzie's childhood home. The house glowed. Light spilled from every ground-level window. Obviously the Cavratt estate remained as prosperous as ever.

The columned portico offered respite from the frigid rain, which had fallen for nearly an hour. No sooner had their rather ancient vehicle passed beneath the stone abutment than a veritable army of footmen descended upon their carriage, handing each of the Kendrick women out in turn and unloading their trunks with unfathomable speed.

Mother rushed up the stone steps quite at her ease in the entirely unfamiliar home. Sorrel, despite being the sole family member with connections to Kinnley, felt less confident. She held back, knowing from experience that Lord Cavratt had very set ideas about propriety and a firm dislike for the overly forward in society. And, of course, steps were difficult to maneuver when one possessed only one fully functional leg.

"Sorrel, you never told me Kinnley was so grand," Marjie said almost reverentially as she helped Sorrel up the steps.

"I never saw Kinnley," she said. "I only ever saw Lizzie in London. Permount House, the Cavratt home in Town, is spectacular in its own right. It is quite arguably the finest home in Grosvenor Square."

"I am happy, then, that Mother insisted I bring my very best gowns." Marjie stared in obvious awe at the enormous entryway of Kinnley.

Sorrel refused to gawk despite the splendor. Marble floors. A grand staircase. Exquisitely carved statues flanking either side of the windowed entry hall. No wonder Lizzie had so sorely missed Suffolk while in Town.

"If you will follow me, please." A silver-haired woman in a serviceable gown and frilled cap led the way up the oaken staircase. "Lady Cavratt has placed you in rooms adjoining one another, if that will be pleasing to you."

"I am certain it will be positively perfect!" Mother exclaimed, her voice unnaturally high as though she were a schoolgirl barely suppressing a fit of giggles. "My son, I am certain you were told, will be joining us shortly. He is at Eton currently."

"Yes, ma'am," the housekeeper replied. "There is a room in the same wing as yours if you would like to house him there. He can also be placed in the nursery wing or in the wing where the Jonquil gentlemen will be staying. You may decide prior to the young Mister Kendrick's arrival."

"Positively perfect!" Mother actually did giggle at that.

Sorrel, with Marjie's help, managed to keep up, though she had to sit the moment she reached her room. She almost instantly resorted to lying on the plush bed while her entire right leg throbbed and pulsated with pain.

She let her eyes lose focus enough for the pale blue bed curtains to grow fuzzy, making it almost seem possible that she were gazing up at a late summer sky. The warmth of the low burning fire made the room nearly warm enough. If not for the lingering chill deep in her joints, Sorrel might have actually believed she'd left winter behind. She might have convinced herself that she remained ensconced in the familiarity of home.

As she lay there, a face flashed through her memory, one with amused blue eyes. She could yet see the flamboyant gentleman's features twist in distaste as she'd suggested that a lady of refinement might use a walking stick. His opinion ought not to have mattered—she would likely never see him again. Yet it more than mattered. It hurt. She knew the mangled mess she had become, all the result of a pointless and devastating accident. To see that deformity reflected in his obviously unflattering opinion had wounded her.

Sorrel swore to herself, as she had countless times since her accident, that no one would ever hurt her again. She wrapped her pride around her like chain mail and prepared to face the other guests, determined that none of them would pierce her defenses as that dandy in Kent had managed so easily to do.

Three

Philip felt suffocated as he sat in his well-sprung, top-of-the-trees, flashy carriage with the Lampton seal proclaiming the superiority of the vehicle and its passenger for any who cared to look (and he knew from experience that plenty did). He would have much preferred making his way to Suffolk on horseback freezing near to death like any self-respecting gentleman. But, he lamented, one must keep up appearances.

Therefore, he traveled in a bottle-green waistcoat, complete with blue-embroidered hummingbirds and enormous silver buttons beneath a coat of matching blue superfine and an outercoat with no fewer than five capes. His high-starched cravat sported a knot of fashionable perfection. A stylish high beaver sat on the seat across from him. His feet were housed in his polished-to-a-mirror-shine Hessians propped up beside his hat. What he wouldn't give to be in his dressing gown and carpet slippers, a luxury in which he seldom risked indulging. Dandies simply didn't wear such things.

Reminding himself that some sacrifices were worth making, Philip glanced out the partially curtained windows of his carriage at the path bending smoothly toward the white stone façade of a house he knew as well as his own: Kinnley.

He'd traveled to the home of his best friend too many times to count since he and Lord Cavratt had met at Eton. Of course, his friend had been only "Crispin" then, and Philip had been only Lord Jonquil, a courtesy title he had preferred to ignore.

"Lud, that was a long time ago." He sighed into the silence of the empty carriage.

Yet Kinnley had not changed: Jacobean architecture with its characteristic flat roof and rounded archways perfectly complemented by an almost naturalistic approach to the landscape. Skeletal trees, stripped bare by the hand of winter, stood in informal greeting on either side of the carriageway. As the final bend brought the path directly in front of the house, the trees gave way to open land with an unimpeded view of the house to one side and the sea to the other.

Philip could easily picture in his mind the large, shallow lake and formal knot garden behind the house and the expanse of rolling fields spreading as far as the eye could see. No. Kinnley never changed. When they were fifteen, Philip had tried to convince Crispin to trade estates when they came of age. The late Lady Cavratt had swooned on the spot. In the end they decided to keep their respective homes.

"Lord Lampton," Hancock, the Cavratt's all-seeing, all-knowing butler greeted from the front door, offering the appropriate, though entirely unnecessary, bow.

"Am I too early for a dramatic entrance?" Philip asked, smoothing the almost imperceptible wrinkles on his coat sleeves.

"I believe the household is gathered in the west sitting room, my lord," Hancock informed him.

"Perfect." With a quick sidestep and the long stride his height afforded him, Philip, twirling his walking stick, easily passed the butler and moved without a single pause to the room Hancock had mentioned. As reported, the entire household seemed gathered there.

Philip immediately spotted Crispin—dark, wavy hair, clothes in respectably subdued tones. No hummingbird motifs for the very sober Lord Cavratt. Beside him stood a lady a few years his junior, with honey-colored hair and a pleasant, quiet air. Crispin's wife had swiftly become one of Philip's favorite people. She smiled at his antics and laughed at his jokes but never laughed *at* him. More important still, she'd made Crispin happy, *truly* happy. If women could be knighted, he would put in a word for her. Perhaps she should be sainted, though Philip knew he had very little influence On High.

His thoughts did not remain on his hosts for long, nor did he do much more than vaguely note the unfamiliar house guests gathered there. The room was positively teeming with his family members, who, as always, grasped his immediate attention. His beloved mother—"Mater," as all the brothers had called her since their childhood—wore her customary elegant black bombazine and black cap. The only splash of color, aside from her bright blue eyes, came from a blue topaz pendant hanging around her neck. How Mater managed to look elegant and ageless in full mourning, Philip would never know. Father had been gone nearly a decade, and Mater had yet to so much as lighten her mourning attire. Sometimes he wondered if she would have recovered from her loss faster if all seven of her sons hadn't been the spitting image of their father.

He eyed the three brothers present. To a one, they sported golden hair, blue eyes, and tall and lean builds. 'Twas no wonder, really, that society made little effort to differentiate them, contenting itself with referring to the collective whole as "those Jonquils." Philip himself mixed their names up on occasion.

Corbin and Jason, the twins—though their resemblance began and ended with their very Jonquil-esque appearance—had arrived at Kinnley and stood in exclusive conversation to one side of the room. "Conversation" was perhaps a stretch. Jason talked and Corbin silently listened, the typical arrangement for those two since nearly birth. Another brother, Stanley, home on medical leave from fighting on the Continent, had come as well. He sat awkwardly attempting to talk to a rather lovely young lady over a game of backgammon. Jonquils tended to make fools of themselves when conversing with ladies. Poor Stanley was probably making a mull of the entire thing.

Philip glanced quickly between his family members. On whom should he swoop down? His customary entrance required both the element of surprise and a certain flamboyant flare. Mater, Philip quickly decided. Definitely Mater. He moved quickly and quietly to the sofa where his ever-dignified mother sat listening to the unceasing chatter of an unidentified companion. He slipped smoothly on to the sofa beside her.

"How about a kiss for your favorite son?"

"My dearest Layton!" Mater exclaimed and turned in Philip's direction.

"*Layton*? *Layton*? You wound me, Mater." Philip clasped a hand over his heart and grimaced as though run through by his mother's words. Laughter that could belong only to a roomful of Jonquils echoed off the walls. "And I had my Hessians champagne-polished and everything."

"You know I am only teasing you, dearest." Mater smiled. "Give your Mater a kiss, then greet your hosts like a proper guest."

Philip pecked Mater's cheek then rose to do the pretty around the room. His hosts merely smiled in amusement when Philip minced his way toward them. One's best friend could not be expected to do anything else. They'd known each other too long for formality.

His brothers' greetings were easy to predict as well, thanks to a lifetime of association.

Corbin smiled but offered no actual words in greeting. Jason looked him over disapprovingly, shook his hand, and quickly took up once more the topic of discussion between him and his twin.

Stanley clasped his left arm around Philip's shoulder, Stanley's right arm apparently paining him again, and welcomed him warmly. "Philip, allow me to make known to you Miss Marjie Kendrick."

The blue-eyed china doll curtsied prettily. She couldn't be more than seventeen, eighteen at the most. Philip hoped, for his own sanity, she didn't giggle. As the very definition of a Bond Street beau, Philip would be positively required to offer endless witticisms and overblown compliments but didn't think he could survive four weeks of schoolgirl giggles.

"A pleasure to make your acquaintance, Miss Kendrick." Philip bowed deeply with a sweep of his hand.

She looked momentarily taken aback by his affected manner but quickly recovered herself. "I am afraid I shall have to be Miss Marjie, my lord. I have an older sister, you understand. *She* is Miss Kendrick."

"Mrs. Kendrick is chatting with Mater." Stanley motioned with his good arm toward the sofa.

Philip eyed his mother's conversational companion. The matron, wearing more frills than a dozen debutantes combined, giggled. Philip raised an eyebrow in surprise.

"My mother is . . ." Miss Marjie paused, looking quite at a loss to describe her mother appropriately. "That is, she . . . Mother is very youthful."

"How fortunate for your mother." Philip offered Miss Marjie a conspiratorial glance, which earned him a soft laugh—not a giggle, he noted with satisfaction.

"Doubles," Stanley called out, pulling his opponent's attention to their game.

Philip made his way toward Crispin's younger sister, Lizzie, having only just spied her across the room. She seemed entirely oblivious to his presence, which was typical. They grew up very much like brother and sister.

"Your husband is a brave man to leave you unattended amongst so many of England's dashing single gentlemen," Philip said with a wink once he reached Lizzie's side.

"Oh, posh!" Lizzie laughed. "Edward knows perfectly well the Jonquils are like brothers to me."

"You don't find us devastatingly handsome?" Philip smoothed his jacket front as he assumed his most self-confident stance.

"What woman wouldn't?" Lizzie smiled obligingly. "The Jonquils have broken half the hearts in England, I daresay."

"Only because there are so many of us."

"Probably," Lizzie replied. "May I introduce you to a dear friend of mine?"

"Of course."

Lizzie motioned to the settee beside her own chair, and Philip turned, his famous smile pasted on his face. In perfect unison, he and Lizzie's raven-haired companion uttered a single word:

"You!"

He recognized the young lady in an instant, the harpy from the inn in Kent! How could the fates be so unkind?

"You two know each other?" Lizzie sounded understandably astounded.

She answered first. "Yes, I have had that misfortune." *Miss SK,* as he'd come to think of her, narrowed her eyes as she gazed critically at Philip. She still found him unimpressive, did she? The lady lounged quite at her leisure on the plush settee, not, apparently, inclined to curtsy or make any true acknowledgment of him. "The gentleman offered me some invaluable insights into fashion," she added dryly, not breaking eye contact with Philip, though her words were supposedly for Lizzie. "Advice, I am told, Brummel himself would covet."

"And yet"—Philip utilized his ever-ready quizzing glass to eye the ivory-handled walking stick leaning conspicuously against the wall beside the settee—"you seem to have disregarded the invaluable lesson."

"We both seem to have disregarded all discouragement of our individual affectations." She pointedly eyed Philip's quizzing glass. "Although I find yours far more ridiculous than my own."

"Naturally." Philip bowed his head toward her.

"Yes, naturally. For *yours* truly is ridiculous."

"And yours is not?" Philip used his most disapproving tone, one that had been known to send grown men running to their lodgings to change an offending neckcloth or horridly clashing waistcoat.

"I fail to see how it is any of your concern." Did Philip hear a hint of emotion in her voice? So the quarrelsome nag could be ruffled, after all.

A high-pitched, overly sweet voice reached them from somewhere behind. "Sorrel!"

Philip's opponent allowed the tiniest of exasperated sighs.

The same unidentified woman, though Philip strongly suspected the voice belonged to the frilly matron, spoke again. "That is no way to speak to the Earl."

Miss SK, *Sorrel,* as he now knew her name to be, raised one sleek, black eyebrow in something bordering on surprise and amusement. "The Earl?" She almost chuckled on the word, watching him challengingly. "The earl of *what,* pray tell?"

Philip would have enjoyed the saucy retort if he didn't already thoroughly dislike the lady.

"Have you any suggestions for an appropriate title?" he asked. *When all else fails, flirt.* The strategy had certainly worked before.

"Plenty, my lord, but my mother has already beseeched me to speak more respectfully."

"The title would, then, have been disrespectful?"

"Naturally." She matched with perfection the tone he'd used to utter the same word moments earlier.

"Pray forgive my daughter, my lord." Philip suddenly found himself accosted by the matron in springtime ruffles and numerous yards of lace, talking in a voice that could not possibly have been so naturally girlish. "Sorrel was not always so insolent, I assure you."

"Thank you, Mother," Sorrel said dryly. "That is infinitely helpful."

"Miss Kendrick seems to have made quite an impression on you, Philip," Mater joined the conversation, looking far too intrigued for Philip's comfort. "Though you seem to be having a disagreement."

"A difference of opinion is all." Philip glanced again at Sorrel—*Miss Kendrick,* he corrected himself—still lounging on the settee, though now avoiding his gaze. Let her squirm a little.

"And what has left you so at odds with this young lady?" Mater asked.

Bless Mater. Leave it to his ever-loving mother to offer up the perfect opportunity to bring a starched-up miss down a peg or two.

"A fashion faux pas, Mater." Philip hooked a thumb in the pocket of his waistcoat, affording the room a view of his exceptionally well-made, if slightly bright, attire.

"Philip *is* known for his sense of the fashionable," Mater said warmly to Miss Kendrick.

"What insurmountable blunder has you at odds?" Lizzie looked between Philip and her friend.

"We were debating affectations," Philip said with a lazy smile. "She objects to my quizzing glass."

"Not an unheard-of mannerism," Lizzie conceded.

Philip nodded his agreement, spinning his quizzing glass on its ribbon. "*Her* affectation is not nearly so commonplace."

"Sorrel has an affectation?" Lizzie appeared doubtful.

"So it would seem. Miss Kendrick and I became acquainted over a walking stick, you see." Philip couldn't help a victorious smile. "It seems she adheres to the Byron school of fashion, carrying a gentleman's walking stick. She guards it quite vehemently, I understand."

"A walking stick?" Lizzie replied with obvious amusement.

"Did she not twirl it at her side when she strolled into the room?"

"She was already in the room when I entered." Lizzie turned back to Miss Kendrick. "You never carried a walking stick that year in London."

Philip leaned casually against the back of a nearby wingback chair. "Perhaps it is a recently acquired—"

"—affectation," several voices finished with him.

Philip raised an eyebrow in challenge. How, he wondered, would Miss Kendrick respond to that? He assumed she'd throw back some biting retort. He considered the far-fetched possibility that she might blush or, even more far-fetched still, that she might smile or look remotely impressed at his quick retorts. He'd held his own, after all. He'd dealt a sound blow in their verbal brawl—a turn of events he doubted occurred often, considering her obviously quick wit.

Her eyes snapped back to his, something sparking in them. She lifted her chin and squared her shoulders but didn't sit up, didn't rise. "A woman fashioning a walking stick offends your visual sensibilities?"

"Soon all of London's fashionable females would be limping through balls and musicales." No dandy would embrace such a thing.

"An impossibility, then," Miss Kendrick replied, her expression all but blank, her tone uninterpretable. "A lady with a limp being considered beautiful."

"In our society, appearance is everything." Philip knew that well.

"On that point, my lord, we agree." Miss Kendrick shifted quite awkwardly until she sat forward, her feet in front of her on the floor. "Now, if you will excuse me, my affectation and I feel the need for a change of scenery."

She grasped her walking stick without hesitation and rose slowly, unsteadily to her feet. A fleeting look of pain crossed her face before being replaced by cool indifference. Miss Kendrick bowed her head ever so slightly before turning away. To say she limped would be an enormous understatement. She leaned heavily on the aforementioned walking stick and moved as one in a tremendous amount of physical agony, as if her right leg functioned only minimally and only with great effort.

Philip watched her go amidst the total silence in the room. His smile vanished. His smug satisfaction dissipated. The entire room watched Miss Kendrick exit.

"Sorrel," Miss Marjie called after her sister.

Miss Kendrick waved off the plea and continued her struggled walk out of the room.

"I had no idea," Lizzie said quietly. "She didn't used to have a . . ." Lizzie looked uncomfortable with the word ". . . a limp."

"Apparently my foot still fits in my mouth," Philip said, resisting the urge to run his fingers through his hair.

Lizzie looked to Mrs. Kendrick. "What happened? She walked without a limp when last I saw her."

"Oh . . . we . . . well . . ." She stuttered and waved her hand in an awkward display of apparent dismissal. "Oh, my, do look. It is snowing." Mrs. Kendrick flitted to the far window, leaving behind a roomful of astonished onlookers.

"We rarely talk about Sorrel's condition." Miss Marjie offered her quiet explanation. "Sorrel rather prefers it that way. Mother quite insists on it."

"An injury?" Lizzie asked.

Miss Marjie nodded. "About two years ago."

"Is that why she did not return to London for her second Season?"

Another nod.

"She never mentioned it in any of her letters." Lizzie's eyes were still glued to the door through which Miss Kendrick had passed. "I never knew."

"If you will pardon me." Philip bowed to the room in general. "I have an apology to make."

Four

INSUFFERABLE, HORRIBLE MAN! SHE SHOULD have forced her walking stick down his dandified throat the first time she met him. The unfeeling, detestable—

"Miss Kendrick."

Sorrel didn't bother to stop or even attempt to turn around. The tap-and-drag rhythm of her walk echoed in the empty corridor. She already felt the awkwardness of her gait; hearing the syncopation of it, too, only added to her frustration.

"Miss Kendrick." Curse his fully functional limbs. The infuriating popinjay arrived at her side before she'd had the chance to escape. "Miss Kendrick."

"You, apparently, have learned my name." How she hoped he heard the acid in her tone!

He stepped around and faced her. "I wish to apologize, Miss Kendrick."

"For being a pompous dunderhead?"

The Earl's jaw tightened momentarily. Did he expect her to simper at his offered regrets? To be won over by an apology he most likely did not remotely feel? Perhaps he simply thought his overly bright sense of fashion would leave her weak in the knees. The fribble!

"For my thoughtless words," he said. "I did not intend to be offensive."

"And I did not intend to be contentious." She would concede that much.

"Shall we cry pax?" He smiled as though it were a settled matter.

"You belittle and insult me before a roomful of people who have yet to form opinions of me and insinuate that my less-than-graceful gait makes me less than ladylike. You make my early moments at a monthlong house party embarrassing and difficult, and a simple 'I apologize' should placate me?" How many ways could this man hurt and belittle her? "Did you not exact enough satisfaction several evenings ago depriving me of my crutch? Why do you find it absolutely necessary to add salt to the wound?"

"I did not realize at the time that you had a legitimate reason for carrying a walking stick."

"No. You assumed I obsessed over my appearance like—"

"Like I do?" The Earl's blond eyebrow arched in obvious disapproval at her insinuation.

"I know a tulip when I see one."

"Perhaps now *you* are the one being judgmental. Assuming based on appearances that—"

"Someone once told me that appearance is everything," she said, not caring for the social niceties at the moment. "I daresay you know precisely what your appearance communicates."

"You know nothing about me, Miss Kendrick." Now the blue eyes were icy cold.

Sorrel didn't flinch. Let him be angry. Let him feel half as affronted as she did. "I know far more than I care to, Lord—" Except she didn't know his name. And he realized it. A smile of satisfaction crossed his unfairly handsome face. Why couldn't villains all be hideously ugly?

"Philip Jonquil, Earl of Lampton." He bowed rather smugly.

"Fop," Sorrel mumbled under her breath.

"I fear we are at an impasse, Miss Kendrick. Could we not reach for a cessation of hostilities?"

"I doubt you would hold to a truce, Lord Lampton. Not with such cannon fodder as I am certain to provide you with." She tapped her walking stick for emphasis.

"Would not my mannerisms prove ammunition for you as well in this war of words?" Lampton smiled smoothly. "The quizzing glass and what."

"The quizzing glass and *what*?" Sorrel asked, determinedly keeping her eyes from his too-easy smile, concentrating instead on his knife-edged words of earlier. "How highly armed am I likely to find myself these next four weeks?"

"I do not believe it a good battle plan to point out my own strategic vulnerabilities to an enemy," he said.

"Am I your enemy, then?" she asked.

"If we cannot trust each other to maintain even a temporary peace, what else could we possibly be?"

She met his challenge with a raise of her chin. "It is to be a battle, then?"

He nodded. "Until one of us cries pax."

"Agreed."

"Agreed." Lampton smiled far too triumphantly. Far too confidently. "Might I offer you my escort somewhere?"

"No." Sorrel knew she must look confused. She *felt* confused. Hadn't they just agreed to be bitter enemies?

Lampton offered a bow before sauntering almost blithely back to the west sitting room. So the confounded man looked forward to the coming clash? Excited about their declared animosity? Sorrel smiled mirthlessly. She knew she could hold her own in a verbal match; bitter experience had taught her to fight tooth and nail for everything.

* * *

Philip stopped at the door of the sitting room and glanced back toward Sorrel. Somehow, he couldn't think of his newly sworn enemy as *Miss Kendrick*. They were at war, after all. No British soldier would use his drawing room manners with Bonaparte.

Lampton War Tactic Number One: Do not think of the enemy as female; think of females as the enemy. Or something like that.

His female enemy slowly, determinedly staggered away down the windowed rear corridor. Admittedly a formidable foe, and a fighter to the core, he'd wager. He certainly felt up for the challenge. He needed a strategy. Philip narrowed his eyes as he watched what he labeled as Sorrel's retreat. Yes, he needed a strategy, and another tactic.

Lampton War Tactic Number Two: If the enemy's hair shines like onyx in the morning sun, it is best not to notice. Or pretend not to. Or at least disregard the shine. And the hair.

Philip's passage into the sitting room came rather abruptly but did not go unnoticed.

Mater wasted no time letting her thoughts be known. "I certainly hope you apologized."

"I did." He offered an abbreviated bow but held back a smile.

"Well." Mater looked duly relieved. "I am happy you are forgiven."

"On the contrary," Philip quickly corrected. "Miss Kendrick"—he would keep tactic number one under wraps: too many females who might misunderstand—"has declared my apology insufficient and insincere and swears she will not forgive me but has every intention of disliking me with a passion."

Jason looked smug. Corbin seemed a little surprised. Lizzie appeared horrified. Mater had that intrigued look once more, so Philip turned abruptly away. His gaze, however, fell on Catherine—sweet Catherine, so like a younger sister to him. She looked concerned, but for *whom,* he couldn't say. A hint of disappointment hung in her eyes, and it cut at him. No wonder Crispin would do anything for his wife. She could pierce with a look. At least Sorrel only pierced with words.

Lampton War Tactic Number Three: It is best not to think of one's relationship with the enemy in the same way one thinks of his best friend's relationship with his wife. Period.

"Now, Catherine," he hastily entreated, "do not look distraught. I only make a spectacle of myself so Crispin will appear to all the more advantage in your eyes. He is rather a bumbling wreck at times, though it pains me to say such about my oldest friend."

At that she smiled and shook her head amusedly. "On behalf of my husband and myself, I heartily thank you."

"Yes. Such a noble sacrifice." Crispin had crossed to his wife's side. "And one you have apparently made often. For I believe you have been making a spectacle of yourself for years."

Philip had to laugh at that. So did the rest of the room, quite successfully breaking the tension. Philip casually crossed toward Miss Marjie, still engaged in a somewhat neglected game of backgammon with Stanley. Philip kept his gaze, however, directed at Crispin and Catherine. Lord Cavratt held his wife's hand quite gently in his own and said something too low to be overheard. She gave him a look of blatant adoration and love. No person had ever looked at Philip that way. The realization rankled.

"Miss Marjie," he addressed the young lady whose side he had reached. "As your sister will not accept, please allow me to offer my apologies to you. I realize my words were unkind and hurtful, though unintentionally so."

"You couldn't possibly have known, my lord." Miss Marjie smiled back. "You, unfortunately, chose a particularly sensitive topic on which to be at odds with Sorrel."

"As I have discovered," Philip acknowledged. "But then I have never been one to do things by halves."

"And neither has Sorrel." She sighed somewhat regretfully. Philip vowed to eventually learn what past discretions had inspired such a tone. "If she has sworn to dislike you, I fear she will."

"I fully believe you." Philip lowered his voice so only she would be privy to his admission. "She has gone so far as to declare the two of us at war. I am to fortify myself against all manner of attacks against my person."

With her voice equally low and her expression entirely serious, Miss Marjie offered a warning. "Do not underestimate Sorrel."

Lampton War Tactic Number Four: When the sister of one's

enemy suggests caution, be cautious.

He spent the remainder of the day on strategy. Philip decided he needed to maintain the upper hand, stay one step ahead of General Sorrel. He knew enough of her quick mind from their two encounters to be certain she would not be easily outwitted. He needed the element of surprise.

Philip wandered to the window of his bedchamber, glancing out across the front grounds of Kinnley and down toward the sea, barely visible as darkness approached. He'd have to be downstairs in a few more minutes for the evening meal.

But how to outmaneuver the enemy? She, he did not doubt, would come to the meal fully anticipating a battle. She would be ready for him. Philip stepped back to the full-length looking glass. He could simply begin talking before she had a chance and not give her a moment to respond. He tugged at the sleeves of his deep-blue coat. No. Rambling would be too transparent.

Perhaps he should ignore her. Philip took another look at his cravat. Avoiding Sorrel would, no doubt, convince her he was afraid or not up to the challenge of facing her. That would never do. If he could predict the direction from which her attack would come, he could at least anticipate her objections and thwart her efforts.

Philip studied his reflection. Brummel would have approved of the more subdued tones he'd chosen for that evening's meal—Philip's usual colorfulness had been the one point of fashion on which he and The Beau did not agree. Sorrel would certainly not find anything objectionable in his appearance.

He could think of a handful of ladies who would not only not object but would have positively fawned on him. That fawning had historically rendered him rather ill, though he always took pains to hide it. That night he might have preferred the simpering. He could have spent the evening spouting meaningless compliments and not worrying himself over the poisonous barbs sent his way.

Philip stopped mid-tug of his butter-colored waistcoat. Meaningless compliments. Flirtations. A mischievous smile spread across his smoothly shaven face. General Sorrel would *never* anticipate that strategy.

She had declared them enemies, predicted their endless brangles, pronounced herself prepared for battle. She would be anticipating an onslaught, an opponent. The she-warrior would get just that, but not in the way she anticipated.

Philip flirted masterfully. He knew how to compliment, how to offer sugary sentiments and bring a smile and a laugh to a lady's lips. He'd wager Sorrel would have no idea how to respond.

Lampton War Tactic Number Five: Always catch the enemy off guard.

Five

He wasn't coming down. Sorrel tried to hide a satisfied grin. Hancock the butler would be announcing the start of dinner, and the puffed-up Earl had yet to appear. She had, apparently, won the first battle. The realization came with a pang of disappointment. Sorrel had, in the short time she'd spent with the Earl, deemed him a worthy opponent, one not likely to turn tail and run.

She mentally shrugged. Yet another man who didn't act the way she expected him to.

Sorrel turned her attention to Lizzie, deep in animated conversation with her husband, Lord Henley. Lizzie had always been so full of life. How fortunate for her to find a husband who accepted that—he seemed to appreciate it, in fact.

Lord and Lady Cavratt chatted quite amicably with Lady Lampton. Lord Cavratt, Sorrel noted, held the bulk of the conversation. Lady Cavratt was, by all accounts, extremely shy. Society generally looked upon tongue-tying bashfulness as a nearly unacceptable flaw in a lady. Yet Lady Cavratt had married a man whose title rivaled almost every other of the Peerage in terms of antiquity and respectability. Lord Cavratt did not appear to merely tolerate his wife and her "shortcomings." He quite obviously adored her.

"Penny for your thoughts, Miss Kendrick," a deep voice whispered at her side, startling her half out of her wits, though Sorrel managed to hide all signs of surprise.

"For a shilling I might share them, my lord," Sorrel replied without so much as glancing at the Earl of Lampton. She'd have recognized his patronizing voice anywhere.

"Are your thoughts so valuable, then?" Sorrel heard him sit beside her.

"The value of any item depends on the amount one is willing to pay for it," Sorrel replied. At this, she did turn toward Lord Lampton, making her statement a challenge. What she expected to see, Sorrel couldn't say precisely, but his smooth smile and twinkling eyes took her by surprise.

Lord Lampton reached inside his perfectly tailored jacket and pulled a silver coin from his waistcoat pocket. He held it out in front of her between his thumb and forefinger. He raised an eyebrow then took hold of her hand resting on the arm of her chair. He turned her hand palm up and placed the shilling in its center.

"Now, what had so occupied your thoughts when I came upon you?" Lord Lampton asked. "You had not yet seen my Weston, so you certainly weren't pondering that piece of perfection."

So, he really was a dandy. The realization was unexpectedly disappointing. "I am still not pondering your attire, my lord."

"I have paid for your thoughts, I will remind you."

Sorrel smiled as innocuously as she could. "When you arrived I was pondering how I might cheat you out of a shilling." She held the silver coin up so Lord Lampton would be sure to see it then slipped it inside her left glove.

He laughed. "Touché, Miss Kendrick. Might I say, a shilling well spent."

"Next time I will have to charge a guinea."

"Next time I will know better than to offer payment for your thoughts," Lord Lampton countered, twirling his confounded quizzing glass on its ribbon. "Especially since I seriously doubt you answered honestly."

"You didn't indicate you were paying for an *honest* answer."

"I see I will have to be more specific in my requests," Lord Lampton said. "Now, it appears Lady Cavratt is coming to claim my arm for dinner, and I believe my brother Jason is come to claim yours. A word of advice, Miss Kendrick: do not bring up his aspiration to become a King's Counsel." Lord Lampton leaned closer to her, bringing with him a pleasing hint of cedar that Sorrel tried hard to ignore, and whispered, "A difficult topic."

Mr. Jason Jonquil appeared at Sorrel's side just as Lord Lampton rose. The eldest Jonquil offered Sorrel a bow and a smile, much to her confusion. Had he so quickly abandoned their feud? Did he fear going to battle and hope to broker a last-minute peace agreement? She'd settle for nothing short of surrender. Life had placed her at a perpetual disadvantage, forcing her to grasp at any victory she could claim.

Sorrel noted with a mixture of disappointment and satisfaction that she and Lord Lampton were seated at enough of a distance to make conversation between them all but impossible. There would be no battle over dinner. There would be plenty of time for armed conflict later, time for deflecting Lord Lampton's obvious attempts to outmaneuver her. If she knew Lord Lampton, and Sorrel felt she'd taken his measure pretty accurately, he had tried to steer her from a conversational topic sure to make the meal more enjoyable. Sorrel took advantage of a lull in conversation after the fish to address her dinner partner. She sincerely hoped Lord Lampton would overhear.

"I understand you have hopes of being a King's Counsel, Mr. Jonquil."

There seemed to be a synchronized intake of breath around the table. Sorrel glanced quickly about. Every member of the Jonquil family gazed, wide-eyed, in every conceivable direction except toward Mr. *Jason* Jonquil, who in the very next moment began a rather impassioned denunciation of those holding the very position he, supposedly, reached toward. As her dinner partner continued his criticism, Sorrel turned in near awe toward Lord Lampton.

The Earl raised his glass in her direction and, with a twitch of his very expressive right eyebrow, smiled rather triumphantly. He'd been honest about this touchy subject. He'd actually been offering helpful advice. He had to have known she would have assumed the opposite. Insufferable!

The rest of the meal proved less disastrous but no more successful. Mr. Corbin Jonquil proved quiet but cordial. Very little conversation originated with him. Sorrel tiptoed around topics with Mr. Jason Jonquil, uncertain what else might be a sore spot with the barrister.

By the time the ladies withdrew to the drawing room, Sorrel wished only to disappear into a corner for the remainder of the evening. She would not be so fortunate.

Lady Lampton crossed the drawing room to sit on the sofa directly beside Sorrel's chair. "I fear my family has not made the most favorable impression on you, Miss Kendrick. My son Jason is well suited to the law, being both astute and well spoken. But he is, I must confess, the least patient of my sons, which has made waiting for promotion to a King's Counsel rather hard for him to endure." She smiled so maternally that Sorrel couldn't help softening toward the woman, even if her eldest son was a rather trying individual.

"And then there is Philip." Lady Lampton hit on precisely the topic Sorrel did *not* want to discuss, or so she told herself. "Each of my sons has his own strengths and weaknesses. Philip's are one and the same." She seemed to sigh as if saddened for her son.

Sorrel didn't ask the obvious question but waited, quite intrigued.

"He is intelligent. Now before you argue"—Lady Lampton held up a staying hand and smiled knowingly—"as you undoubtedly have reason to, Philip has a quick intellect. It is that sharpness of mind that tends to get him into trouble. He cannot pass up an intellectual challenge, though that is not always the best way to make friends."

"Rather the opposite, it seems."

"Yes. Your war." Lady Lampton smiled at her. "Philip will take this seriously, you know."

"As will I."

Lady Lampton watched Sorrel rather closely. "You, too, have a sharp wit—I have seen evidence of it. I believe you and Philip have the potential to wreak havoc on one another."

"You believe I should back down?"

"Good gracious, no!" The countess looked shocked at the very idea. "As the only female in a household with eight males, I long ago became a rather vocal advocate of a woman holding her own." With her silver eyebrows raised and her mouth in the early stages of a grin, Lady Lampton looked positively mischievous.

"Have you come to plead for your son's welfare, then?" Sorrel asked, a smile spreading across her face.

"Precisely." Lady Lampton chuckled lightly.

Sorrel joined her laugh to Lady Lampton's. How she enjoyed a friendly companion—she'd seldom had an agreeable conversational partner in the past two years.

"Dare I beg a seat beside you lovely ladies?" Lord Lampton's arrival quickly dispelled Sorrel's lightened mood.

"Of course, dearest." Lady Lampton patted the sofa beside her. "The gentlemen certainly didn't linger over their port this evening."

"I could not resist the ever-increasing pull of the drawing room." Lord Lampton flashed a smile that Sorrel could only interpret as flirtatious. That made no sense. He couldn't have done so for the benefit of his mother. Yet he certainly would not flirt with his sworn enemy.

"Jason still appears a tad blue-deviled," Lady Lampton remarked, her gaze fixed across the room on the son in question.

"He muttered something about idiots being permitted to practice law as we left the dining room." Lord Lampton shrugged and smoothed the sleeve of his midnight-blue jacket. "So perhaps he is still obsessing over his unrealized ambitions. Although I am certain he is simply depressed because I refused to allow him use of my quizzing glass. I do not believe he has the self-possession to do it justice."

"If you and Miss Kendrick will excuse me, I will see what I can do for Jason before he infects the entire party with his gloomy mood." Lady Lampton rose from her seat, Lord Lampton standing as well.

"Perhaps you could promise him a quizzing glass for Christmas." Lord Lampton looked entirely serious. "But only if he is a very good boy and doesn't badger the bar with his disappointments."

Lady Lampton shook her head amusedly but otherwise ignored her eldest son's comment and crossed the room. Lord Lampton retook his seat at the end of the sofa closest to Sorrel.

"I feel I should tell you"—Lord Lampton addressed her with an even expression—"when conversing with Corbin it is best not to bring up Jolly Jaunt, a thoroughbred of his with which he is currently none too happy. Stanley"—he nodded toward the youngest Jonquil present—"does not appreciate discussing Orthez, having been injured during that battle. When Harold arrives from Cambridge, be advised he feels rather strongly about the excesses of society, having set his sights on the Church. Charlie, who will descend upon us from Eton at any moment, sorely dislikes his status as 'the baby' of the family."

Sorrel refused to look at him. Lord Lampton was obviously trying to further embarrass her. "There are certainly quite a few topics best avoided among the Jonquils."

"There are quite a few Jonquils," Lord Lampton said. "I imagine, though, every family has its sore spots and difficult memories."

"Some more than others."

"Indeed, some memories are more difficult than others. Mrs. Kendrick seemed quite intent this morning on avoiding a topic that seemed uncomfortable for her."

"My mother avoids all topics that are uncomfortable for her," Sorrel retorted. "In fact, she avoids people who make her feel the same way. My mother does not believe in being uncomfortable."

"She is a creature of comfort, then?"

"No more than some." She eyed Lord Lampton with an accusatory expression.

"You believe, then, I am overly concerned with my comforts."

"In my experience, most gentlemen are," Sorrel answered. "Especially those for whom shallower pursuits are paramount."

"Dandies, in other words."

"Dandies. Fops. Rakes. What are they but seekers of their own comfort?"

"Which of these less-than-dignified descriptions suits me best, Miss Kendrick? I should like to know your impression of me."

He wished for her opinion? How would he feel should she offer criticisms as biting as those he'd delivered? His precisely expressed opinion that a lady with a limp could not be considered beautiful still stung every time she recalled it.

"Only a dandy would sport an Oriental at a simple country dinner." She pointedly eyed his cravat, which had bothered her from the moment he'd made his appearance earlier in the evening. "Though your attachment to your quizzing glass tends to push you beyond dandified toward the foppish. As to your being a rake, I cannot say. Except that I seriously doubt Lord Cavratt would remain close friends with a dissolute gentleman. Whether he is simply deceived in your character remains to be seen. After all, he has maintained his connection to a gentleman who is, apparently, obsessed with his appearance and unnaturally attached to his affectations. That doesn't, precisely, reflect favorably on his taste in friends."

Lord Lampton's expression tightened, his lips setting into a firm line. For a moment he said nothing, and Sorrel began to feel uncomfortable. Her words had not been kind. She knew her tendency to speak bitingly when she felt vulnerable.

"It seems," he finally said, his tone almost cold, "I have made a very shrewd purchase, Miss Kendrick. For my shilling I have received a quid's worth of your thoughts."

"You did ask for my opinion, my lord," Sorrel replied.

"I had best request no further revelations from you. I fear I can ill afford the onslaught."

In one smooth movement, Lord Lampton reached his feet, offered a stiff bow, and walked away. Sorrel had the distinct impression she had offended the Earl. She had, perhaps, been blunter than the situation warranted. But a war of words did not abide inconsequential conversation.

Lord Lampton's dissatisfaction clearly represented little more than the sulking of the defeated. Sorrel would certainly have been declared the winner in this first battle despite her earlier blunderings. Yet watching him walk away, she did not feel triumphant.

Six

War is not for the feeble hearted.

Philip pushed Devil's Advocate harder, running neck-or-nothing across the snow-dusted hills of Kinnley. Nothing like an ice-cold wind biting at one's face to clear the head. Of course, a dandy would have objected to the destruction such an activity brought to one's coiffure. Fashion dictated one appear windswept, not actually *be* windswept.

Contrary to the declarations of General Sorrel, however, Philip was no dandy. Not truly. He certainly did not qualify as a creature of comfort.

The black gelding's breath came in visible puffs, its sides expanding with the effort of running so hard for so long. Philip brought the magnificent beast back to a trot and pulled his caped coat more closely around him.

The last evening's conversation still echoed in Philip's mind. A gentleman intent on nothing but his own enjoyment, she'd labeled him. *For you, shallower pursuits are paramount.* What did Miss Kendrick know of him? On what evidence did she base such outlandish evaluations, he would like to know.

Philip answered his own question. *Observation.* Outwardly he gave every indication of being a dandy. The carefully calculated ploy had reaped rewards but had come at a sacrifice, as well. No one really knew him. He couldn't allow them to.

Philip sighed, oblivious to his surroundings and hardly noting the cold. He'd rather not think of the years he'd spent under the

guise of a dandified fop nor the opportunities it had cost him. The loss would be worth it, he vowed, even if the likes of Sorrel Kendrick failed to understand.

She felt his friendship reflected badly on Crispin, which it didn't. At least he hoped it didn't. Crispin hadn't chosen to cut the connection despite five years of rather absurd behavior on Philip's part. There had always been loyalty between them. Hadn't he salvaged Crispin and Catherine's marriage when no one else had seemed able to—had even played a role in saving their lives? That had certainly not been the act of a man concerned solely with shallow pursuits.

Philip jerked the reins, and Devil's Advocate obeyed with agitation. At a more sedate pace than Philip would have preferred, but necessary if he were to regain his composure, he began returning to the house.

There were certainly any number of ladies who'd been unimpressed by him in the past, turned off by his seeming belief in the importance of appearance above nearly all else. And, he added with emphasis, there were quite a few who'd found him dashing and amusing and excellent company.

So why did General Sorrel's disapproval bother him so blasted much? The argumentative, sharp-tongued lady's opinion ought to have blown past him like the cold wind. Instead, it clung to him like a damp cloak.

Shallower pursuits? Seeking only his own comfort? What could be further from the truth? He acted as the head of a family, of an *enormous* family! What man with six younger siblings had time for selfish concerns?

He'd dropped the appropriate comments in the right ears to pave the way for Jason's career to progress as far as it had for one so young.

He had called in favors and seen a veritable parade of the most sought-after stallions make their way to Corbin's property in Nottinghamshire to ensure the success of that brother's lifelong ambition of breeding race horses.

Layton, the second oldest and the closest to Philip's age, weighed particularly heavy on Philip's mind. A mere five years earlier, Layton had been settled and happy with a prosperous future stretched out in front of him. Now? Philip let out a deep breath, clouding in the cold air in front of his face. He supported his brother the best he knew how, but Layton's troubles went too deep for Philip to alleviate. Lud, he wished he could.

Stanley worried Philip as well. No one knew the depth of sacrifice Philip had made from the time that army-mad brother had left to fight for his country. So desperate had he been to see the war end swiftly, before it claimed Stanley as it had so many other young men, that Philip had volunteered his services to the Foreign Office in the hope that he might help end the conflict. He'd given up years of his own life trying to help secure peace. For five years he'd daily dreaded hearing that his brother would not return home, that his own risks and efforts wouldn't be enough to bring Stanley home alive. The memory of that anguish still brought a sting to Philip's throat.

Would a true dandy worry so much? He doubted it.

His youngest brothers were still young, but Philip stood by them, supported them in their pursuits. He corresponded faithfully, staying abreast of their experiences and disappointments. He visited them regularly at school.

He was a good brother, by George! His family had their difficulties, but he would not abide a razor-tongued female faulting him for those struggles. Heaven knew he'd done all he could.

Kinnley loomed large in front of him without Philip having noted his approach, so lost he'd been in his own reflections. "Come," he instructed his obedient mount. "I think that is plenty of exercise for one morning."

He turned toward the stables in time to spy the retreating figure of his adversary slowly straggling toward the house. Had the general been for a ride? She wasn't dressed for it and looked far too pristinely put together to have been for a jaunt. As he approached, Philip thought he detected an uneasiness in her countenance.

Curious. What could be disturbing the unflappable Miss Kendrick? Perhaps her inaccurate portrayal of him from the evening before troubled her conscience. Not likely. She didn't seem the sort to be concerned over any wounds her words had inflicted.

Had he actually decided to flirt with her? Ha! He'd have likely had as much success, and enjoyment, snuggling up to a hedgehog.

After thoroughly brushing and rubbing down his faithful horse, Philip made his way to the house cold and hungry. Seeing Miss Kendrick at the breakfast table, he continued on undetected to his room without stopping to break his fast. He wasn't running away, he told himself sternly. He simply did not feel like brangling.

"A tray, my lord?" Wilson, his valet, asked after helping Philip from his riding coat.

Philip silently nodded his assent, and his man disappeared without another word. He tossed his loose cravat onto the bed and began fumbling with the top buttons of his lawn shirt. Next came the buttons at his wrists. Finally he pulled off his riding boots.

There. Philip breathed deeply. Much better. No immobilizing collars or heavy boots. He stood in his stockinged feet, his shirt loose and untucked.

A folded letter on his bedside table caught Philip's eye. It hadn't been there when he'd left for his ride that morning. He took it in his hand and spun it around. Philip knew the handwriting: Garner. This would be news from the Foreign Office.

He sat quickly in the ladder-back chair beside the spindle-legged writing desk beneath the long, western facing window and broke the seal.

Lampton,
Sorry you couldn't be in London just now.

Philip automatically decoded the message: the Foreign Office did not wish him to return to Town.

At a particular gathering not two days past, a splash was made by a much emulated gentleman.

The Foreign Office felt Le Fontaine would be at the coast soon.

There were but two persons present who could come close to matching him in appearance. He was unfortunate enough to have chosen the very event where those two distinguished gentlemen were previously engaged to be.

Garner would be joining him in Suffolk, possibly at Kinnley. It seemed Le Fontaine had likely chosen a nearby landing place.

The newcomer ought to have anticipated the presence of his competition, as the event has, in the past, been attended by those same gentlemen. All in attendance are still in an uproar.

Ipswich. They had nearly intercepted Le Fontaine in Ipswich before. The Foreign Office seemed anxious.

Philip walked to the fireplace and tossed the seemingly innocent missive inside, waiting to see that it disintegrated into cinders before walking back to the window.

Le Fontaine in Suffolk. Philip's heart pounded a little harder at the thought. Le Fontaine had eluded capture for years, but now he was nearby. Too nearby. Philip had never tailed the elusive French spy in such close proximity to his family.

"Your tray, my lord." Wilson set the food-laden tray on an end table. "Would you prefer to dress before or after you've broken your fast?"

"After, Wilson," Philip replied, wanting the comfort his current dishabille granted him. He would don his dandy costume soon enough. "After."

Philip rubbed his eyebrows with his thumb and forefinger. Nothing could be done until Garner arrived. There were some things that simply couldn't be communicated in writing, not even in code.

"Lud," Philip muttered. "Garner's right. I am too old for this."

Couldn't Le Fontaine have at least taken a break for the holiday? Didn't the man know Philip had enough to deal with already? He was in the midst of a war, for heaven's sake!

Lampton War Tactic Number Six: Females are, by default, the most dangerous of enemies, as evidenced by their tendency to declare war at the most inconvenient times.

He had an enemy somewhere along the coast, as well as one in that very house. Philip began to understand how Wellington felt.

First order of business: eat his breakfast. Then: a dandified transformation followed by a return to the domestic battlefront.

Lampton War Tactic Number Seven: War, like charity, begins at home.

After breakfast, Philip closeted himself in Crispin's vastly impressive library, pretending to read a recently published treatise on the famed Battle of Trafalgar. He was dressed to the nines and completely uncomfortable.

My mother does not believe in being uncomfortable. General Sorrel's declaration entered unbidden into his thoughts.

Philip shook his head in agitation. She would, no doubt, be surprised to learn that his persona often left him deucedly uncomfortable.

Setting aside the book he'd little more than glanced at, Philip made his way to a western window and gazed out over the formal knot garden that had been the pride and joy of the late Lady Cavratt. Winter had bared the bushes sitting beneath blankets of white snow, broken only by the precisely cleared paths.

A brisk walk in the winter sun would be just the thing to clear his mind, Philip mused. But dandies didn't get their boots muddied. Lud, he'd grown tired of the charade. Years of acting the fop were taking their toll. He reminded himself, for what felt like the hundredth time in recent months, that he had good reason for assuming the frustrating role he had.

Movement down one of the garden paths caught Philip's attention. Had someone actually braved the elements? Gone traipsing through the mud? A moment more of watching and the brave soul came into view.

Philip narrowed his eyes to be sure of what he saw. Then, in a moment of determination, he went for his overcoat. No amount of dandification could keep him from that garden.

Seven

Philip reached the garden more quickly than he would have thought possible considering the coldness of the air and the decidedly muddy state of the grounds—Wilson would likely tender his resignation when he caught sight of Philip's mud-caked Hessians. He'd simply have to explain to the man that such things happen in war.

He turned the first corner of the winter-stripped garden in time to hear a rather unladylike curse muttered in a decidedly feminine voice. So Sorrel not only fought like a soldier—she had the vocabulary of one. That ought to put to rest any worries he had of offending her sensibilities.

He rounded the next corner fully expecting to find his opponent ready for a brawl. Philip had not thought to find her standing stock still, leaning heavily on her cane, her gloved hand rubbing at her right hip. He could tell the instant she became aware of his presence. She rose up to her full height—an inkling of pain entered her expression that he vaguely remembered seeing before—and glared at him.

"Lord Lampton," she offered with cold civility.

"Miss Kendrick," Philip replied, matching her tone. "I see the cold has not kept you indoors as it has the rest of the party."

"I found myself in need of exercise."

"You are an advocate of exercise, then?" Philip tried to look his haughtiest, lest she think she'd gotten the upper hand with her underhanded comments the evening before.

Sorrel let out a small puff of air and shrugged dismissively. "I have little choice," she replied and resumed her slow, awkward walk.

"And how is it, Miss Kendrick, that you find yourself forced into exertion?" Philip easily caught up with her and curtailed his stride to match hers, swinging his quizzing glass as he sauntered.

"I have discovered in recent years that limps are rather like dogs, my lord," Sorrel answered. "If they aren't regularly walked, they tend to act up."

"So you are here at the behest of your limbs."

"My aching, throbbing, uncooperative limb, yes." Sorrel seemed to grimace but immediately recovered. "That and the fact that I cut quite a dash with this cane of mine."

Philip almost allowed a smile. He'd made similar inane comments thousands of times, though he always managed to keep all hints of bitterness out of his voice. Sorrel hadn't been able to. How was it possible that she could be so very frustrating and intriguing at once?

"I have to concede that you do have very good taste in canes," Philip said, indicating his own nearly identical one.

Sorrel looked at his cane and then into Philip's face, and, for a split second, he thought she would smile at him. She didn't.

Lampton War Tactic Number Eight: One must contemplate a new strategy when dealing with an enemy whose smile, or *almost smile,* throws off one's equilibrium, no matter how briefly.

Perhaps he needed to embrace anew his former strategy. Sorrel had nearly smiled at him. She'd been borderline friendly. Maybe flirtation would be the best tactic, after all. Let her stone-cold heart flutter a little—it would do her good. It would do *him* good. She'd be forced to reevaluate her hasty opinion of him, or at least her own superiority, if she found herself entranced by a dandy. Ha!

"I understand your brother will be joining our ranks soon." Philip dumped his cursed quizzing glass back in his waistcoat pocket and pursued an overtly friendly topic.

"He will be traveling with *your* brother, I believe," Sorrel said. "Though I do not believe they were well acquainted before the journey was arranged."

"Charlie is a good gun." Philip allowed himself to smile at the thought of his youngest brother. "He'll likely have your brother sworn to some mischief or another before their arrival."

A noise strangely like a feminine chuckle escaped seemingly without Sorrel's knowledge. She continued walking without acknowledging her strategic misstep—enjoying the company of the enemy was not a wise move. Philip reminded *himself* of that fact. Twice.

"One thing about your brother's arrival intrigues me, Miss Kendrick." Philip spoke as though they were the most unexceptional of companions with only friendly feelings between them.

Sorrel didn't ask the obvious question. So she wouldn't take the bait? Fine. He'd simply press on.

"You are named Sorrel. Your sister's full name, I seem to remember, is Marjoram. Both herbs, I believe."

"You have discovered our family secret, my lord," Sorrel answered dryly. "We are all of us named for herbs. My father"—Now why had that word brought bitterness into her voice again?—"decided that his children would be named for something useful in the hope that we would emulate our namesakes."

"Many parents name their children with just such an end in mind. Did your father's plan prove more successful than most?"

"Ironically, yes."

Why ironically? Philip wondered.

"Marjoram, the herb, is sweet, rather universally liked, and is soothing to even the most dyspeptic of individuals." Sorrel sighed rather wearily. "Marjoram, my sister, is exactly the same."

"And what of sorrel?"

"Sorrel is known for being bitter and astringent. I am sure you will find the name and the description rather fitting."

How did one respond to that? They continued in silence. Philip listened to the muffled sucking sound of Sorrel's heavy-laden cane being thrust in and out of the mud and searched for something more to say. He couldn't seem to bring himself around to flirting once more. Sorrel was supposed to be standoffish and contrary but seemed almost vulnerable in her self-castigation.

"Let me see if I can guess your brother's name." Philip assumed a very speculative look. "I've got it! Horseradish."

"Horseradish?"

"Knotweed, perhaps?"

"Really, my lord."

"Nutmeg? Peppermint? Poppy?"

"Why on earth would my brother be named Poppy?"

"You said your brother was also named for an herb. Though I believe a poppy is really a flower."

"Poppy?" Sorrel said with an amused tremor in her voice. "Poppy! He would be mortified."

Then, stopped still in her tracks, she laughed. A shoulder-shaking, grin-inducing laugh. Philip couldn't help joining her.

"Poppy wasn't right, then?" Philip pushed out amid his laughter.

Sorrel shook her head, her smile still brightening her face. Philip did his utmost not to notice her dimples. "Fennel. His name is Fennel."

"And does his name suit him?" Philip still hadn't wiped the smile from his face—he couldn't seem to manage.

"Fennel was once believed to improve one's sight, and my brother, I assure you, sees far more than one realizes—more than he ought to, in fact."

"A visionary?"

"An astute observer."

"Younger brothers do have a tendency to unearth secrets," Philip replied.

"You have so many younger brothers you must have no secrets left."

Referencing his brothers at first raised Philip's hackles—Sorrel had accused him of being an irresponsible brother—but her smile appeared so genuine, he couldn't help thinking she'd meant no affront.

"Not nearly as many secrets as I would have otherwise."

Their walk continued in companionable silence, Sorrel's expression oddly pleasant. Her cane continued poking holes in the soft soil, and her walk remained every bit as awkward as before, but she seemed more at ease.

His flirting tactic seemed to be working. Philip had to admit he wasn't actually flirting but simply having an unexceptional conversation, which made it all the more exceptional. He was casually conversing with the enemy. The enemy!

Lampton War Tactic Number Nine:

No tactic existed for the unexpected situation. He could think of no immediate explanation or safeguard.

The arrival of a liveried footman saved Philip the bother of examining his unexpected situation. The footman bowed and held a folded piece of paper out to Philip. He took it and waited until the servant had made his way from the garden before eyeing the missive.

The letter had no direction scrawled across the front, no seal along the back. It hadn't been posted. Only the name *Philip* graced the front of the page. He unfolded the note and read the few sentences inside.

Philip,
Charlie and Fennel Kendrick have just arrived. Your youngest brother seems quite anxious to see you. Let us hope he has not concocted another of his schemes.
Mater

"Well, Miss Kendrick, it appears our brothers have descended upon us from Eton." Philip refolded the note and slipped it in his coat pocket.

"Fennel?" An uncharacteristic eagerness entered Sorrel's eyes. Philip found the change strangely endearing. He hadn't yet seen Sorrel look pleasantly excited about anything. Was it possible there was a warm-hearted woman underneath the prickly exterior?

She spun around as if to head back toward the house. After a sudden, strange catch in her movement, Sorrel's right leg seemed to give out and she crumpled to the ground. Another expression with which she ought not to have been familiar slipped past her lips. She cast her cane to the ground in front of her in obvious frustration and remained half-sitting, half-sprawled, on the ground.

"Miss Kendrick." Philip squatted in front of her and held out his hand, an unspoken offer of assistance.

He expected some gratitude for his gesture. After their friendly chat, he assumed she'd smile the way she had before, dimples and all, and accept his offer. She didn't.

Sorrel looked from Philip's outstretched arm to his face, and her expression set in a scowl. As if Philip had never made his offer, Sorrel shifted very awkwardly forward, took hold of her cane, and struggled to her feet, all the while ignoring Philip's very existence.

"Do you think that was absolutely necessary, Miss Kendrick?" Philip asked after Sorrel had settled herself on her feet. "I assure you I am quite capable of assisting a young lady to her feet."

"And *I* am quite capable of getting to my own feet, Lord Lampton," she snapped back. Her jaw appeared to clench, her glove pulled tight around the obviously tensed hand gripping her cane.

"Are you always so stubborn?" Philip demanded.

"Are you always so condescending?" she shot back.

Well, General Sorrel had returned with a vengeance.

Lampton War Tactic Number Nine: Ignore the smile. The enemy is always the enemy.

* * *

"Sorrel!"

She recognized Fennel's voice immediately. Sorrel had hoped to change out of her now mud-stained coat or at least put more distance between herself and Lord Lampton, who would enter the house at any moment, before greeting her baby brother.

"You slipped?" Fennel eyed the enormous swath of mud across the side of Sorrel's coat. "Our traveling coach spent half the journey sliding all over the roads. Charlie pulled out a bag of marbles, and we spent the last hour or so wagering in which direction they'd roll."

"You wagered?" Sorrel asked in some alarm. She'd never known her brother to engage in anything remotely reckless.

Fennel grinned at her. "I have scandalized you, I see." He slipped an arm around her shoulder; despite his being her baby brother, at fifteen Fennel already surpassed her in height. "We staked only the distinction of guessing correctly. Half the time we both predicted the same direction so it hardly mattered."

"Yes. Well, Charlie *is* a great gun," Sorrel replied with a minute roll of her eyes.

Fennel laughed. "Where'd you learn cant like that?"

"Charlie's brother described him thus," Sorrel answered.

"Which brother?" Fennel asked with obvious amusement. "According to Charlie, he has several dozen."

From the doorway a familiar voice answered. "It often feels that way."

Sorrel stiffened, knowing Lord Lampton had entered behind her. Fennel turned back toward the new arrival but kept a supportive arm across Sorrel's shoulders, forcing her to turn as well.

"And which of the hundreds of Jonquils is this?" Fennel asked her with a smile.

"Fennel, this is the Earl of Lampton." Sorrel made the introduction but avoided Lord Lampton's gaze. "Lord Lampton, this is my brother, Fennel Kendrick."

Fennel extended his free hand and heartily shook Lord Lampton's. "Charlie speaks highly of you," he said. "Highly and often."

"There *is* a great deal to admire." Lord Lampton shrugged as if praise of himself were an everyday occurrence.

Sorrel bit back a sharp reply. Fennel laughed.

"You, my lord, are precisely as Charlie described."

"He mentioned my yellow waistcoat?" Lord Lampton tugged at the aforementioned article of clothing.

Fennel laughed once more. *Why,* Sorrel wondered, *does he find Lord Lampton so amusing?*

"Charlie's been anxious to see you, Lord Lampton," Fennel said through his remaining chuckles. "He and Lady Lampton were on their way to the west sitting room, I think they said."

"Thank you very much, Poppy," Lord Lampton said, offering a quick bow and beginning to walk past them.

"Poppy?" Fennel repeated, still smiling as broadly as before.

"Your sister"—Lord Lampton inclined his head toward Sorrel—"told me your name was Poppy."

"I did not," Sorrel hotly replied.

"I am quite certain she did," Lord Lampton said. "I tried to tell her that no self-respecting young man would appreciate such a pet name being generally known."

"What a load of rubbish," Sorrel grumbled.

"Perhaps, Miss Kendrick, you may add my tendency to tell a good tale to my otherwise humble list of affectations." Lord Lampton winked at her and continued his exit.

Fennel chuckled. "Charlie said his oldest brother always says the most absurd things. He said the Earl is a good enough actor to grace Drury Lane if he wanted to."

"Actor?" Sorrel asked, a little intrigued. "Do the Jonquils play a lot of charades, then?"

"I don't know," Fennel replied, walking toward the wide, wooden stairway with his arm firmly clasped around Sorrel's shoulder. "Charlie just said his brother Philip is a good actor. I will confess I wanted to meet him just to figure out what Charlie meant."

"I'd like to know that myself," Sorrel mumbled.

"Now, which way to your room?" Fennel asked as they climbed more stairs. "I am certain you wish to change."

"Another flight, I am afraid," Sorrel said. "Then down the corridor to the left."

Her hip ached horribly by the time they completed the climb. She had twisted or at least bruised it in that embarrassing fall in the garden. Why couldn't Lord Lampton have stayed inside like any normal person? She'd gone out in the morning hoping the rest of the household would stay in until the weather warmed a bit. She'd hoped to work out the kinks in her joint without anyone witnessing such obvious evidence of the state in which life had put her.

"Any idea where I am being deposited?" Fennel asked as they neared the door of Sorrel's room.

"You've been given a few options, I believe. There is a room in this wing where Mother and Marjie and I are staying. Or you can choose a room one floor down in the same wing as the Jonquils. I think Lady Cavratt thought you would enjoy some male company."

Fennel silently walked Sorrel to the powder blue settee and stood nearby until Sorrel had managed to lower herself onto it. He then strode with all the self-assurance of a fifteen-year-old to the bell pull beside the mantel and gave it a tug.

"You should go have some tea," Sorrel said. "I am certain you must be famished."

Fennel laughed. "I am always famished."

"I know."

"So good to see you again, Sorrel." Fennel smiled sincerely. He waved before disappearing through the door.

Sorrel let out a deep, tired breath. She missed Fennel when he was away at school. He alone chose to neither avoid her entirely nor treat her like a useless child. Fennel treated her just the way he always had, except that he became a bit more solicitous when he thought it necessary. He had kept his arm around her shoulder to help her up the stairs when her hip gave her trouble or stayed nearby as she struggled to sit down. He helped but never forced that assistance on her.

Why couldn't more people be like Fennel?

"'Ow was yer walk, Miss Sorrel?" Jenny, her abigail, asked, entering into the room. "Feelin' any better?"

"I accomplished nothing except falling on my backside." Sorrel rubbed her aching hip.

"An' I am that sorry 'bout it, too, miss." Jenny smiled. "How's about a nice warm bath?"

"That would be wonderful, Jenny."

Twenty minutes later, soaking in a tub of refreshingly warm water, hair pinned up to keep it dry, Sorrel closed her eyes and tried to calm her weary mind. Why did nothing in life unfold the way it ought?

She and Lizzie had spoken again and again during that Season long ago in London about the lives they intended to lead, the desperate love they meant to inspire in the hearts of their future husbands, the envy such devotion from two top-of-the-trees gentlemen would inflict upon the other young ladies of the *ton*. Sorrel had before dreamed only of a happy life with an agreeable gentleman. Lizzie had inspired her to new heights during those months of fast friendship.

Now Lizzie lived those very dreams. And Sorrel? Sorrel had learned quite quickly not to dream.

She shifted in the fast-cooling water, her hip aching as much as ever. She'd have to end her bath soon—tepid waters seemed to make the stiffness more profound.

For not the first time, Sorrel contemplated settling in Bath, where warm waters and a bevy of physicians could surely render her life a little less miserable. The average age in Bath must have been nearly seventy. Had she disintegrated so very much? Her future reduced to a lifetime of socializing with people fifty years her senior?

Sorrel clenched her jaw against a sudden rush of emotion. Why must life be so exceedingly unfair? Once she'd been hopeful, optimistic. Hard experience, however, had taught her that dreams, especially dreams of happiness, did not come true. Not for her.

Eight

Philip had watched Fennel Kendrick's attentions to Sorrel with a great deal of approval. Sorrel was all prickles and spines where everyone else was concerned. Yet young Mr. Kendrick had stood with an affectionate arm around his sister's shoulder for the course of an entire conversation.

Philip had but offered his hand to help her up from the muddy ground in the gardens, and she'd rebuffed *him* as though he'd offered her maggoty mutton.

He didn't think young Kendrick's attentions were more acceptable simply because they had come from a relative. Sorrel had waved off Miss Marjie's concerns on more than one occasion.

What had Sorrel said about her brother? He saw "far more than one realizes." So what did Fennel "see" that afforded him such geniality with his sister?

Suddenly realizing the direction of his thoughts, Philip shook himself and turned his attention back to his tea. Of what possible benefit could it serve to know how Fennel had gained his sister's trust? Philip had no desire to be counted among Sorrel's friends. Did he?

"Fennel," Charlie called out enthusiastically. Philip looked up to watch the youngest Kendrick enter the room as Charlie continued. "Come have a sandwich. Lord Cavratt's cook sent them up special for the weary travelers." He finished with a chuckle and a feigned look of suffering.

Mater laughed lightheartedly as she always did when Charlie acted theatrical.

"Did you find your beloved sister?" Charlie asked Fennel between mouthfuls with a smile that said they had discussed the Kendricks during their journey.

"I did," Fennel said.

"And had she fallen ill as you had feared?"

Fennel shook his head and smiled. "She had, in fact, fallen. But not ill. Sorrel emerged from the out of doors decidedly muddy."

Fennel and Charlie laughed, and Philip found himself chuckling along with them. His reaction seemed to catch Fennel's attention, as the young man chose a seat near Philip.

"My sister did not actually tell you my name was Poppy, did she?" Fennel smiled broadly over his cup of tea.

"She did not."

"You were teasing her, then?"

"I suppose."

"I am glad of it," Fennel said, his expression sobering somewhat. "Sorrel needs teasing. She needs someone who does not think she is . . . fragile."

"Fragile?" Philip sputtered. "Your sister is about as fragile as the foundations of this very house. I doubt I have ever met a female less fragile than Miss Kendrick."

Fennel's expression grew far too insightful for a fifteen-year-old. "May I trust you to be honest with me, Lord Lampton?"

"Of course."

"Do you think my sister is . . . contentious?"

"Contentious?"

"Unapproachable? Unfeeling, perhaps?"

"I . . ." Philip hesitated. An honest answer would require a great deal of tact. "Miss Kendrick is far from *un*feeling. She seems to have little trouble communicating her feelings. In my experience, those feelings are not overly tender nor gentle."

Fennel sobered further at the description, and Philip wondered for a moment if he had offended the lad. "She was not always that way, my lord," he said rather regretfully. "I don't mean to imply that she ever simpered or anything, but she was not so . . . bitter."

Philip shifted awkwardly in his seat. Such private information was seldom imparted to strangers.

"I am grateful you and she have formed some sort of friendship." Fennel took a generous bite of his sandwich. "She would strangle me for saying so," Fennel said after swallowing, "but Sorrel is in desperate need of a friend. One who does not think of her as an invalid."

The invalid did not make an appearance downstairs until dinner. Her absence had given Philip the opportunity to ponder Fennel's intriguing evaluation of his sister's situation. Fennel described his sister in terms that sounded lonely and vulnerable. General Sorrel? Vulnerable? Perhaps brotherly affection had tinted Fennel's vision of her.

The wilting flower arrived for the evening meal every bit as standoffish as she'd ever been. She remained polite but withdrawn amongst the company in general. For Philip she hardly spared a glance. If he didn't know better, Philip would think he had offended her. That hardly seemed likely. They hadn't spoken more than a handful of words, and he'd said nothing provoking.

"Friends," Crispin's voice carried across the drawing room. "My wife has agreed to indulge her poor-mannered husband and grant a particular request of mine."

Philip felt a smile sneak across his face. What was Crispin up to?

"I have never been one for the strictures of society when among friends and family," Crispin went on.

That was doing it a bit brown, Philip thought. Crispin usually held rigorously to the rules of society. It had always seemed to Philip something of a defensive mechanism.

"So, rather than insist we proceed to our meal according to rank and other such nonsense, I would invite you to simply choose a partner and proceed."

A general murmur of approval passed through the room. Philip kept his gaze on Crispin and Catherine. No sooner had the announcement been made than Catherine, cheeks flushed, offered what appeared to be a thank-you to her husband. Not one to let curiosity go unacknowledged, Philip made his way to where the host couple stood.

"Bad form, Crispin," Philip said with a drawl. "If you had wanted to accompany your wife rather than force her to hang on my arm, I would have gladly obliged you."

Catherine blushed more deeply and Crispin chuckled. "I *was* rather desperate to have Catherine sit beside me."

"You've been married more than two months," Philip pretended to scold. "Certainly you've grown weary of each other's company by now."

"Not remotely," Crispin answered and kissed Catherine's hand, causing her cheeks to burn crimson.

Philip chuckled as he bowed and turned back to the room in general to claim a companion for supper. Stanley, as always, had sought Miss Marjie Kendrick's company. Jason was deep in conversation with Mater. Corbin, he could see, seemed headed in Sorrel's direction.

A strange desire to land his brother a facer suddenly seized Philip. Unable to make sense of the sensation, Philip did his best to dismiss it as he hurried across the room. "Miss Kendrick." Philip dipped his head to her. "Might I accompany you in to supper?"

She simply stared back, her eyebrows snapped in concentration as though his words made no sense.

"I promise not to offer to assist you in any way," Philip replied dryly.

Any other woman would have laughed at the witty rejoinder, or at least have taken offense at a perceived slight. Sorrel seemed almost relieved by it, and, as though that were the only situation under which she would have done so, she accepted his offered hand. He quite suddenly became aware of the fact that Sorrel smelled of limes. *The crisp, slightly tart scent matches her quite well,* he thought. *Nothing overly sweet or soft for a warrior!*

"Mr. Kendrick," Philip heard Charlie spout in an exaggeratedly deferential tone. Philip turned to see Charlie bowing deeply beside Fennel. "Would you walk in to dinner beside me. It seems there are no ladies for the Nursery Set."

"Of course, my good man." Fennel bowed back, equally overdone.

The two walked from the room with an air of self-importance that would have put Brummel to shame. Philip offered his arm to Sorrel and caught the last remnants of a smile on her face.

"Charlie and Fennel seem to have become fast friends," Philip observed. "Neither should be lonely during the holiday."

"I should hope not." Sorrel's expression turned suddenly somber. "I would not wish loneliness on my worst enemy."

She did not speak another full sentence for the remainder of the evening. Her reticence held through the next day, and the day after that.

Philip decided Sorrel's lack of conversation did not indicate that he had come out victorious in their battle. Rather, he felt certain she was either avoiding him or was upset. He found, to his surprise, that both possibilities bothered him.

* * *

She wasn't avoiding him nor was she upset. Sorrel told herself so for the hundredth time, it seemed, four days after her ill-timed fall in the gardens. She simply didn't like the man. Philip Jonquil was arrogant. And vain. Self-absorbed. Shallow. Handsome.

Sorrel admitted the last fact with a sigh of resignation. How could a woman *not* notice hair the color of gold, eyes the color of a summer sky, and a tall, lean form? Of course, he was also a dandy of the worst sort. The man had worn a teal jacket and deep orange waistcoat to supper the night before. Who *thinks* of such a combination let alone *wears* it?

She let out a breath, which instantly condensed in the air before her, and continued her slow, lopsided walk to the stables.

She had come to the stables every morning since arriving at Kinnley a week earlier. Each day she ventured further inside. Lady Cavratt, who had asked Sorrel to call her Catherine, had offered Sorrel the use of her mare, Fairy Cake, whenever she liked. Sorrel had thanked her but had yet to ride.

Fennel had come upon her only the morning before as she stood gazing at the bay-colored mare. A magnificent-looking animal. At least fifteen hands high. Sleek. Young. Undoubtedly a fine galloper. Sorrel's heart raced in excitement every time she came to watch the horse.

"She'd give you a good bruising ride," Fennel had said, startling Sorrel.

"That is precisely what I am afraid of," Sorrel had replied. "I am bruised enough as it is."

"Still smarting from your slip the other day?"

Sorrel didn't reply. She smarted, all right. Her hip hurt. Her backside hurt. Neither, however, had suffered as acutely as her pride. How she loathed looking incompetent!

"You really should consider trotting out on Lady Cavratt's mount," Fennel encouraged. "It has been far too long since you rode."

"I do not want to ride, Fennel."

"Then you come out here for the witty conversation?" Fennel motioned at the stalls of horses.

"Fennel."

"The mare's bound to be a good trotter. Probably a smashing good galloper, too."

"Watch your language, Fennel."

"This coming from a lady who can swear like a sailor." Fennel raised his eyebrow knowingly.

"Yet another reason to spend less time in the stables," Sorrel replied and made her way back toward the house.

"You didn't used to be a coward, Sorrel." Fennel's voice carried from the stable door.

Sorrel stopped in her tracks: The disappointment in Fennel's tone cut her to the core. Her brother didn't say anything else. Eventually they parted in silence.

Those words echoing in her memory, Sorrel watched the bay mare with a touch of anxious excitement. Sorrel wore Marjie's pale blue riding habit. Pastels did nothing for her complexion. Between the two of them, Marjie had the beauty. She also had the kind, affectionate nature.

Sorrel, on the other hand, had always been the strong one, the brave and daring one. That made Fennel's declaration hurt more.

She had never been a coward. Dressing that morning, Sorrel had vehemently told herself that she hadn't lost that distinction. Standing in the stables, though, Sorrel felt like a lily-livered weakling. Fairy Cake made her a touch nervous, but the animal corralled a few stalls down positively terrified her. She hadn't seen that particular horse in the Kinnley stables before.

The black gelding stomped and jerked impatiently. Its ears twitched and nostrils flared. A white star, perfectly symmetrical and centered on its sleek nose, broke the blackness of its coat. If not for that star, Sorrel would have run, to the degree she could run, straight back into the house and would have given up for good. She'd done little more than stare for fifteen minutes.

"We'd almost given you up, m'lord," a groom's voice called out from the far end of the stable.

"Was deucedly cold yesterday morning. I thought today I'd set out later and see if I can return without my rump frozen to the saddle."

Sorrel recognized Lord Lampton's voice and felt her jaw tighten. What disparaging remark would he produce that morning? Not that she couldn't offer a resounding set down of her own. She simply had enough on her platter at the moment without adding his acidic comments.

"'ll you be wantin' ta saddle Devil's Advocate yerself, m'lord?"

"As always."

Sorrel had a difficult time imagining the lazy Earl doing any kind of manual labor, even something as trivial as saddling his own horse. Yet it seemed he did so regularly.

The next moment Lord Lampton, impressive in a dark-green riding coat, strode into sight. He took almost immediate note of Sorrel's presence, though he did not appear surprised.

"Miss Kendrick." He offered a bow.

"Lord Lampton." An awkward curtsy.

"You appear to have decided to ride today." Lampton's gaze swept over her, making Sorrel every bit as nervous as the black gelding nickering loudly nearby.

"I am still in contemplation," Sorrel countered.

Lord Lampton's eyes seemed to narrow as if he were assessing her.

"Shall I saddle up Fairy Cake fer ya, Miss Kendrick?" the groom who'd followed Lord Lampton offered. "Lady Cavratt gave strict orders ta letcha ride iffen ya ever got the inklin'."

"I . . . uh . . ." Sorrel hadn't anticipated retaking a saddle in front of an audience, least of all the overly critical Earl of Lampton: as if the man hadn't seen her physically defeated already. "Perhaps another day."

"Actually, Sam," Lord Lampton stopped the groom. "Saddle up Fairy Cake. I have a feeling Miss Kendrick will mount yet."

"I do not see how that is any concern of yours," Sorrel snapped, shifting her weight and grasping her cane tighter. She'd been standing in one place too long and her joints were objecting.

"It probably isn't," Lord Lampton replied, stepping confidently into the stall of the midnight-black gelding, rubbing its nose and murmuring soothingly to it.

Sorrel's breath came a little faster, and her heart pounded at the sight of anyone standing near the overpowering animal. The memory of a black, four-legged form stomping and jerking, its rage-filled eyes rolling back into its black head, came unbidden into her thoughts. She did her best to shake the memory out. Sorrel swiped at a trickle of sweat suddenly running down her forehead.

The sound of horse teeth grinding hay grew to an unnatural volume; her nose seemed to imagine anew the pungent smell of a stable hand Sorrel hadn't seen in years. She could feel nonexistent fog, could conjure up the taste of air thick with the threat of rain. Voices shouted frantically. The earth shook with the sporadic pounding of hooves. Sorrel wiped at more perspiration, trying to rid her mind of that day, those memories.

"All ready iffen you've decided to ride, Miss Kendrick," Sam said.

"I don't—"

"Come, Miss Kendrick," Lord Lampton added his voice. "Since when do you back down from a challenge?"

Sorrel clenched her hands in indignation. To make her hesitancy sound like mere sheepishness! To reduce years of suffering to "a challenge"! Well, she certainly did not need Lord Lampton's high-in-the-instep evaluations of her character to make her decisions for her. Sorrel would ride if she chose to or decline if it suited her. At the moment, she far favored declining.

Sam led out the very docile mare. Sorrel found herself wavering. The mount seemed gentle enough. The only docile horses at Kendrick Hall were the ponies, and Sorrel refused to lower herself to that level. To ride such a magnificent and suitable animal would be . . . wonderful. Wonderful and terrifying.

"You can always keep to the stable yard, Miss Kendrick. Practice your figure eights and what." Did she hear a hint of condescension in Lord Lampton's tone?

"I have not limited myself to a stable yard since I was five years old," she corrected him none too gently.

He produced a look of obviously feigned contrition. "Forgive my inaccurate evaluation, then. I suppose I mistook you for a novice."

"On what grounds, I would like to know," Sorrel demanded, following Sam and Fairy Cake into the stable yard.

"No true horsewoman would turn down the opportunity to ride such a remarkable piece of horseflesh." Lord Lampton led his own sleek, black mount into the yard. "Crispin purchased her for his lovely bride at quite a substantial sum, and well worth every pound. You would be hard pressed to find Fairy Cake's equal."

"If I had not found the mare impressive, my lord, I would not have returned after my first encounter." The nerve of Lord Lampton assuming she knew nothing about horseflesh.

"The horse is not objectionable. The company certainly cannot be." Lord Lampton offered a ridiculously self-assured smile. "The weather is holding. The roads are drier than they have been all week. I cannot see a single objection."

Sorrel could think of several, but none she would admit to. Before she had a chance to object, a second groom had arrived with a mounting block, and she was being assisted into her saddle.

For the briefest of moments, Sorrel thought she might faint—she who abhorred fits of the vapors and women who indulged in them. The mare shifted beneath her. Sorrel held her breath.

"You are making her nervous," Lord Lampton said. He watched her from astride his own intimidating mount.

"She is making *me* nervous," Sorrel countered, trying to accustom herself once more to the feel of a sidesaddle. It felt more awkward than she remembered, more uncomfortable, more uneven. Perhaps *she* had grown more awkward, uncomfortable, and uneven.

"So, to the back meadows or to the seaside?" Lord Lampton asked, barely managing to keep his anxious horse from carrying him away.

"I have no need of your supervision," Sorrel said as confidently as she could manage.

"You forget, Miss Kendrick," Lord Lampton replied, tall and confident in the saddle. "We are at war, you and I. One should always keep an eye on the enemy."

"That is your war tactic, then?"

"One of several." Why did Lord Lampton seem to hide a smile at that admission? "The meadows or the seaside?"

Sorrel watched her foe for a moment, wondering if this were some strange attempt to befuddle her or see her disgrace herself once more. Perhaps Lord Lampton really did not believe she was much of an equestrian. She had her own doubts. There had been a time . . .

Lord Lampton continued to watch her with the patience of a saint. Somehow Sorrel would not have believed patience to be one of his strong points.

"I was born and raised in Kent, Lord Lampton. At the seaside. I confess I thoroughly enjoy the sounds of the tide."

"The seaside it is, then."

Nine

Lord Lampton guided his mount out of the stable yard, and Sorrel urged Fairy Cake to follow. The first few moments of movement were difficult, to say the least. She adjusted as well as she could to the gait of the horse, trying to negotiate her balance. Her right leg, wrapped around the pommel of the sidesaddle, ached from the awkward position. Her right hip sharply protested the effort needed to maintain a proper riding posture. Perhaps this hadn't been such a good idea, after all.

"There is a very direct route to the sea," Lord Lampton said, having slowed his mount to allow Sorrel to catch up. "But the view from the east end of the Cavratt holdings is far superior."

Sorrel began to seriously doubt her stamina. They'd gone only a few yards. She felt every bounce and jar.

"Of course if you cannot keep up . . ." Lord Lampton gave her a smile of challenge. He tipped his head in her direction, threatening to set his already jaunty beaver at an almost absurd angle.

"You continue to question my equestrian skills?"

"Simply giving you the opportunity to retreat."

"I never retreat."

Why did Lord Lampton look as though he doubted her declaration? She, of course, couldn't care less about the Earl's opinion of her. And yet she couldn't let the slight pass. She had at one time been regarded as having as good a seat as any man of her acquaintance. Lord Lampton thought her unequal to a short ride?

A few colorful words from her infamous vocabulary came to mind. She refused to give the Earl the satisfaction of thinking he had the upper hand.

Lord Lampton kept his obviously anxious animal at a sedate trot. Sorrel thought she knew how the gelding felt, wanting to push beyond the bounds dictated to it but unable to do so.

"I do not believe your horse enjoys trotting," Sorrel observed after a few minutes of silence between herself and her riding partner.

"Devil's Advocate hasn't a mild bone in his body." Lord Lampton patted the neck of the thoroughly bored horse.

"I have never encountered so many oddly named horses as I have here at Kinnley." Sorrel tried to sound lighthearted despite the pounding in her hip.

"Like Fairy Cake, am I correct?" Lord Lampton remained even with her. "That, I believe, is some kind of private joke between Lord and Lady Cavratt."

"And why did you choose the name Devil's Advocate?"

"There were a couple of reasons."

He flashed a smile different from his usual one. It did not drip with vanity or egotism but rather communicated amusement, ease, even apparent humility. Sorrel couldn't help herself; for some reason she refused to dwell on, she quite suddenly wanted to hear the reasons behind the name.

"For one thing, he is the most contrary, disobliging creature in all of creation." Lord Lampton laughed.

"Strange. I thought *you* were the most contrary, disobliging creature in all of creation." Now why had she said that? Why did Lord Lampton seem to force the most spiteful words from her?

"I am a very close second, I assure you," came the laughing response. "Perhaps that is why Devil's Advocate and I get along so famously."

"Undoubtedly." Sorrel shook her head the moment the word passed her lips. Why did he bring out this side of her?

Lord Lampton simply chuckled amusedly, looking as confident and self-assured as ever atop his graceful mount. "He takes it upon himself to question every direction I give him. So, you see, he lives up to his name."

"He could be a Kendrick, then. We all live up to our names." Sorrel thought she sounded less like a spiteful spinster than usual. A hint of amusement even colored her tone.

"What do you think, old man?" Lord Lampton leaned closer to the horse's head. "Would you like to be a Kendrick?"

The horse flicked his head and nickered.

"Settled!" Lord Lampton chuckled. "I shall send you to Kent at the first opportunity," to which the horse responded by leaping; its back arched. Lord Lampton seemed unconcerned with the show of impatience. Sorrel, however, pulled Fairy Cake to an abrupt and complete stop, watching the flailing black gelding with growing discomfort.

"No one will ever take you if you act like that, you great beast." Lord Lampton cheerfully chastised the horse. "It is no wonder your sire is unwelcome in so many places. You're both too hotblooded by half."

His words more or less flooded over Sorrel, not sinking in or impacting her. She simply watched the horse, convinced it would never settle down—Lord Lampton would never get it under control. She vaguely noted that her head hurt—it had ached for a day or so but had grown more pronounced. Her right leg throbbed horribly from hip to ankle.

Sorrel tore her gaze away from the now trotting horse beside her and tried to focus on the road ahead.

"Where in Kent do you reside, Miss Kendrick?" Perhaps the aching in her head had played a trick on her—Lord Lampton's question sounded almost friendly.

"The nearest town of any note is Dover," Sorrel replied rather mechanically—her brain seemed to be dozing off, rendering her thoughts unclear.

"I have been to Dover many times," Lord Lampton said. "A beautiful area of the country."

Sorrel replied with a nod.

"And you have lived there all your life?"

Another nod. Blast, her leg hurt!

"Are you unwell, Miss Kendrick?" Lord Lampton asked. "You do not seem quite yourself."

"I am fine." Did he notice the grimace she had desperately fought to hide?

"Now it is your turn to pry into the details of my life." Lord Lampton's teasing tone seemed a bit forced. "I assure you it is best to know as much about one's enemy as possible."

"Another war tactic, no doubt."

"You have no idea the extent of my war tactics." A self-effacing chuckle accompanied his words.

"Your brother, Jason, tells me the Jonquils hail from Nottinghamshire." That simple sentence had taken far more effort than Sorrel would have guessed. She tried to covertly rub her right hip in a vain attempt to soothe it.

"The closest thing we have at Lampton Park to a seaside is the banks of the Trent," Lord Lampton replied amusedly. "That quite often proved a battlefield as much as the Continent has at times. With seven of us, and all boys, there were plenty of wars reenacted at the Park over the years."

Sorrel smiled. She and Fennel had staged a few reenactments of their own. She had always regretted, for Fennel's sake, that there were no other brothers in the family. Sorrel had, in many ways, been as much an older brother to him as an older sister. She had taught him to ride and fence and climb trees. How she missed those days!

"You seem to have had a very happy childhood." She tried to ignore the pounding in her head.

"My parents doted on one another and on all of their children," Lord Lampton said. "It was a rather picturesque upbringing, I suppose."

"Must have been wonderful." Sorrel wasn't entirely sure she'd kept the remark to herself. If she had spoken aloud, she sincerely hoped she'd kept the wistful tone out of her voice.

"There are days when I would gladly go back to romping around the grounds. Back when life was simpler and all my brothers were happy and carefree."

"Are they so unhappy?" Sorrel asked. She continued rubbing at her almost unbearably painful leg.

Lord Lampton shrugged. "Probably no more so than most people." His nonchalant mannerisms and tone were underscored by a look of concern that flitted momentarily across his face.

Sorrel tried to shrug off the look. She'd come to think of Lord Lampton as a self-absorbed fop and didn't feel ready to reevaluate that opinion, especially with her head throbbing and her vision spinning.

They continued riding without speaking. If the silence bothered Lord Lampton, Sorrel didn't notice. Perhaps she simply wasn't paying enough attention. Staying mounted required all her concentration.

Despite the late December weather, Sorrel felt clammy. She was in pain and dizzy and had begun to shake. What was wrong with her? Being on horseback wasn't as unnerving as she'd expected it to be, and yet she was falling apart.

Lord Lampton said something beside her, but Sorrel couldn't make sense of the mumbled noise. She put a hand to her temple, attempting to hold her head still. The landscape around her swayed so much her head had to be swaying as well. Why in heaven's name couldn't she focus on anything?

Sorrel thought she heard Lord Lampton's voice again, though farther off. Blast the man! Had he gone on without her? Not that she cared. She just . . . just . . .

Unable to put together a coherent thought, Sorrel tried to say something, call out for help, as she felt herself falling.

Ten

"Sorrel!"

She was falling off her horse!

He tried again. "Sorrel!" She didn't reply, didn't acknowledge he'd spoken despite having used her Christian name. If she were as fine as she'd earlier claimed, General Sorrel would have given him a stinging set-down.

Having dismounted and wrapped the reins of Devil's Advocate around an obliging tree limb, Philip rushed to where Sorrel swayed in her saddle and plucked her off Fairy Cake's back. Disturbed by how light and fragile she felt, Philip attempted to set her on her feet, but she seemed entirely unable to stand.

Doing the only thing he could think of, Philip swept her into his arms and carried her to the base of a tree and set her gently on the ground. She seemed completely unaware of everything around her.

"Sorrel," Philip said firmly, looking into her glazed eyes with alarm. "I am taking unforgivable liberties with your name. Aren't you going to snap at me? Tell me I am a presumptuous lout?"

Her brows knit in obvious pain. Each breath came out ragged and labored. The color had all but drained from her face. Her nearly colorless lips twitched a moment. In a voice no more than a whisper, she quite unexpectedly pleaded with him, "Help me, Philip. Please."

For a moment he froze. What had happened to the warrior he'd been brangling with for a week? She had no right to be

vulnerable and broken! He found to his further confusion that her razor-sharp tongue could utter his name in a way that tugged at his very heart.

"Please." Her voice had grown even quieter.

Sweat beaded on Sorrel's forehead. Sweat? Outside in December? He placed a hand cautiously to her forehead then shifted it to her cheek. She was burning up.

"Blast you, Sorrel," Philip grumbled. "You told me you were fine."

"Leg."

"What the devil kind of response is that?" His mind spun, trying to decide how to get Sorrel back to the house as quickly as possible.

"Leg."

"If you are trying to secure a victory by completely confusing your enemy, congratulations. You win." Philip worked at unbuttoning his overcoat. Sorrel, in the midst of her incoherent mutterings, was shivering. "Although I think contracting a fever is a rather underhanded strategy."

Philip draped his coat over her, feeling the cold almost immediately. Now, how in heaven's name ought he to get her back? They'd gone too far to carry her himself. In her condition, Sorrel would never stay mounted.

"Did anyone ever tell you that you are a great deal of trouble?"

Sorrel nodded.

"And I will have you know I am no hero," Philip told her.

He wiped a trickle of sweat from Sorrel's eyebrow. What had he gotten himself into? The house could only be reached on horseback. Sorrel would not stay mounted for more than a moment unless she rode back with him. Philip knew instinctively that offering such monumental assistance to his prickly adversary was tantamount to laying his head under the guillotine blade. Once Sorrel came to her senses, she'd slaughter him.

"Don't you know dandies are never intrepid?" He brushed a stray strand of obsidian black hair from her tightly closed eyes.

After pulling his coat more snugly around Sorrel's shoulders, Philip tied Fairy Cake's reins to the pommel of his saddle. Devil's Advocate was being unusually docile. Now would be the best time to mount.

Philip knelt beside Sorrel once more. "Sorrel." He touched her face—something he found he enjoyed more than he ought. "You are going to have to help me with this."

Her eyes fluttered open. She watched him with an intensity he hadn't anticipated. The obvious pain in her eyes made Philip question her lucidity.

"Come on, then." Philip lifted her from the ground, still startled at her frailty. Somehow he'd pictured his adversary as something of an Amazon: sturdy, warrior-like. A stab of some emotion struck him as he carried her. Guilt, perhaps? It didn't feel precisely like guilt. Philip told himself he'd think about it later.

Getting Sorrel on the back of Devil's Advocate proved a bit awkward. Philip breathed a sigh of relief as he set his feet in the stirrups and put a steadying arm around Sorrel's waist. He nudged the unusually cooperative horse forward.

Sorrel's fever had not, apparently, impaired her alertness as Philip had guessed. She managed to keep a distance between them even while sharing a saddle, though she swayed precariously. Stubborn woman! Didn't she realize she was making their journey far more difficult than it needed to be? If she would just let him support her!

Rolling his eyes at her obstinacy, Philip closed his arm more closely, forcing her to lean against him. For a moment she seemed to struggle against the new position but quite suddenly gave it up, leaning heavily against his chest.

"That isn't entirely unpleasant, now, is it?" Philip smiled to himself, knowing full well it would kill her to admit as much.

"Thank you, Philip," she whispered, but Philip easily heard her over the pounding of hooves.

Quite suddenly he didn't feel so cold. Words couldn't be warming, could they? Lud, he needed to lighten the mood!

"That is the second time you have used my Christian name, I will have you know," Philip said, the smell of citrus in her hair teasing his senses. "I do not recall giving you permission to do so."

"I feel blasted awful."

Why the sound of Sorrel uttering a less than dignified word made Philip laugh, he couldn't say. "I can honestly say no woman has ever told me *that* while we were out for a ride." Philip held her just a little more tightly to him, because she was unwell, of course. "You have wounded my pride, I will have you know."

"How much farther?" She did not sound well at all.

"Not much farther, Sorrel. Not much farther."

Philip pushed Devil's Advocate ahead faster. Their arrival at the Kinnley stables instigated a flurry of frantic activity. Grooms appeared seemingly out of nowhere helping him dismount and seeing to Sorrel's needs. Leaving the two positively spent horses in the capable hands of the Kinnley stable staff, Philip retook possession of Sorrel, who obediently put her arms around his neck as he carried her anxiously into the house.

As luck would have it, the first people he came across were Miss Marjie and Fennel. Marjie's "Good gracious!" mingled with the young man's "What's happened?"

"She grew feverish during her ride," Philip answered quickly. "She seems to be in quite a lot of pain."

"She rode?" Fennel asked, looking both disbelieving and excited at the same time.

"I have told Sorrel so many times to be more careful of her health," Miss Marjie interrupted with a look of disapproval for Fennel. "The fevers have been less frequent. Why did she have to put herself in peril?"

Miss Marjie laid a hand on Sorrel's forehead. In the first show of life Philip had seen in his armful in some minutes, Sorrel swiped her sister's hand away. Now *that* was the Sorrel he knew! Miss Marjie was not remotely deterred but continued her attentions.

"As much as I enjoy displaying my not insignificant strength," Philip said, "would one of you be so kind as to direct me to Miss Kendrick's chambers? I believe she would greatly appreciate being set down."

Miss Marjie pinked then spun around to lead the way. Philip shifted his hold on Sorrel, and she winced.

"My apologies," he whispered to her. "I told you I was no hero."

Sorrel offered no reply, verbally or otherwise. Philip found he rather preferred when Sorrel snapped at him or offered rather unflattering assessments of his character. The silent, feverish Sorrel worried him more than he cared to admit.

"One more flight," Miss Marjie called over her shoulder as they finished their first ascent.

"You go up and down this many stairs every day?" Philip gazed into Sorrel's face. It was a wonder she hadn't collapsed a few days sooner.

"My leg hurts."

"She is not terribly coherent," Philip told Fennel, who had followed.

"It's the fever," Fennel said quite matter of factly.

"This has happened before?"

"Quite often, ever since her unfortunate incident."

He'd heard that phrase before: "unfortunate incident." Philip could only guess they were referring to however Sorrel had sustained her disabling injury. He thought it odd her family never discussed it beyond that evasive title.

They reached the next landing. Philip followed Miss Marjie to the left all the way to a door, which she opened. Philip stepped inside. Miss Marjie flitted to the bell pull and tugged, watching anxiously as Philip laid Sorrel on her bed. Sorrel looked miserably ill.

"Should I seek out your mother?" Philip offered, still watching Sorrel. She lay perfectly still except for the slow rise and fall of her chest.

"No," both Fennel and Miss Marjie answered in unison.

"She might appreciate knowing." Philip couldn't imagine Mater not wishing to know if one of her children were as ill as Sorrel appeared to be.

"Mother finds these episodes quite uncomfortable," Miss Marjie explained while fussing over Sorrel once more.

Mother does not believe in being uncomfortable.

"What can I do?" Philip offered, noting with growing discomfort that Sorrel no longer objected to Miss Marjie's attentions.

"She will need bandages and fever powder," Miss Marjie replied without blinking an eye—the Kendricks had obviously been through this before. "Her abigail, Jenny, will have the recipe for the plaster Sorrel requires."

"Shall I have Lord Cavratt send for a physician?" Philip pressed. Sorrel looked more ill by the moment.

"Only if he does not believe in cupping," Miss Marjie insisted quite decisively.

Fennel stepped closer to Philip and, sotto voce, explained, "About a year after her accident, Sorrel was suffering with a bout of fevers. The physician who attended her advocated cupping. She nearly died before we insisted he stop bleeding her. Afterward she quite quickly recovered. Marjie and I are convinced Sorrel ought not to be cupped."

"I have never been convinced that bloodletting is as beneficial as it is generally believed to be," Philip said.

Fennel hadn't taken his eyes off Sorrel. He looked concerned but not panic-stricken. Was that Fennel's natural, easygoing nature? Or was he, who had seen Sorrel suffer through similar episodes, not overly anxious about her recovery?

A young serving woman entered the room, her face immediately betraying her confusion.

"Sorrel's having one of her fevers, Jenny," Miss Marjie explained.

Understanding dawned on Jenny's face. She turned to Fennel and Philip. "'Taint no place for the two of you." She motioned them to the door. "Miss Sorrel will be right as rain soon 'nough."

Philip offered a bow to Miss Marjie and looked once more at Sorrel, hoping Jenny's assessment was accurate. The door closed firmly.

"She actually rode?" Fennel didn't wait a single moment to accost Philip.

"That hardly seems consequential considering—"

"It is beyond consequential, Lord Lampton," Fennel countered. "She hasn't ridden since her unfortunate incident. She hasn't gone anywhere near horses. She used to practically live in the stables."

"Her return to horseback did not seem to do her a lot of good." Philip had quickly come to regret his role in goading her to ride.

Philip thought he saw Fennel roll his eyes. "The fever has been coming on for days. She hides it well, but I can always tell. She'd have been in the throes of it whether she'd stayed to the house today or not."

It was only a minor comfort. She could have been safely indoors when the fever hit. She could have been spared the further ordeal of getting back to the house. At least she was warm and cared for now.

Walking determinedly down the corridor in search of Crispin, Philip decided he would apologize to Sorrel as soon as she recovered enough to comprehend what he said. Although playing the humble repenter while Sorrel remained only marginally lucid seemed a much safer plan. Once she recovered, she'd probably despise him more than ever.

For some reason, the possibility made Philip's insides wrench.

Eleven

"I hope Miss Kendrick is feeling better this evening," Crispin said to Mrs. Kendrick in the west sitting room that night after supper.

"Oh . . . well . . . It's nothing, really." Mrs. Kendrick waved a hand. "Just a trifle . . ."

Miss Marjie and Fennel looked immensely uncomfortable as their mother muttered on. Philip watched the family in confusion. *Just a trifle?* Sorrel had nearly fallen from her horse. She'd been incoherent with fever. Mr. Ryder, the physician, although reassuring them Sorrel would be quite fine, indicated she would need to remain abed for several days. 'Twas certainly more than *just a trifle*.

Catherine, who had been visibly interested in the answer to her husband's inquiry, seemed equally surprised by Mrs. Kendrick's dismissive words. She turned to Miss Marjie with a look that practically pleaded for explanation.

"She is improved," Miss Marjie reassured the listeners. "By tomorrow she will probably be anxious to be up and about. Another two days and she will undoubtedly be herself again."

"I am very relieved to hear that," Crispin said.

"She seems remarkably unconcerned," Stanley whispered at Philip's side with a pointed look in Mrs. Kendrick's direction. "Those kinds of fevers are anything but *trifling*."

Stanley knew the truthfulness of his statement. Philip had personally nursed Stanley through one particularly difficult fever,

which the doctors attributed to the wound he had received during the Battle of Orthez. According to every medical opinion Philip had managed to procure, Stanley would be subject to intermittent bouts of infection-induced fevers for the rest of his life.

"It seems," Philip whispered back to his brother, "Miss Kendrick's sister has developed quite a knack for treating the fevers. She predicts the invalid will be up and about in only a few days."

"A vast improvement over the two weeks *I* spent with the same ailment," Stanley said pensively.

"Perhaps we should investigate their treatment method," Philip suggested.

Stanley's eyes slid to where Miss Marjie stood conversing quietly with Catherine. The unmistakable longing in Stanley's look struck Philip with tremendous force. Had Stanley developed a tendresse for Miss Marjie? After a moment of hurried reflection, Philip decided his brother had indeed fallen under the charms of the younger Kendrick sister. The two had been in each other's company quite a lot since the Kendricks' arrival.

Miss Marjie was a pleasant sort of girl, pretty, with a kind disposition. She didn't have her sister's striking beauty, but— Philip stopped on the instant. *That* thought didn't warrant further speculation.

"I am certain Miss Marjie would impart her wisdom," Philip rather heavily hinted. Stanley's obvious infatuation with the younger Miss Kendrick was a far safer topic than his own heretofore unacknowledged attraction to the older sister.

"She is a good and kind-hearted lady." So why did Stanley seem so decidedly *un*happy?

"You could at least inquire after her sister," Philip said. "It is as good a way to start a conversation as any."

"I could just as easily ask *you* how Miss Kendrick fares." Stanley eyed him with something akin to an accusatory look.

Philip smiled. "I am flattered that you think me clairvoyant, dear brother."

"Not clairvoyant, just—" Stanley seemed to search for a word but in the end simply shrugged.

"What is that look supposed to imply?" Philip tried to keep his tone light but didn't think he succeeded.

"Are you and Miss Kendrick still at war?" Stanley seemed honestly curious.

"Of course we are. I am certain Miss Kendrick dislikes me as much as I do her."

Stanley smiled rather impishly. "I am certain she does. Every bit as much as you dislike her."

Philip had a feeling that, inside, Stanley was laughing. Laughing at him! Philip found nothing amusing. War was not funny!

At three o'clock the next afternoon, Philip came across Fennel making his way up the stairs to visit his sister. Sorrel's welfare had been inexplicably on Philip's mind all day.

"How is Miss Kendrick, Poppy?"

After a smile at the nickname Philip had refused to drop, Fennel invited him to check on Sorrel himself.

"Are you sure?" Philip didn't want to give anyone else the wrong impression—Stanley had been looking at him a little too suspiciously lately. "I have no desire to make myself a nuisance."

"If you are there, Marjie might not lecture me."

"Why would she lecture you?"

"Like a fool, I told her I had encouraged Sorrel to ride," Fennel admitted uneasily.

Philip felt a touch of uneasiness himself. "Was her riding so foolish, then?"

"No," Fennel replied immediately. "Not at all!"

Philip smiled at the unabashed confidence in Fennel's tone.

"Sorrel was the best rider in all of Kent before her incident," Fennel pressed on as they reached the first landing. "She could even outride our Father and did on at least one occasion . . ." Fennel's voice trailed off as his thoughts seemed to take precedence over his words. Nearly to the top of the remaining flight of stairs,

Fennel picked up the conversation again. "Sorrel always loved to ride. She needed to again. I had hoped that, away from Kendrick Hall, she might have a go at it. I didn't realize the fever would come on as quickly as it did. Fortunately, you were nearby." Fennel ended with a flourishing smile for Philip.

"It wasn't exactly a coincidence," Philip said. "I goaded her into riding and then had the great honor of paying for my mischief by having to return her to the house barely conscious."

"She won't exactly thank you for that, you realize." Fennel paused in front of Sorrel's door.

"For forcing her hand and getting her to ride when she probably did not truly want to?" Didn't Fennel realize that Philip expected repercussions?

"If you think Sorrel's hand can be forced in any way, you don't know her very well. I meant she won't be too happy about your carrying her back to the house."

"She would rather I had left her out in the cold, unconscious and fevered?"

"She would rather have been *alone* in the cold, unconscious and fevered," Fennel corrected.

Before Philip could probe for an explanation, Fennel reached for the doorknob. Philip stopped him. "Would you ask first if I would be welcome?"

"Of course you would—"

"Humor me, Poppy."

Fennel shrugged and disappeared inside. Philip smoothed the arms of his jacket and tugged his waistcoat into place. Only a moment later, Miss Marjie appeared in the doorway, her porcelain features lit with a bright smile. "Of course you may come in. You save Sorrel's life and then expect us to shut you out?"

"I have every confidence Miss Kendrick would have contrived some means of returning herself to the house without my assistance," Philip replied amusedly. "She is, as I am sure you know, quite resourceful and abundantly independent."

"And inordinately attached to her walking stick," a familiar voice added dryly.

Philip turned toward the oversized bed and barely managed to keep his mouth from gaping open. Sorrel sat watching him, propped up by mountains of fluffy white pillows, her dwarfed frame wrapped in a silken robe of ruby red.

Red is her color, Philip thought. She looked stunning.

A single ribbon tied back Sorrel's ebony hair, though several stubborn tendrils escaped to frame her pale face. Her nearly black eyes were darker than ever and seemed to pull at him. Philip couldn't tear his eyes away.

Lampton War Tactic Number Ten: Never visit the enemy on her deathbed. Ever. *Ever.*

"You appear to have survived your ordeal," Philip offered by way of a greeting.

"Sorry to disappoint you." Amusement touched her reply.

"It would be a fairly easy way to end this war of ours," Philip said.

"Dying is not nearly as easy as you seem to think."

Philip watched her more closely for a moment. She certainly didn't look on the verge of dying. As a matter of fact, she smiled quite mischievously at him.

"Obviously you are feeling better." Fennel chuckled, giving his sister a peck on the cheek.

"None of that, Fennel." Sorrel pushed him away, though Philip detected a glimmer of gratitude in her eyes. General Sorrel, it seemed, wasn't as prickly as she let on. The thought brought a smile to Philip's face, which he quite quickly held back.

"Wasn't it kind of Lord Lampton to come check on you?" Miss Marjie spoke rather pointedly to her sister.

Sorrel, obviously far from flattered, turned a challenging eye toward Philip. "Lord Lampton came simply to inquire after my health?" She obviously didn't believe a word of it. "How extremely thoughtful of him."

"Actually, I wanted to ask your opinion on the lay of my cravat," Philip answered, lifting his chin to allow a better view. "My valet came up with the knot himself."

"Flamboyant, overdone, and positively out of place in your current setting," Sorrel replied without missing a beat.

"Surely the fever is still affecting your vision, Miss Kendrick." He feigned indignation. In all truthfulness, he completely agreed with her.

"I assure you I can see it plainly," she said.

"And I assure *you* that you most certainly have not seen it at all, else you would have nothing but praise for my valet."

"I could not possibly see it better if I were wearing it myself."

"It has been my experience that it is impossible to see a neckcloth hanging around one's own neck."

"Regardless of where that particular cravat were hanging, it would be out of place, sirrah, and entirely too ostentatious."

"Come, now!" Philip protested, crossing to the head of her bed. "A closer look, I beg of you. I refuse to believe my indispensable Wilson is anything short of a genius."

He thought he saw Sorrel roll her eyes, entirely annoyed. Why did he enjoy ruffling her feathers so much?

"Very well," Sorrel grumbled. "Let me see this mark of perfection."

Smiling inwardly at the first hint of concession he'd ever had from Sorrel, Philip sat on the edge of her bed and held his chin up quite proudly for her inspection.

"I was wrong, Lord Lampton," Sorrel said a moment later, much to Philip's surprise. "It is far *more* ridiculous than I first believed."

"It is not so bad as all that." Philip dropped his chin and his pretensions quite immediately. "A bit over—" He stopped short as their eyes met. He couldn't finish his sentence. He couldn't quite seem to remember what he had intended to say in the first place. He could only sit frozen in place. Her eyes were black as a moonless night and yet something fiery and intriguing sparked in their depths.

Sorrel broke their eye contact. She looked away almost bashfully, and a completely uncharacteristic hint of a blush stole across her cheeks. Philip couldn't think of anything except how exceptionally beautiful she looked in that moment, followed immediately by the thought that he'd entirely lost his mind.

"Add this particular knot to my list of affectations, Miss Kendrick." Philip finally managed to speak, hoping his voice didn't sound too strangled. "I intend to make it part of my signature look."

"That is hardly surprising." The look of impatient civility had returned to Sorrel's face, but the color in her cheeks had not fled. It softened her response in a way Philip would not have expected. Could it be that Sorrel did not hold him in such deep antipathy as she'd professed?

"I am happy that you are recovering quickly," he added quietly before rising and making his way to the door. "Thank you for allowing me to visit," Philip said to Miss Marjie, who, along with Fennel, watched him rather too pointedly for comfort.

Philip had a very strong feeling that he'd made a major strategic error. The challenge, of course, came in identifying exactly what error he'd committed.

* * *

"How kind of Lord Lampton to come see you," Marjie exclaimed the moment the door closed behind Sorrel's unexpected visitor.

"Very uncharacteristic," Sorrel said. "What do you suppose motivated such a . . ." How did she possibly put into words the confusing turn of events? ". . . an inconvenient . . . excursion?"

"Perhaps Lord Lampton is not so unfeeling as you suspect," Fennel suggested. As usual, he sounded far older than his mere fifteen years, far more knowing than a gangly youth ought to be.

"I never said he was unfeeling," Sorrel defended herself, though she knew she'd implied just such a thing that first evening Lord

Lampton had been at Kinnley. She'd accused him of being entirely self-absorbed.

"That could almost count as a compliment," Fennel said as he plopped onto the foot of her bed and gave her a look of amusement. "Lampton's top o' the trees, Sorrel. Charlie says he's fantastic. The best older brother a fellow could ask for."

Now *that* sounded more like a fifteen-year-old.

"I am glad Charlie likes his eldest brother," Sorrel replied dryly.

"Because you don't?" Fennel spoke almost critically.

Why was he attacking *her*? What had Sorrel done to deserve her brother's derision? "Lord Lampton has given me absolutely no reason to like him, Fennel." She knew she sounded defensive. She didn't care.

"How can you say that, Sorrel?" Marjie said. "He sat beside you at supper only the other evening . . ."

Forced his company on me, Sorrel silently corrected.

". . . rode with you only yesterday . . ."

Tricked me into getting on that blasted horse!

". . . kept you from falling off your horse when you grew ill . . ."

Sorrel stared at her sister in shock. She had no memory of her ride after leaving the stables, the fever having clouded her recollection. She had assumed she'd returned herself to the house. What was this about falling from her horse?

". . . He brought you back to Kinnley, carrying you *personally* to your bedchamber. Called for the doctor. How can you dislike a man like that?"

Sorrel came perilously close to tears. She never allowed herself to cry! She could picture herself slumped over Fairy Cake's neck, shivering with fever, heavy and limp in the arms of a man who, no doubt, found her helplessness and broken state terribly humorous. Yet another thing that made her vulgar and unworthy in the eyes of the world. If a woman with a limp could never be fit for society, a woman with a tendency toward fevers and falls qualified as positively revolting.

"I should never have gotten on that horse," Sorrel whispered, her heart dropping. "I should have stayed in the house."

"I have told you so these two years, Sorrel." Marjie laid her hand on Sorrel's just as she would have done to a tiny toddler who had finally acknowledged the superior reasoning of her parent. Sorrel hated being treated like a child simply because she struggled to walk. A broken hip did not automatically mean a broken brain!

Sorrel pulled her hand away perhaps a touch too forcefully. Marjie's lips pursed in disapproval. "It seems you have overtaxed yourself," she suggested. "Time for a nap, I think."

"Marjie," Sorrel protested the patronizing tone.

"Can I talk to Sorrel for a minute?" Fennel requested. "Alone?"

"She needs to rest, Fennel."

"Only a minute, Marjie. Then I'll let her have her *wittle nap*." Fennel said the last two words precisely as a four-year-old would, and Sorrel couldn't help but smile. Fennel knew *exactly* how Marjie made her feel. Marjie did not miss his tone, either.

"Well," she said, rather vexed. "Forgive me for being a bother. I suppose you would prefer I ignore Sorrel the way—" She stopped short, but Sorrel knew what Marjie had been about to say. *The way Mother does.*

"Of course you are no bother," Sorrel said placatingly. "I am simply a difficult patient. You know I always have been."

Marjie smiled again and shook her head almost amusedly. "You promise to rest after Fennel leaves?"

"On my word of honor."

Her air of maternal regard fully restored, Marjie pulled Sorrel's blanket more closely around her, adjusted the drapes so no rays of light would fall across Sorrel's face, smiled fondly at her older sister, and slipped from the room.

"She is going to drive me mad, Fennel," Sorrel declared after Marjie's departure.

"Marjie cares about you. She never quite got over nearly losing you. We all felt that rather acutely, you know."

"Yes, but even Mother doesn't hover the way Marjie does."

"Perhaps that has something to do with *why* Marjie does," Fennel mumbled, as he always did when making an observation he thought should have been apparent. He abruptly switched topics. "Why do you hate Lampton?"

That was blunt.

"I do not hate Lord Lampton."

"Dislike, then?"

"I . . . that is . . ."

"You don't even *dislike* him, do you?"

"He . . . just . . ."

Fennel watched her quite patiently. Sorrel was sorely tempted to change the subject, but Fennel, she knew, would never allow it.

"He is aggravating and arrogant and . . ." Sorrel continued searching for the right word but couldn't seem to wrap her mind around it. She found Philip Jonquil entirely maddening but couldn't begin to say why. Nor did she know why she found his aggravating company oddly enjoyable at times. Ever since pulling out of her fever earlier that day, she'd found herself missing him, wishing he'd come argue with her. Marjie treated her like spun glass. Lord Lampton treated her like . . . like a worthy opponent, like a human being. Few people did anymore.

Suddenly realizing she'd been wool gathering in the middle of a conversation, Sorrel turned her eyes back to Fennel. He watched her with a barely masked smile she recognized. He assumed that expression whenever he discovered some secret or solved a mystery he did not intend to reveal. All of their larks had made his insightfulness well known to his oldest sister. At times, like now, she found that tendency a touch aggravating.

"I really hope you aren't actually going to stop riding," Fennel said quite unexpectedly. "Lampton said you were riding quite well before you took ill."

"Then he is not very observant," Sorrel countered. "I rode awkwardly and slowly, and it hurt like bloo—"

Fennel's laugh stopped the words before they left Sorrel's mouth. "If Father had known the stable hands were teaching you to talk like that, he'd have dismissed the whole lot."

"Before or after thoroughly birching me?" Sorrel asked with a touch of bitterness she didn't like hearing. "'Have to beat the devil out,' he'd say. There were times I hated the man." She suddenly remembered she was speaking to her younger brother, a young man who ought to be permitted to retain some of his naivety. "Sorry, Fennel. I had no right to say that."

Fennel managed an obviously forced smile. "None of us were exactly overcome with love for him."

A heavy silence hung over the room. Sorrel tried to force away the constriction that always seemed to seize her chest when her thoughts turned to her late father. Fennel seemed to be reliving a few unpleasant memories of his own.

"How did . . ." Fennel pulled his legs up onto the bed in front of him, looking more five years old than fifteen. "Father was so . . . horrible, sometimes, but you never . . . broke down. You never cried even once, not like his son, the 'watering pot.'"

Sorrel flinched at Fennel's well-known quote—her father had detested the very tears he'd routinely brought to Fennel's eyes. He'd minced no words when berating his son. Father's repeated insults flung at Fennel were part of the reason she despised her father's memory so much. "He was arrogant, pompous, and entirely without basic human compassion, despite his professed piety. I refused to be humiliated by a brute. I promised myself I would never retreat."

"So your first war, then, was with Father?"

"I suppose so." Sorrel felt drained again.

"You look tired, Sorrel."

How does Fennel always seem to know precisely how I feel?

She nodded. Fennel jumped from the bed much more himself than he'd been moments before. "Marjie'll skin me alive if I interrupt your nap time." He grinned then turned to the door. His hand on the knob, Fennel turned back to her. "You know, Sorrel," he said with the look of a discerning gentleman, "Lampton is *not* Father."

"I know that," Sorrel replied, completely baffled.

"No. I don't think you do." A moment later, he was gone.

Lampton is not *Father. What does he mean by that?*

Twelve

PHILIP WINCED.

Lizzie's voice could probably be heard throughout Kinnley. "Edward! Come see. Hanover is here!"

Her exceptionally patient husband arrived on the scene and shook his cousin's hand. "What brings you to Kinnley?"

Philip kept his grimace inside. Hanover Garner, despite being an invaluable agent, could not fabricate a believable story any more than he could stitch a decent sampler. He could shoot the spade out of an ace of spades from across a room, in dim candlelight. He had an almost unfathomable mind for strategy. But the man struggled with the slightest of fibs. If not for that quirk, Garner would have been the best spy in England—that and the fact that spying made him nervous and being nervous made his nose run. Philip had every intention of giving Garner a box full of handkerchiefs for Christmas.

"I was headed to Lowestoft to visit my Aunt Harriet," Garner told his cousin. Philip tried not to smile when Garner sniffed—his sinuses were giving him away already. "I heard you were at Kinnley for the holidays and hoped to impose on your hospitality for a day or so."

"Of course you must stay!" Lizzie declared.

"That, I believe, would be up to your sister-in-law," Garner reminded her gently.

Lizzie blushed. Philip barely managed to not laugh. Catherine was, as mistress of Kinnley, the true hostess of their gathering, though she had relegated most of the planning and carrying out to Lizzie. Catherine most likely preferred it that way.

"You are quite welcome, sir," Catherine assured them all a few minutes later.

Philip saw the look of relief that crossed Garner's face. The man needed to work on a more neutral exterior. Introductions were quickly made. Garner wrinkled his nose—he had to hold back a drip, no doubt—when Lizzie "introduced" him to Philip. Perhaps they ought to have devised a different strategy.

Knowing Garner would probably contract an inflammation of the lungs if their first "chance meeting" were left in his hands, Philip skillfully arranged to bump into his handkerchief-clutching partner as he returned from checking on his horse in the Kinnley stables.

"A fine afternoon," Philip observed casually. "And my waistcoat matches the sky perfectly. I thought it would be a shame if I did not take a walk under such astounding conditions."

"I could use a walk myself." Garner sniffled. "Mind if I join you?"

Fifteen minutes later they were circling the banks of Kinnley Lake, out of earshot of the house and entirely alone. Garner's nose had stopped leaking.

Philip dropped the dandified tone he'd grown to loathe over the years. "So, Ipswich?"

"Precisely. Though our sources seem to think it is merely a temporary stop-off." Garner thrust his hands into the pockets of his greatcoat, a sign he was deep in thought. "He is passing off information sometime in the next weeks, but somewhere other than Ipswich."

"It is left in our capable hands, then, to discover in whom he is confiding, where they will meet, and the exact date and time?" Philip raised an eyebrow at the improbability of their task. "Is that all? Perhaps we can cure the King's madness in our spare time."

Garner chuckled. "We are supposed to meet with one of our contacts in Ipswich three days from now. With any luck, that meeting will prove beneficial."

"But how to make the trip without raising eyebrows?" Philip pondered the dilemma. He doubted Mrs. Kendrick nor Miss Marjie would think anything of their leaving. Lizzie might shrug before turning her attention to her party. But Sorrel would not only notice, she'd be suspicious from the beginning and would quite likely nose about in search of answers.

He barely registered Garner's chuckle. As he seemed to do alarmingly often the last day or so, Philip was thinking of Sorrel. She'd been almost friendly the afternoon before when he'd visited her in the sickroom. Sure, she'd scoffed at his cravat, but in the same visit, she'd smiled at him. She'd been so deucedly adorable dwarfed by the enormous four-poster bed. The way she'd blushed—

"This isn't such a difficult problem." Garner interrupted Philip's dangerously deviated thoughts.

"What isn't such a difficult problem?" Philip asked, masking his alarm. Had he unknowingly spoken aloud?

"Getting to Ipswich," Garner answered. "We simply say we haven't finished our Christmas shopping."

"Shall I supply you with yards of linen for that bouncer?" Philip eyed Garner amusedly.

"I have a few things to pick up." Garner shrugged. "I can offer the excuse honestly. No dripping."

"Suppose there are others who feel inspired by our outing and wish to come along?" Philip asked. Lizzie could never pass up an opportunity to shop.

"We needn't shop en masse," Garner said. "We'll agree to meet up again at a certain time, in a certain place—after we've met our contact."

"It is plausible."

"And, might not even be necessary. Everyone else may have planned ahead better."

* * *

With the absence of Sorrel and the addition of Garner, the numbers at supper were decidedly lopsided. Obviously at a loss as to how she might maintain the partnering up that Lizzie had, no doubt, convinced her all formal meals required, Catherine looked over the male-heavy gathering with an expression of utter bewilderment.

"The numbers will grow more uneven, I fear." Philip shrugged from his position beside their hostess. "Two more Jonquils will arrive within the week—we are all male in my family, you know."

"I don't imagine your mother would entirely agree with your generalization."

Philip smiled. Catherine, though the quietest woman of his acquaintance, could hold her own when she chose to. "I will apologize to Mater quite promptly for my unintended insult of her femininity," he said.

"Though that will hardly solve *my* problem." Catherine's attention turned to Crispin, as it always did. Lud, those two were decidedly too happy for company. They were making Philip rather ill and, though he shuddered to admit it even to himself, slightly jealous.

"We are all friends here, Catherine," Crispin answered. "No one objected the last time we chose a more casual approach. Simply let them wander in and sit wherever they'd like."

"And suppose I would like to sit *on* the table?" Catherine asked with a look of such feigned innocence it was all Philip could do to pretend he couldn't overhear what had quickly become a private conversation.

"You know the punishment for outrageous behavior, Lady Cavratt," Crispin replied with a playful raise of his eyebrow.

"Oh, dear, not the dreaded lake." Catherine clutched a hand dramatically to her heart.

Crispin smiled amusedly. "It is not yet frozen over, you know."

"I suppose I will have to sit demurely, then." Catherine almost managed a repentant look.

"Not too demurely, my love." Crispin took Catherine's hand and kissed it with enough fervor to make Philip step away, but not before he heard Crispin whisper, "I love you far too much when you are mischievous."

Philip would forever be glad he had interfered in that marriage. If he hadn't played matchmaker, they might never have stayed together. Philip smiled but doubted the gesture reached his eyes. He was happy for his friends but found their contentment hard to stomach at times. Not that they weren't circumspect in their shows of affection—Catherine would be mortified if she knew how much Philip had overheard of their most recent conversation. What ate at Philip felt more like loneliness.

I wouldn't wish loneliness on my worst enemy, Sorrel had once said.

Too bad, General Sorrel, Philip mused. *Your worst enemy is, at the moment, quite lonely.*

He'd have been glad for a good argument just then. Miss Marjie had informed him in no uncertain terms that Sorrel was not well enough to appear downstairs just yet.

Catherine invited the guests to make their way into the dining room with as much disorder as Crispin had earlier suggested. Philip dragged his feet. *What is the matter with me?* he wondered. His recent bouts of discontent seemed to have given way to full-on discouragement the past couple of days.

Dandies are never blue-deviled. Philip really needed to get himself under control. Pulling himself up to his most ridiculously composed manner, he stepped out of the drawing room behind all the others.

As the group's footsteps and conversations began to fade into the dining room, Philip distinctly heard a strange thumping. He paused mid-stride and listened. Thump. Pause. Pause. Thump. Pause. Pause. Thump.

"What the devil?" he muttered.

The sound came from behind him. Rhythmic and growing louder.

Philip retraced his steps, moving in the direction of the noise. Thump. Just as enough time passed for the next thump he heard, instead, a scrape and a thud. Then, in a voice he would have known anywhere, came a decidedly lower-class expression that would have made Mater blush. To Philip, it was music.

He grinned. "Sorrel," he mouthed silently as he picked up the pace.

Turning the corner leading to the massive front staircase, Philip found Sorrel struggling to regain her feet.

"Alas. Someone has overwaxed the floor again," Philip said as dolefully as he could manage.

Sorrel's head snapped up, and her eyes met his, her surprise quite obvious. She would be angry with him, take a verbal bite out of his proverbial backside—something he looked forward to, strangely enough. The shock in her eyes, however, gave way to what Philip could only describe as mortification.

"Oh, Lud! Not you!" she muttered, looking down at the floor.

Now why did that reaction sting when a razor-sharp cutting remark would have been welcome?

"I am afraid so, Miss Kendrick." Philip did his best to maintain a lighthearted reaction, even though all the while *Not you!* echoed in his mind. "Shall I fetch your walking stick?" He motioned toward it where it lay just out of her reach.

Sorrel nodded mutely but did not return her eyes to him.

Why not me? he demanded silently.

Philip retrieved her walking stick then squatted before her, holding out his hand to offer assistance.

She obviously saw his gesture from the corner of her eyes. "I do not need your help, L—"

"Blast it, Sorrel!" Philip snapped. "I only want to help."

"I am a perfectly capable person, despite—"

"I am certain you are under normal circumstances. But you were thrown about on that ride, regardless of your valiant efforts to hide the grimaces. You have been laid up with a fever for two days and, according to your sister, ought not to be out of bed yet."

"Marjie would have had me in bed every day for the past two years if the decision had been hers."

"Sorrel."

His use of her given name brought those ebony eyes to his. Confusion, pleading, defiance, even a hint of pleasure lurked in their depths. Her every emotion seemed readable in her eyes. Including a great deal of pain, and he didn't think it was entirely physical. Obviously, she struggled with admitting she needed help. She needed a way of accepting without admitting she'd given in. What had she said to him? *I don't retreat.*

"All I am asking is that you allow me to help you to your feet," Philip told her plainly. "I am not implying you are lacking in capability or that you require my assistance in any way. Not even necessarily in *this* way. I offer only because I am the victim of a rather unfortunate upbringing."

She was curious—Philip could see it in her face.

He shrugged as casually as possible. "Father and Mater raised us to be gentlemen. A gentleman offers his arm to a lady at every possible opportunity."

"I would be insulting your honor as a gentleman by refusing?" Sorrel eyed him a touch suspiciously.

"Precisely," he answered as seriously as he could.

"I would not want your mother to think she'd failed you." She knew he had offered her a way around her pride. He could tell she knew. She didn't seem angry at the subterfuge. She seemed almost grateful. "Very well. For your sake."

Philip smiled. Her hand slipped inside his own, and he began to rise. In less than a moment he realized Sorrel needed more help than she'd let on. Simply offering a hand to hold would hardly do the trick. Philip took back his hand and placed in hers the walking stick before putting his arm around her waist and lifting her to her feet.

When she began to protest, he stopped her by declaring, "I must as a gentleman."

"Of course. Wrapping one's arms around a lady is a regular requirement of gentlemanly honor." Sorrel eyed him shrewdly.

"Is it?" Philip asked, not releasing her. Feeling strangely determined to pound someone, he demanded, "What *gentleman* told you such rubbish?"

"Only you," Sorrel answered, and a smile seemed to sneak into her eyes. "Your gentleman's code seems nearly as elaborate as your war tactics."

"Like keeping an eye on the enemy," Philip said, feeling relieved. "At the moment I am fulfilling both my code and my strategy."

"Your proverb refers to your eyes, not your arms, Lord Lampton," Sorrel pointed out.

"Philip." He ignored the pointed reference to his arms, still supporting her, though she hardly needed it any longer. "I would like you to call me Philip. It is so much simpler to be on a first-name basis with one's enemies."

"You seem to have more experience with war than I do." She hadn't attacked him for his rather forward request and hadn't pulled away.

"Perhaps I do." Philip shrugged. "Or maybe I simply have more enemies."

"*That* I believe." But her tone was teasing. Teasing? Sorrel?

"Actually, you are quite possibly the only person I have ever met who disliked me from the very first."

She looked at him doubtfully.

"I am generally considered witty and engaging." Philip smiled smoothly, rather enjoying her signature scent of limes. "And devastatingly handsome."

She didn't deny the claim, he noticed.

"So why do you dislike me so vehemently?"

She opened her mouth to say something, but the remark seemed to die unspoken. Instead she watched him rather intensely. All the animosity, all the prickles, vanished, as if she searched for the answer to his question but couldn't find it, or couldn't express it. There was a vulnerability to her that she so seldom let show. It made her so human, so reachable that, without thought, Philip inched closer to her.

Sorrel Kendrick was stubborn and razor-tongued, but there was no denying she was beautiful and captivating. And, in that moment, entirely kissable.

His eyes focused on that enormously captivating mouth of hers as he leaned ever closer. Mere inches separated them. Then less. Then—

"Where in heaven's name has that boy gotten off to?"

Mater. Philip let out a breath of disappointment, the tension of the moment gone as he stepped back from Sorrel.

He cleared his throat a little awkwardly and led the way into dinner, all the while avoiding Sorrel's eyes and keeping his mouth shut. He'd very nearly made a fool out of himself.

Lampton War Tactic Number Eleven: Kissing the enemy is generally considered a strategic misstep.

Thirteen

Life was entirely unfair.

Sorrel had promised herself as a child that she would never allow an arrogant, self-absorbed man to hurt her. She'd gone to extraordinary lengths to put up impenetrable barriers, to hide all weaknesses. Her father had never been permitted to see anything but the confident, independent side of her. The stable hands knew her as a bruising rider and take-charge lady. She never allowed any vulnerabilities to show.

Yet in the previous week she'd allowed the cockiest of coxcombs to see her fall *twice,* to apparently witness her disintegration into fever, to encroach on her sickbed. Standing there in that moment in the corridor, she'd been too addlepated to extract herself from his arms, too distracted by a sense of comfort she'd never felt in all her life to simply step away. She'd nearly allowed him to kiss her. Indeed, his mother had only barely prevented that disaster.

Standing there, balancing precariously on her walking stick, Sorrel reached the horrible realization that she had grown dangerously defenseless. "Lampton is not Father," Fennel had said. But he easily could be. He could tear her to pieces with a word.

"Miss Kendrick." Lady Lampton obviously found Sorrel's presence as shocking as Sorrel had found Philip's sudden appearance a few moments earlier. "We were told you would not be joining us this evening."

"I desperately needed a view other than my own bed." Sorrel tried to respond cheerily. Her well-laid plans for joining the party for dinner seemed less wise by the minute.

"And a grand entrance it will be," Philip assured her.

"I hadn't planned such a dramatic arrival." Sorrel sighed, wishing she'd stayed in bed. "The stairs were harder than I had anticipated."

"Sorrel," Philip softly scolded, "you could have asked for—"

"I do not need help." She was sick to death of looking like a fool in front of this man!

"I will tell Lady Cavratt you are coming," Lady Lampton said then disappeared far too quickly for any objections.

Feeling herself scowl, Sorrel began a begrudging trek to the dining room. Philip stopped her after one step.

"Sorrel, I . . . about the, uh . . ." He looked decidedly uncomfortable. She should have been glad to see it but, instead, felt something akin to empathy for the maddening man. "I know I . . . it was . . . ungentlemanly . . ."

"I understood you were raised to be a gentleman above all else." Sorrel raised a questioning eyebrow. "The very reason you intend to offer me your arm, I am certain."

She hardly required an escort to supper, nor physical support, but she hoped to interrupt what she feared he was about to say. If she had to listen to an awkward apology for temporarily losing his senses long enough to nearly kiss a lady as undesirable as she, Sorrel would positively whack him with her walking stick. Let him make of the affectation what he would after that!

With a smile that seemed to communicate gratitude, Philip bowed and offered his arm. They walked slowly—her hip ached already—toward the sound of conversation ahead in the dining room.

"We have a new member of our party. I don't know if you have heard."

"Another brother?" Sorrel asked.

"Not for a few more days. This is a cousin of Lord Henley's. A Mr. Garner."

"Marjie did not mention him. Apparently he does not hold a candle to your Stanley. She does not seem to notice anyone other than him."

"I have noticed a similar affliction in Stanley," Philip said with an amused smile.

They continued for a brief moment in silence. Sorrel wondered if anything would come of the budding romance between their siblings. She wondered if Philip were thinking the same thing.

"Mr. Garner seems a likable enough gentleman," Philip said. "Lizzie assures us he will be a welcome addition."

"Sorrel!" Marjie's shock was unmistakable.

Sorrel silently sighed. They'd barely entered the dining room and her sister was nearly hysterical already.

"You should not be up and about," Marjie said.

"I feel fine other than a little ache." Sorrel kept her voice low in the hope that Marjie would follow her lead.

"You are in pain?"

"You know perfectly well I am always in pain."

Philip's grip on Sorrel's arm seemed to momentarily tighten. Certainly Sorrel had merely imagined it.

"I still cannot like that you came all the way down here on your own."

"As you can see, Miss Marjie, she is not alone," Philip said with a look of immense satisfaction. "You certainly cannot object to my attentions. I believe I am capable of seeing that a young lady comes to no harm on her way to dinner."

Marjie's lips moved silently as if searching for an answer. She finally settled on "Of course" before returning to her seat.

"How did you do that?" Sorrel whispered to her unexpected rescuer as he slid her chair under her. "I can never seem to bring an end to Marjie's distress over my health."

"It is the cravat, Sorrel," Philip replied perfectly seriously. "I tried to explain to you yesterday in your room. The knot, an original, you will remember, communicates my authority in ways mere words never could."

"I noticed the knot." Sorrel cocked her head. "The only thing it communicated to me was its own ridiculousness."

A smile seemed to twitch at the corner of Philip's mouth. She fought down an answering smile of her own.

"You really should try something more fitting," she said.

"What would you suggest, my dear? I am certain my valet would eagerly accept your advice."

My dear? Sorrel knew some gentlemen used the term rather generally. So why did Philip's use of it seem to render her temporarily speechless? She tried to cover her affected state by looking ponderous.

"I have the very one," Sorrel said once she'd regained her voice. "The Horse Collar."

His mouth dropped open just as she'd expected it to. "My valet would literally fall down dead if I even suggested such a thing. Perhaps you do not realize it is so unrefined even the costermongers are forswearing it."

"I had no idea." Her sarcasm dripped like rain.

A grin split Philip's face. He took hold of her hand and squeezed it in a decidedly friendly gesture. "I have missed you these last two days, Sorrel. No one else would have dared suggest such a thing to me, dandified as I am. I believe you shall keep me humble yet."

"I am no miracle worker, Philip."

With a low chuckle, Philip tucked into his fish. Sorrel hadn't quite recovered her appetite, so she merely picked and nibbled. Her attention kept returning to Philip. He'd missed her? Why? And why did she enjoy hearing him say so? She did not easily trust people. Perhaps Philip was more trustworthy than he appeared.

"That is our newest arrival." Philip nodded toward the head of the table where Lizzie spoke animatedly with a man whose slightly balding head Sorrel could barely see.

"Mr. Garner, I think you said," Sorrel remembered.

"That sounds right."

A moment later the newcomer turned to speak with Lord Henley. His face came fully into view, and Sorrel's stomach leaped into her throat. She had always had an astounding ability to remember faces, and she knew that man. He had been at the inn back in Kent where Philip and she had first come across each other. This Mr. Garner and Philip had been in the same private dining parlor in an obscure, out-of-the-way inn several days' journey from where they were both now residing.

Sorrel glanced across at Philip, now listening to his brother Jason talk about something or other. Suspicions began creeping into Sorrel's thoughts. Philip had said, or at least very heavily had implied, that he did not know Mr. Garner. Indeed, he had acted as though he wasn't even sure of the man's name. Yet Sorrel knew they'd spent at least one evening closeted in an all-but-empty inn. Even if that meeting had been a coincidence, they couldn't help but have become acquainted under such circumstances.

Something was decidedly havey-cavey. Why would Philip pretend to not know a man with whom he was obviously at least minimally acquainted? Surely the two men would recall having met. So why the secrecy? Why the act?

"Certainly that dissatisfied expression is not still for my ostentatious cravat." Philip's laughing voice interrupted her thoughts. "It is not so overdone as all that."

Sorrel could only manage a silent nod of her head. She seriously suspected Philip was hiding something. She'd learned long ago not to trust gentlemen with an exaggerated opinion of themselves. So why did learning Philip might not be entirely trustworthy sting so acutely?

Fourteen

"There! I see it!" Fennel's enthusiasm flowed unrestrained. "The outer edge of Ipswich."

Sorrel had found the perfect opportunity to make the trip she'd been anticipating ever since Lizzie's invitation had arrived so many weeks earlier. She'd been trying to think of a way to get to Ipswich for nearly a year.

Stanley and Philip had suggested a trip to Ipswich to obtain a few remaining items on their Christmas gift list. With Christmas a mere week and a half away and the arrival of the remaining Jonquil brothers expected in a matter of days, this would be the last opportunity for such a distant excursion until after the first of the winter holidays.

Fennel and Charlie had wrangled their way into the traveling group, followed by Lord and Lady Cavratt and Mr. Garner. Sorrel had talked Fennel into securing her a seat in one of the carriages with the stipulation that he not mention a word of it to Marjie. Instead she'd left a note. Marjie would lecture her unrelentingly when they returned. It would be worth every word.

"How fortunate the weather held," Catherine said after their group alighted in Ipswich.

Sorrel nodded her agreement.

"You seem particularly grateful to arrive," Catherine whispered. "Yet somehow I do not think you are obtaining a gift."

Sorrel turned to her. Catherine was nearly silent in most instances, but Sorrel had come to recognize the sharp intellect at work behind the timid countenance.

"I have a rather important errand here in Ipswich," Sorrel admitted sotto voce. "I am hoping to convince Fennel to accompany me. With there being no room for my lady's maid—"

"Charlie and Fennel will be off on a lark before you have a chance to ask, I daresay." Catherine eyed her regretfully. A smile of unmistakable genuineness crossed her face. "Could Crispin and I accompany you?"

"The errand is of a rather . . . um, personal nature." Sorrel shifted uncomfortably.

"You cannot walk the streets of Ipswich entirely unaccompanied," Catherine warned. "It is certainly not so unforgivable as it would be in London, but Crispin does not believe it entirely safe."

Sorrel mulled the dilemma over in her head. She would never have another opportunity to pursue a possibility that had been little more than a distant hope until a month earlier. "Would you promise not to tell my sister?"

Catherine's suspicions were obviously raised.

"I am doing nothing objectionable, I promise you."

Catherine smiled kindly. "Crispin and I will prove the very souls of discretion."

"Thank you."

Less than one-quarter hour later, Catherine and Crispin walked Sorrel to an unassuming door not far from the shops of Ipswich without any questions other than when they should return for her and to mention they would be nearby. Sorrel took a reassuring breath and watched as Crispin walked up the steps, her card in hand, and knocked. He'd laughed, saying he would enjoy "playing footman."

"This young lady is expected, I believe," Crispin informed the imposing butler who opened the door. The man took the card and disappeared inside.

A manservant, Sorrel noted. That was a promising sign. A moment later the butler returned. "Dr. Darrow says to come in directly."

Sorrel took the steps with what little dignity a woman dependent on a cane could muster. Crispin and Catherine looked curious but honored their word to not press for information. The door closed behind Sorrel, and she suddenly felt a whisper of misgiving.

Sorrel followed the butler's retreating steps past the door to what appeared to be an informal sitting room. The tastefully decorated corridor boasted freshly cut flowers sprinkled about in cut-glass vases. Dr. Darrow must have been relatively wealthy to afford hothouse flowers in the dead of winter. Ahead, the butler opened a heavy oak door and held it, waiting for her.

"Miss Kendrick," he announced.

Sorrel stepped across the threshold into a cozy library, lit and warmed by a welcoming fire. She felt more at ease immediately. The books lining every wall appeared to be organized by color—odd, she thought, but thorough.

"Your letter intrigued me, Miss Kendrick," Dr. Darrow admitted after the butler stepped out. The physician's voice made his Scottish heritage clear. "Please have a seat." He motioned to a nearby chair. "I have many questions for you."

Sorrel nodded and limped her way to a very sturdy-looking armchair and sat rather anxiously.

"This is Mrs. Darrow." He indicated a stout, bright-faced woman of indistinguishable years seated near the fireplace.

"Pleased to meet you," Sorrel offered.

"Your letter indicated multiple breaks to the right leg." Dr. Darrow immediately took up the topic at hand. "How many, precisely? And where?"

"I will tell you what I know," Sorrel prefaced—she possessed no medical expertise. "In the incident my ankle was broken, both bones below the knee, and a break in the hip of the right leg."

"The incident?" Dr. Darrow pressed. "Explain that."

"I was—" Sorrel swallowed back a lump. She hated talking about that day.

"Knowing how it happened is generally vital."

"I was trampled by a horse," Sorrel blurted, hoping to get the words out before they registered.

"The bones, then, may have been crushed and not merely broken." The doctor's quill scratched as he wrote something on a piece of parchment. "Is there residual pain?"

"Constant."

"Where?"

"Mostly in my hip. Also in the lower leg if I walk for long or put weight on it repeatedly."

"Your letter indicated the leg was not straight. Was this true before the trampling? A club foot perhaps?"

Sorrel shook her head. "I do not believe the bones healed in proper alignment."

"May I see the leg?"

A well-bred young lady did not, generally, show her leg to an unknown male. The man in question, however, was a doctor, and Sorrel desperately needed his expert opinion. She'd read in *The Times* months earlier that he had saved the leg of a child struck by a carriage. How she hoped he could help her!

Skirt hiked to her knee with her leg stretched out on the brown velvet sofa, her stockings and boots removed, Sorrel kept her eyes fixed on the doctor. She had absolutely no desire to see her gnarled, twisted leg again. He didn't seem to enjoy the sight any more than she did. Sorrel appreciated the professional curiosity in his bespectacled eyes.

"The doctor that set this ought to be drawn and quartered," he finally pronounced, taking a seat beside the sofa. "A stable hand could have achieved better alignment."

"It was never set." Both Darrows looked at her with astonishment. Sorrel took a deep breath and explained. "My father took a rather severe view of life. He felt accidents and illnesses were judgments from God and that suffering would purge one of sin. He wouldn't allow the breaks to be set."

Dr. Darrow snorted his derision. "A zealot, was he?"

Sorrel didn't reply. She preferred not to think of her father.

"Does he disapprove of your being here?"

"My father has since passed away."

"Can you walk unassisted?" The doctor returned to the interrogation.

"A few steps. I need my walking stick for anything more than that."

"Lack of balance or pain?"

"Both. Balance presents the first difficulty. The pain always follows."

Dr. Darrow sat silently for a moment. "The bones healed so misaligned," he finally said, "you have been left, essentially, clubfooted. The leg bows as well."

The catalog of deformities was not pleasant to hear. It was no wonder Philip had so quickly decided she could never be beautiful. Sorrel dismissed the thought, determined to focus on the interview at hand.

"That, along with what is probably a shattered hip, accounts for the pain and balancing difficulties," the doctor said.

"Can anything be done?" Sorrel hoped she didn't sound too desperate. The thought of living out her life in constant, unrelieved pain was almost too much to bear.

Dr. Darrow pushed his spectacles back up his prominent nose. "It is possible, if the bones were rebroken and then set properly, that the alignment could be improved."

The bones rebroken. She remembered all too vividly the pain of the initial break to think on such a thing with any degree of equanimity. It would be agonizing. Yet if it worked, she'd endure it. Her entire body tensed at the drastic procedure, but she could not deny that it was the first ray of hope she'd had in months, years.

"That, of course, would not entirely cure the limp," Dr. Darrow said.

Her heart instantly dropped. A piece of that momentary hope dissipated with his words.

"The hip is part of the overall problem," the doctor explained, "and rebreaking will not address that injury."

"You said 'not entirely.'" Sorrel needed to know what benefit she could reap from his suggestion.

"A straight leg would alleviate some of your struggles and might reduce your dependence on the cane."

"I see." Every promise came with a clause. It *might* work. It *could* help. Sorrel wasn't sure what she wanted: a painful operation that might do nothing at all for her or living the rest of her life utterly broken.

"I know of a surgeon, a skilled and respected surgeon, who could offer you a more definite answer," Dr. Darrow said. "He has performed several similar procedures."

That sounded at least a little promising. "I would appreciate his direction," Sorrel said, "and your permission to name you as my reference."

Dr. Darrow nodded. "I will write to him myself, as well."

Sorrel reached the Darrows' front door just as Catherine and Crispin ascended the outer steps. They dutifully asked no questions about her appointment.

Crispin broke the silence some five minutes later. "It is nearly time to meet for luncheon. Perhaps we should begin walking toward the Dove and Crow? The rest of our group should arrive within moments."

Sorrel glanced at the slip of paper in her hand on which Dr. Darrow had scrawled a name and direction. A Dr. MacAslon in Edinburgh. Edinburgh! How in heaven's name was she supposed to get to Scotland?

The question lingered in the back of her thoughts as she unseeingly ate the thick fish stew served at the Dove and Crow. A trip to Scotland in her condition could take weeks. She'd discovered during the journey from Kent that, though thirty miles a day was possible the first day or so, her stamina dropped off rather quickly after that. By the last day of their travels, she'd been completely undone within two hours.

Edinburgh was nearly four times as far from home as Kinnley. If she somehow managed to convince her sometimes-suffocating family to allow her to make the journey and undergo the treatment, would she be able to endure two weeks of carriage travel? Could she complete the trip to Scotland healthy enough to go forward with a surgery? Where would she stay once she arrived? Who would stay with her? Who would care for her while she recovered? Who would watch over her family while she was gone?

Her hopes dimmed as the difficulties of the undertaking sunk in. Still, she couldn't completely shrug off the possibility of being freed from even some of her burden. She might emerge with less of a limp, perhaps even less pain. She might depend less on her walking stick. How she longed to regain *some* of her independence, some of her self-respect.

If only she had someone with whom she might discuss the situation. Her thoughts immediately turned to Philip. Despite her initial doubts, his mother had been quite correct about him. Philip was intelligent, sharp-witted. If anyone could help sort out the logistics of such a thing, he could.

Catherine's voice broke into Sorrel's reflections."Just as soon as the rest of our party arrives, Crispin will call up the coaches."

"Have you any idea what is keeping Lord Lampton and Mr. Garner?"

"Likely the same thing that has delayed your brother and young Charlie—Ipswich offers too many diversions."

"I am going to take a couple of turns in the corridor while we wait," Sorrel said. "I need to stretch my legs before confining them to the coach for two hours."

"Certainly." Catherine smiled kindly at her. "Travel must be uncomfortable for you."

"Far more than I like to admit." Sorrel, walking stick in hand, limped from the room.

The first turn down the empty corridor proved slow and awkward—the cold combined with her stretch of immobility at lunch had stiffened her joints considerably. She began her second turn but came up short at a door near the back end. A serving girl stepped from the taproom into the corridor, and Sorrel was obliged to wait while she passed.

As she stood there, leaning precariously against the wall, her eyes and ears turned toward the public room and the gathering of humanity stretched out before her. Boisterous conversations mingled with laughter. Men of obvious means drank beside the lowliest of stable hands. Nearest the door, leaning over tankards of ale, two men were engaged in an intense conversation.

The man who sat in her line of sight, his face turned toward her enough to be seen, seemed particularly consumed by their tête-à-tête. His rugged, sun-darkened face bore heavy creases, as though he spent an inordinate amount of time in the sun. Perhaps he was a farm worker or a sailor.

"North of Brownlow," the tanned man said to his companion.

The second man's head shook back and forth in obvious disagreement. "No place to make port," he said.

"Then make port up shore and row down." The first man sounded agitated. "You *will* be there."

"Of course," came the reply. "Twenty-ninth. Double twelves."

A grunted confirmation escaped the first man's throat before he downed the remainder of his tankard.

"What do I tell Bélanger?"

"Pêchez de le fontaine." The tanned man's French accent was perfect. Too perfect, in fact.

Sorrel stared for a moment. His English was infallible, yet he spoke French like an émigré. Something about his statement struck her as strange. What, precisely, bothered her about it, she couldn't immediately say.

Sorrel turned back toward the front of the corridor and limped heavily back to the parlor. The party would be ready to leave soon. She refused to be caught eavesdropping. Philip may very well have returned and would never let her hear the end of it. Somewhere in the last few days, his opinion of her had begun to matter. She had yet to decide whether that was a good development or bad.

Fifteen

Philip kept to his extensive portrayal of a care-for-nothing dandy even as he took careful note of every person he passed on the streets of Ipswich. He sauntered about and checked his reflection in an obliging window. The women he passed received a tip of the hat or a deep bow or a particularly dapper smile. He made a point of passing through shops, even purchasing an item that caught his eye. If anyone were suspicious of his presence in Ipswich, they'd find ample evidence that he'd come for nothing more or less than a leisurely shopping trip.

After thirty minutes of painstakingly creating a pretext for the trip, Philip encountered Garner outside a haberdashery. The time had come to attend to weightier matters. Without any acknowledgment beyond a civil nod, they parted ways. Philip slipped down a narrow gap between two shops up the street, following it to a back alley. He'd undertaken searches in Ipswich before.

He doubled back. Garner met him directly behind the shop where they'd passed one another. The man held out a dark overcoat. Philip couldn't help an appreciative smile.

"You object to my choice of attire?" He picked at an invisible fleck of lint on his Weston jacket.

"Your taste is impeccable, as always," Garner said. "But draws too much attention."

Philip pulled on the oversized overcoat. He knew the routine as well as Garner did, but enjoyed pricking that man's patience. He

opened the top of a crate tucked behind several barrels and piles of discarded paper. Their associate in Ipswich would have placed a few things inside to help Philip appear less flamboyant.

"Has Ol' Rob received any information about a meeting place?" he asked, buttoning the overcoat.

Garner nodded. "Word is, Le Fontaine is passing information to a contact at the Drake and Crown within the next half-hour."

"Thirty minutes?" Philip switched out his shiny hessians, with Garner's assistance, for a scuffed pair of well-worn boots. "Remind me to thank Rob for giving us so much warning."

Garner didn't respond beyond a poorly hidden sniffle. He wasn't anticipating the coming encounter with any excitement. Philip merely wanted the information he needed to finish this last mission. He wanted to be done.

His watch and fobs went into the crate, as did his walking stick and tall hat. He plopped atop his head the very unexceptional headwear waiting inside. So long as he kept the coat buttoned, his startlingly white shirt and extremely colorful waistcoat might go unnoticed.

"We'd best walk quickly," Philip said, doing just that. "I hope you brought a handkerchief. All that sniffling will make people think you're weeping like a baby."

They emerged from the back alleys a stone's throw from the Drake and Crown. The area was not as fine as the section of town they'd just left, but far from the worst Philip had seen. Le Fontaine was playing the game by his usual rules. He seldom lowered himself to meetings amongst the very dregs of humanity but made a point of avoiding the most elevated. The Drake and Crown fit that description nicely.

Philip and Garner stepped into the taproom with all the ease of regulars. Nervousness or lofty airs would draw too much notice. They took seats at a corner table. Garner made a point of regularly declaring his dislike of their work, but the man had a knack for it. To all the world he must have appeared to notice nothing beyond the somewhat questionable pint of beer sitting in front of him. Philip, however, knew a perusal when he saw one.

"Well?" Philip asked in a low voice.

Garner knew the question behind the single word. "Fewer patrons than I expected," he replied, leaning over his tall glass. "And none show the slightest discomfort. None are speaking in low tones nor seem to be having an important conversation."

"Though some appear to have gone through more than their share of ale." Philip eyed a man struggling to stay on his chair and another who'd already lost that battle. "You seem cold," Philip said, giving Garner a very weighted look.

He received a nod of understanding. Casually and as natural as breathing, Garner wandered toward the large fireplace. He would be listening to the voices he passed, searching their words for telltale phrases.

Philip pretended to devote himself to the joys of watered-down ale. His acting abilities barely proved sufficient. Rather than play the role of a devoted drunkard, Philip opted for "man with a great deal on his mind." He found, though, his mind had but two things weighing on it: Le Fontaine and General Sorrel, the latter being far more pleasant to ponder.

The one and only thing he'd purchased in Ipswich he meant to give her as a gift on Christmas. Had she thought of him during her stay in the town? What would she think of his offering? He allowed a small smile. Sorrel would certainly not be indifferent to his gift. She might very well beat him with her walking stick.

Why did he enjoy her company so much? She had fire and spirit and determination. She was also stubborn and contrary and . . . lovely.

Philip pulled himself back into the moment only to realize Garner had wandered back without his noticing. He needed to focus.

"Feeling warmer?" he asked.

"Not particularly." Garner hadn't heard anything suspicious, then.

"Blast," Philip muttered. "Have you missed anyone?"

Garner nodded as he raised his glass to his lips. "The table closest to the door." He spoke almost from within the glass.

That would be harder to listen in on. The only reason they could possibly have for passing that table was leaving the pub entirely. Not having found Le Fontaine, they couldn't do that yet.

A quarter-hour passed without anyone new joining the small group in the tap room. Philip and Garner had required nearly ten minutes to walk there. The time frame given for Le Fontaine's meeting had nearly passed.

Philip pulled a few coins from his pocket. "Shall we make our way out? Slowly?"

They did just that. Philip took a long moment to toss the barkeep the coins he owed him, all the while keeping an ear on the only conversation in the room Garner hadn't listened to.

"Tell yer woman that a man's gotta 'ave a pint with his friends now and then. Can't expect ye to spend all yer wakin' hours tied to 'er apron strings."

A discussion of marital discord? Philip could have groaned. Was there no one in the entire establishment who meant to discuss matters of international concern? Philip had a spy to track down and hadn't managed a single piece of solid information in months.

"Fiend seize it," Philip muttered under his breath as they stepped out into the cold. Had he truly just wasted a half-hour in a run-down tap room? He'd parted company with his family and friends in order to pursue this tip. He might have spent the afternoon happily brangling with Sorrel.

"So did we miss him, or was he never here in the first place?" Garner shoved his hands in the pocket of his coat.

"It matters little either way. We still have no reliable information on when or where he might make another appearance."

They made their way slowly up the street, sauntering as if they hadn't anywhere to be.

"How long before our party will be expecting us?" Garner asked.

Philip rolled his shoulders, trying to work out the tension he felt there. "I find myself without a watch at the moment. If I had to hazard a guess, I'd wager we haven't a great deal of time."

"It is unfortunate Le Fontaine didn't choose the Dove and Crow to meet up with his comrade." Garner's sniffles had cured, but his attitude hadn't grown sunnier. "We might have taken luncheon with our friends. Lord Cavratt meant to reserve a private parlor."

Philip's frustrations took firm hold of his own attitude. "How precisely did you mean to overhear a conversation in a tap room from within the walls of a private parlor? Have you abilities you're concealing from me?"

Garner ignored the comment. Not twenty yards from the point they meant to slip once more into the back ways and return to their own part of town, a man not quite as tall as Philip but more solidly built stepped directly into their path. He sported a great deal of dirt, a very small collection of teeth, and, more to the point, a rather vicious-looking club.

"Not again," Philip mumbled. He'd been set upon by footpads the last time he'd gone after Le Fontaine.

"There be a toll for passin' this way," the man informed them.

"How much?" Philip asked.

"Wha'ever ye got, cove."

"Very well." Philip shot Garner a knowing look. "I think I've a coin or two." He pretended to pull something from his pocket and extended his closed fist.

When the man moved forward to retrieve his bounty, Philip came at him with the other hand, landing a solid blow to the man's middle. Garner knew his cue. With the thief bent over from the impact of Philip's punch, Garner threw his elbow into the back of the man's neck. As he reeled forward, Philip easily took the club from the thief's loosened grip.

"That, my friend," he said, "was 'wha'ever I got.' I hope it proved sufficient."

He received only a groan in response. Philip and Garner left the man to contemplate a change of occupation. The club found a new home tossed into a rubbish pile somewhere between that less savory part of town and the crate where Philip's things were hidden.

He changed quickly into his usual attire, speaking in low tones to Garner. "Let Ol' Rob know we found nothing. We'll have to send word to the Foreign Office."

"I don't understand it," Garner said. "More than one source felt certain Le Fontaine would be here today. Rob's information seemed good."

"Blame it on my luck lately," Philip offered. "I can't seem to get the upper hand on any of my enemies."

"You have so many, do you?"

"Enough, Garner. More than enough."

Sixteen

"We are fortunate Lizzie did not come along," Crispin said to Philip as they watched James Driver attempting to make room in the carriage's storage box for the group's parcels. "She'd most likely have placed her purchases inside and attempted to fit *us* into the box."

"That would have been positively ruinous for my cravat," Philip scoffed, smoothing his neckcloth as if it had already endured such a disfiguring experience.

"Your cravat could use a little destruction." Crispin eyed him critically.

"You and Sorrel have no appreciation for the fashionably inventive."

"Took you to task, did she?" Crispin seemed far too pleased with the idea. Philip offered no response.

"Seems to be coming on to rain," Garner noted as he walked past the spot where Philip and Crispin stood.

"Snow a week ago, now rain?" Philip glanced at Crispin. "What kind of party are you hosting, Cavratt?"

Crispin smiled at the friendly jab. "Perhaps we should leave for Kinnley before the weather thwarts us further."

In an instant, Catherine and Sorrel emerged from the warmth of the Dove and Crow. Crispin handed his wife into Philip's carriage, his being the better sprung of the two vehicles they had taken to Ipswich. Philip smiled to himself, noticing Crispin kept hold of Catherine far longer than necessary.

Perhaps I ought to walk back to Kinnley, Philip mused. The newlyweds might not prove enjoyable traveling companions.

"Do not be daft, Sorrel." Fennel's voice broke through Philip's thoughts.

"I will beg you to cease berating me and help me inside." Sorrel's tone was tight and tense.

"Lord Lampton's carriage rides smoother. If you think I am going to return to Kinnley just to explain to Marjie why you are too sore to move, you are much mistaken."

"I will be fine, Fennel."

"You are not fine *now*. I don't know what was so important to bring you all this way, but I won't—"

"Perhaps I may be of assistance," Philip offered, not liking the mutinous look on Sorrel's face and not wishing to see Fennel bashed across the head with that lady's walking stick. "I am quite an expert at sibling disagreements, I assure you."

Sorrel pressed her lips more firmly together. Fennel gave Philip an almost desperate look. This was, apparently, more serious than he had realized. "Now what seems to be the difficulty?" Philip asked.

"Sorrel is stubborn as an old mule." Philip tried not to smile at Fennel's assessment—cutting remarks seemed a family talent.

"I rode *to* Ipswich in this coach, and I see no reason why I shouldn't *return* in it." Sorrel eyed Fennel with all the inflexibility of a . . . well, a mule.

"You would be more comfortable in the other carriage."

"If you are so enamored of Lord Lampton's vehicle, perhaps *you* should ride in it."

"It is rather remarkable, I must admit." Philip shrugged.

"Which is why Mr. Garner ought to be permitted to return in it, just as he arrived," Sorrel argued. "I have no intention of putting him out."

"Mr. Garner does not require a gentle ride," Fennel countered.

"Neither do I," Sorrel declared defiantly.

"Blast it, Sorrel!" Fennel snapped at her. "I have no desire to endure Marjie's tears over your state when you return."

"I could sneeze, and Marjie would cry over my fragility."

"You are growing ill again, Sorrel." Fennel ignored his sister's effort to redirect the conversation. "Do not attempt to deny it, you know I can tell. This is twice within a single week. I will not spend another Christmas seeing you delirious with fever and writhing in pain."

Philip had never seen Fennel anything but even-tempered, but at that moment he would not have been surprised to see steam rise from the lad's ears. He was angry and frustrated. If Philip didn't miss his mark, Fennel was worried, more so than he'd been the day Sorrel had been so ill that Philip had been required to carry her back to Kinnley. Sorrel did not seem as bad off as she'd been that day, but Fennel's reaction contradicted that assumption.

"I believe Catherine would appreciate your presence," Philip told Sorrel. "Otherwise Crispin and I are likely to lead the conversation into completely disreputable territory: fisticuff matches, horse races, that sort of thing."

Sorrel did not offer an immediate reply. Her gaze dropped to the ground around her feet. She let out a huff of breath. "I am so weary of all this." The whispered words broke with some deep, pervading emotion.

Philip had the sudden, almost overwhelming urge to pull her into his arms. Prickly, unapproachable Sorrel suddenly seemed all glass and china: delicate and breakable.

Fennel reached out to her, laying his hand gently on her arm. "I know," he said quietly. "I know."

"Poppy, why don't you and Charlie ride back with Mr. Garner. I will see your sister returned as comfortably as possible to Kinnley."

When Sorrel offered no objection to Philip's presumptuous interference nor his nickname for Fennel, Philip's concern grew. He'd fully expected to have to argue his point even as the only other carriage rode out of sight, perhaps having to carry her kicking and screaming into his vehicle complete with stares from the crowd that would gather to witness such a display. He even thought he might have enjoyed coming out the victor in that encounter.

Fennel seemed to hesitate. Philip motioned the boy toward the waiting carriage with a flick of his head. No grown woman's pride could possibly survive being ordered about by a fifteen-year-old, especially her own brother. Sorrel's pride, Philip had begun to realize, was more battered and sorely protected than most.

With a smile of obvious gratitude, Fennel disappeared inside the Cavratt equipage, which almost immediately began its journey. Sorrel stood perfectly still, not looking at Philip, not watching the departing carriage.

"I think he means well," Philip said after a heavy silence.

"My entire family 'means well.'" Sorrel sighed. "I'd rather they think of me as a capable, intelligent, grown woman."

"*I* think you are a capable, intelligent, grown woman." Philip put two fingers beneath Sorrel's chin and gently turned her face up toward him. "Fennel is young, yet. He is still learning how to go about in the world."

"He should not worry himself over—"

"Compassion is as much a part of his nature as independence is a part of yours," Philip said. "But when you fight him so much, he has little choice but to fight you back."

An alarming quiver seized Sorrel's lower lip. Philip felt himself panic. He knew he was absolutely unprepared for a teary Sorrel—he hadn't yet adjusted to her easy acquiescence only moments before.

"The weather may not hold out much longer," he blurted. "We should be going."

But Sorrel took sudden hold of Philip's hand, her sable eyes locked intensely on his. "Philip," she said in a pleading tone completely foreign to their usual encounters. The only other time

Philip had heard her sound so beseeching was when she'd been shivering with a fever. Maybe Sorrel truly was growing ill again. "Do you think I am frail?"

"Frail?" Philip chuckled. He brushed Sorrel's cheek with the hand she was not holding. "Sorrel, if you were any *less* frail, I wouldn't stand a chance in this war of ours. You'd positively fillet me."

"Yes, I would," she replied with a hint of a mischievous smile, the lightness returning to her tone. "And I am afraid I would enjoy it."

Philip allowed his hand to slip to her chin, which he cupped as he smiled back at her. "You are a truly dangerous enemy."

A blush stole across Sorrel's face, completely ruining Philip's declaration. This "dangerous" enemy was absolutely charming.

"She will freeze to death, Philip," Crispin called from the waiting carriage. "Kindly quit accosting her and allow Sorrel to come in out of the wind."

"I see the troops are rallying behind you, General Sorrel." Philip chuckled as he handed her into the carriage. "Should I be worried?"

"Immensely," she replied over her shoulder.

Crispin and Catherine occupied the rear-facing seat, leaving Philip to share the forward bench with Sorrel, and they looked far too pleased with the arrangement. Philip probably should have objected or at least wondered at his friends' intentions. Instead he found himself feeling entirely satisfied.

Philip pulled out a carriage blanket and began unfolding it for Sorrel. "Not an offer of assistance," he said at the moment she got that militant look in her eyes. "I just know if you catch your death of cold on the way home, I will have every female at Kinnley declaring war on me. At the moment, you are the only combatant I can handle."

Sorrel laughed and shook her head. "Losing your touch, then?"

"Afraid so."

Sorrel accepted the offered blanket and pulled it over her shoulders. So she was colder than she'd let on? Philip suddenly wished he'd requested a third brick for the carriage. Another blanket was stored beneath the driver's seat. Philip shook himself. When had he become the overly attentive traveling companion?

Within ten minutes, rain began to fall outside. He could see trees whipped by recurrent gusts of wind. The road to Kinnley would be anything but easy.

You are growing ill again, Sorrel. Fennel had looked so worried. Philip began to feel concerned himself. Sorrel sat quietly watching the scene outside. Did she look a little peaked? Philip thought she looked pale.

"How are you feeling?" he asked softly, leaning closer to her.

"I am a little tired," she admitted with a sigh. "Frailty, I suppose." A hint of frustration colored her tone.

Philip shook his head mutely. Sorrel was far too critical of herself. "It is nearly two hours to Kinnley," he reminded her. "Not one of us will think less of you for catching some sleep."

Her countenance fell. "I didn't . . . A day trip didn't used to . . ."

Philip impulsively took hold of her hand poking out from beneath the carriage blanket. "Ten minutes in my company would wear out Wellington."

A crooked, half-forced smile flitted momentarily across Sorrel's face before her gaze returned to the worsening weather outside. Something was obviously gnawing at her. But Sorrel, as always, was a closed book when it came to emotions. Philip seldom found himself at a loss for words but couldn't in that moment think of a single thing to say. Why in the world did he wish he had some words of comfort for her? Something to lighten her obviously heavy mind?

Philip tucked her hand back beneath the carriage blanket then turned his attention to the opposite window. Sorrel seriously disturbed his peace. He had enough on his mind without worrying over the difficulties of a woman who'd been a stranger to him only two weeks earlier.

A deep chuckle from across the carriage caught Philip's attention. He glanced over at Crispin caressing and kissing Catherine's hand, smiling at her like a lovesick puppy. She watched her husband with obvious adoration. The two were oblivious to the world around them, absolutely besotted with one another and ridiculously happy.

Philip let his eyes wander back to the window. He wasn't jealous. Not much. He had enough going on in his life without the added complication of love. He had his brothers to worry over, his estates to manage. Parliament. The messy business of spying. Le Fontaine. His work had always been satisfying, knowing he was making a difference—improving, perhaps even *saving,* lives.

That was a noble, worthy ambition. He'd get around to marriage and the succession eventually. But, he demanded of himself, what woman in her right mind would set her cap for a shallow dandy? Being regarded that way had never bothered him so much before. It was necessary, after all. But lately . . .

Philip rubbed his face with his hand, feeling twice his twenty-eight years. Maybe Garner had the right of it, after all. Perhaps he was getting too old for the life of an agent.

"Are you feeling well?" Apparently Crispin's awareness of his surroundings surpassed Philip's estimation.

"Just tired from all that shopping and what," Philip answered.

Crispin chuckled his obvious disbelief. "I don't believe I saw a single parcel on your person."

"It was a small item," Philip answered mysteriously, with a pat at his pocket.

"Really?" Catherine looked far too intrigued, so Philip shot her a guilty smile and a raise of his eyebrows. She laughed lightly. "I can see how that could be exhausting. Now we need to find out what has drained dear Sorrel."

Philip turned his eyes to the woman who seemed to occupy his thoughts more often than not the last few days. Despite her earlier declaration that she felt only "a little tired," Sorrel's head bobbed repeatedly to one side, her eyes already closed, her posture slumped.

"I hope she can sleep," Catherine said compassionately. "She has been looking pale today."

"Fennel thinks she is ailing again," Philip remembered aloud, watching her closely and not liking what he saw. Her face looked pale as parchment, dark circles marring the skin under her eyes. He didn't like seeing her look so decidedly unwell. "If she weren't so ridiculously stubborn, she'd have stayed at Kinnley instead of traveling all this way."

"Please don't scold her about this." Catherine watched him with concern. "I think her reasons for coming were quite pressing."

"Pressing enough to risk a fever hours from civilization?"

Sorrel could be so deucedly stubborn at times. First jaunting off on horseback while unwell, then hying herself to Ipswich a few days later at the onset of yet another illness.

"Seems she came to Ipswich to—" Crispin began, but Catherine placed a halting hand on his arm.

"Crispin," she protested. "We promised."

"We promised we wouldn't tell *Miss Marjie,*" he corrected.

"How can we know Sorrel would want Philip to know?"

"It is Miss Marjie's pity she doesn't want," Crispin said. "Philip's not the pitying kind."

Philip smiled. "Piti*ful,* maybe, but not pity*ing*."

Catherine offered an obligatory smile at the pun. Her gaze, however, returned to Sorrel, and Catherine looked concerned. Philip's attention returned to his seat partner, as well, pale but peaceful in her sleep.

She really is beautiful, he admitted to himself yet again.

"It is a shame she dislikes you so much." Crispin seemed to grow contemplative.

There was no safe answer to that statement.

"Sorrel does not dislike Philip, at all," Catherine said.

Philip begged to differ. So did Crispin, which wasn't encouraging in the least. There were many evidences of Sorrel's feelings. Crispin took it upon himself to list them. After five or six examples, Catherine stopped him.

"She does *not* dislike him."

"Have you been listening to anything I have just said?" Crispin replied a bit critically.

Catherine's lips pressed together, and her face blanched slightly. Feeling decidedly out of his element, Philip looked away from the suddenly tense couple and found himself watching Sorrel instead. She seemed to be shivering. Philip pulled her blanket more snugly around her. The movement pulled her partly from her slumber, and those sleepy black eyes gazed up at him.

Lud, he hoped she really didn't dislike him.

"How are you feeling?" Philip whispered.

Sorrel didn't answer beyond a feeble smile, her eyes slowly closing again. Her head bobbed once before resting against his shoulder. The faint scent of limes wafted through the air. Philip quite suddenly hoped the journey to Kinnley took longer than anticipated. A true dandy would have objected to the crease that Sorrel's head would leave on his jacket sleeve. Philip didn't give a fig about wrinkles.

"For mortal enemies, you two are terribly cozy," Crispin said with a raise of his eyebrow.

Philip bit back a laugh. "Only because she is asleep," he said. "And unless you want to spend Christmas fussing over my funeral, I suggest you not mention *this*"—he motioned with his head toward Sorrel—"to my 'mortal enemy.'"

Catherine looked between Philip and Sorrel then back at her husband, and with the slightest exasperated shake of her head, she looked away from them.

"Please don't be angry with me, my love." Crispin reached for Catherine's hand but was denied.

Philip silently encouraged his friend—interfering would mean moving, and, quite frankly, Philip had no intention of so much as shifting his weight. *Limes,* he thought with a smile.

"You know I am a bit of an idiot at times." Obviously Crispin had experience apologizing. "You can always throw me in the lake when we get home."

"Or poison your tea," Catherine answered, as though that were the most logical conclusion in the world.

"Hmm . . ." Crispin looked ponderous. "The tea." He nodded for emphasis. "It is too cold for the lake."

Catherine turned her face back toward Crispin and studied him a moment. Crispin appeared the very embodiment of contrition. Philip barely managed to hold back a laugh. Catherine exhibited no such self-control.

"I never can stay mad at you, Crispin."

"Something I am grateful for daily."

The journey continued silently after the reconciliation. Crispin and Catherine sat snugly near one another, his arm draped affectionately across her shoulders as she leaned securely against his side. The two could have posed for a portrait—they made such an idyllic scene.

Philip himself sat beside a stunning, dark-haired beauty and didn't dare move lest she awaken and beat him senseless for being within touching distance. *It is a shame she dislikes you so much.*

Yes. A deuced shame.

Seventeen

Waking up with her head resting quite intimately on Philip Jonquil's shoulder was not an entirely unpleasant occurrence, which worried Sorrel greatly. Perhaps her repeated fevers were beginning to affect her brain. The way her wits went begging when he smiled at her as she awoke disturbed her more than anything. What was the matter with her?

"I guess I fell asleep," Sorrel said lamely, for some reason not yet lifting her head from its rather comfortable position.

"You have been asleep for more than an hour," he replied quietly. "And I am happy to inform you that you do not snore."

"That is a relieving thing to hear." Sorrel couldn't help a chuckle.

"Crispin, on the other hand . . ."

Philip's words pulled Sorrel's eyes away from his handsome profile and across the carriage to Crispin and Catherine. The couple slept quite unabashedly in a cozy embrace, her head fitted snugly beneath his shoulder, his arms wrapped possessively around her, the carriage blanket covering them both.

Just as Sorrel silently declared the scene alarmingly perfect, a nasalized buzzing filled the vehicle's interior. Her eyes widened, then her lips twitched, followed by a laugh bubbling dangerously near the surface. She looked up at Philip, and all self-control dissipated. His laughter quickly joined hers. Neither Catherine nor Crispin stirred.

"Poor Catherine." Sorrel chuckled. "How does she put up with it, I wonder."

"That is simple enough, Sorrel."

She turned her eyes back to him, looking up into his face. "Is it?"

He nodded, his gaze resting on her. "She loves him."

Sorrel couldn't look away. This man, who could anger her like no one else she knew, held her spellbound as the carriage flew smoothly over what must have been extremely rough road. *She loves him.* He'd spoken with so much authority and conviction and . . . something else. Something she couldn't put her finger on. Wistfulness, perhaps? Or longing?

Philip, it seemed, believed firmly in love. Sorrel distrusted the entire emotion. Her parents had never cared for one another, let alone shared any more tender feelings. She had no experience with love.

"How can you tell she loves him?" Sorrel regretted her question almost immediately. If ever she were in a more vulnerable situation, she couldn't recall it. She'd left herself entirely exposed to this man who thought of her as his enemy.

She expected a stinging reply. A set down. Laughter. Something. Philip answered with silence and a look of intensity she found unsettling.

"I suppose there is no guaranteed way of knowing one person's feelings for another." Philip's gaze never faltered. Sorrel's breathing grew more labored. "Instinct, I suppose."

"You have an instinct for ascertaining a person's feelings?" Would he mind explaining hers? Sorrel couldn't make heads nor tails of the sensations tying her in internal knots.

"Generally I am quite good at it."

"Generally?" Was it her imagination or had Philip moved closer to her? Was that even possible? She sat inches from him as it was.

"Lately I seem to be . . ." he had definitely moved his head closer ". . . losing my touch."

"Are you surrounded by so many mysteries, then?" He was so close her breath fluttered the golden hair falling across his forehead.

"I . . ." His eyes flickered across her face, as if he were searching for something, a look almost of confusion marring his handsome features. "Sorrel . . . I . . ."

A sudden snort made Sorrel jump.

Across the carriage Catherine whispered, obviously half-asleep yet, "You are snoring again, darling."

Crispin answered by shifting his position, without awakening nor releasing his wife, and he promptly settled back in.

Sorrel turned her gaze back to Philip, wondering how he interpreted the cozy scene playing out across from them. He, however, had not looked away from *her*. She felt terribly conspicuous under his scrutiny.

"Are you truly growing ill again?" he asked with a quiet determination, pushing her back from him enough to make a visual assessment of her.

Sorrel opened her mouth to deny the charges, but the lie died on her lips. She shrugged then nodded. "I was a little achy this morning."

"Why in heaven's name did you make this trip if you are not well?"

"I had to," she insisted. "It was of utmost importance."

"Surely whoever you were shopping for would far prefer to see you well than to receive whatever present you went in pursuit of."

"I did not buy anything, Philip," Sorrel said. It was the perfect opening to talk with him about Dr. Darrow and the operation. "I went to . . . to see someone."

Philip seemed to stiffen at her explanation. "Really?" His tone grew suddenly quite cold. "A . . . friend?"

Sorrel shook her head, confused by his displeased expression. "Someone with whom I have been . . . corresponding."

He seemed to scrutinize her. "Was your 'correspondent' all you hoped he"—that word seemed to come out as a question—"would be?"

Dr. Darrow hadn't precisely been brimming with good news, but the visit hadn't been an entire waste. He'd offered her hope, something she'd been sorely short of the past two years. "Yes, I suppose he was."

"A gentleman, then?"

"No." Sorrel wondered at the question. Dr. Darrow was a surgeon, not a gentleman, per se, but respectable just the same. This conversation was not going the way she would have expected.

"Was the visit worth the risk?" Philip shifted his gaze to the growing darkness outside, a sudden distance between them that was not entirely physical.

"I am not sure yet." Why did Sorrel get the impression they were not both having the same conversation?

"Yet?" He snapped his head back to regard her in amazement. "You plan to continue this . . . *correspondence?*"

"Certainly." Why shouldn't she? If Dr. MacAslon could help her, Dr. Darrow would be the surest way to secure his services.

"*Certainly.*" Philip's jaw seemed to tighten as he turned away again. "Your family will object, you know."

"They probably will," Sorrel conceded. Mother would object to the inconvenience. Marjie would object to the pain. Fennel would object to the risk. She'd simply have to find a way to convince them.

"But you plan to persist?"

"As far as I can see, it is the only option I have."

"Blast it, Sorrel. I took you for an intelligent woman, not a fool."

"You think it rash of me to grasp at what few straws I have left? A person has to have hope."

"Hope, yes. But not desperation!"

His words cut her to the core. "I did not think it so farfetched as all that," she muttered, beginning to feel the cold of winter seeping into her bones once again.

"It is utter nonsense." Philip crossed his arms against his chest, his jaw set in determination.

So he thought her a fool, too? He certainly wasn't the first. She doubted he'd be the last. Still, his thorough thrashing of a strategy she had been quite seriously considering pursuing hurt horribly.

Philip had been one of the few people she'd encountered since her "unfortunate incident" who took her seriously, who saw past the broken bones and deformities. But he found her daft just like so many others. How could she possibly hope to convince her family to go ahead with a somewhat risky surgery if the one man she'd thought might stand as her ally found her plan so ridiculous?

Sorrel tucked herself into the corner of the carriage and closed her eyes. Perhaps the idea of trying to fix what remained of her had been daft, after all. She ought to simply accept what she had become and resign herself to the pain.

The sights and sounds of her childhood flooded over her with alarming speed and clarity as she sat silently. She truly was falling ill again. Only in her fevers did she relive a time of life she'd much rather forget. She could see Fennel's downcast expression, hear her father's harsh words of criticism directed at her, feel the pain his words had inevitably inflicted. At one time, she'd looked to him, hoped he'd prove an ally. That hadn't worked out either.

Her trip to Ipswich, it seemed, had been for naught. She'd accomplished little but sore joints, a faster onset of symptoms, a less-than-promising interview with Dr. Darrow. Follow those insignificant experiences with a spirit-dampening conversation with a gentleman who had the unnerving ability to break down her carefully erected defenses, and Sorrel had to admit to herself that the entire trip had proven little better than worthless.

Life was slowly draining every ounce of hope she had.

* * *

So, General Sorrel had a "correspondent" in Ipswich, did she? Philip paced the length of the library one more time. That didn't bother him, he silently declared. Hadn't even crossed his mind since they'd returned to Kinnley late that afternoon. Hadn't entered his thoughts in the two hours since dinner. Not at all. He rapped his knuckles on the oak writing desk as he passed.

She'd gone to see this bounder despite his not being a gentleman, despite knowing her family would object. Sorrel was intelligent, fiery, independent. Why the devil would a woman like that settle for some low-class lout!

"Ol' Rob might not have had much for us, Philip, but there's no call for getting furious about it."

Philip had almost forgotten Garner's presence in the room. "I am not furious."

"I have never seen you so discomposed," Garner said. "The Foreign Office won't expect miracles. There is no possible way to know when or where Le Fontaine's next exchange will take place. We simply cannot do it."

Philip grumbled an incoherent reply *he* didn't even listen to. His thoughts were too full of Sorrel, of the picture she'd made leaning against his arm, too full of the idea of her arranging a clandestine meeting with some profligate who certainly didn't deserve her. If ever a dandy wanted to plant someone a facer, it was then, and he didn't even know *whom* he wanted to knock down.

"Unless some new information surfaces, I am afraid Le Fontaine has slipped from our grasp again." Garner sounded almost relieved at his own declaration.

For Philip, the thought of the dirty spy getting away yet again simply added to his list of grievances. He'd all but decided that Le Fontaine would be his last case. He needed to reclaim his life, to hand the reins over to someone with more enthusiasm.

He'd only begun this work with the Foreign Office as a means of helping bring an end to the war he had feared would cost him his brother. With Stanley home safe, if not entirely sound, and more than half a decade of thankless risk-taking under his belt, Philip wanted to be finished. He *needed* to be finished. Le Fontaine, it seemed, didn't intend to let him.

"Lizzie has invited me to stay through Christmas," Garner said, breaking into Philip's thoughts. "I think I might take her up on the offer. In fact, I think I'll go tell her so now." Garner rose from his seat and left the room.

Philip nodded mutely and wandered to the library window. Why did his thoughts seem to fly of their own volition to Sorrel? He wondered how she fared after their journey from Ipswich. She should never have undertaken the journey to begin with. Had she grown ill? Philip rubbed his face. It would never do to dwell on her.

As if to mock his determination to turn his thoughts, the library door opened, and the lady herself stepped inside. Philip cursed his blasted high shirt points—he'd had to turn his entire body to see who had entered.

"Oh," Sorrel said, obviously startled by Philip's presence. "I am not intruding, am I?"

Philip simply said no then turned back toward the window without another word. A moment of awkward silence passed in which Philip felt sorely tempted to turn back around. Just as the temptation proved almost too great to ignore, he heard the swish of her skirts and the thump of her walking stick as she stepped inside. Her gait sounded more uneven, slower than usual. The thought that she might be in pain sat uncomfortably in the back of his mind. So did the knowledge of her unworthy "correspondent."

He didn't turn around.

Every few moments he heard her move. What was she doing? A strange rustling preceded another period of silence. Philip forced his mind to focus on the black night outside. No stars were visible—the sky must be cloudy. Perhaps it would rain more overnight. Or snow.

There. Nearly a minute without a single thought of Sorrel. He was every bit as impartial to her as he'd always claimed. Philip shook his head at his own insistence. A minute of forced reflection on Suffolk's changeable weather hardly established his disinterestedness.

Not that he needed proof. Sorrel Kendrick was a casual acquaintance against whom he was waging a war. Nothing more. Nothing less. He was entirely impartial. Unaffected. Unconcerned.

"Philip?"

Perhaps not entirely unaffected. The quiet pleading way Sorrel uttered his name made his heart clench in an almost ridiculous way. But, he told himself quite severely, *she* would never know how much she'd cut into his peace.

Assuming his most aloof expression, Philip turned back toward her. She sat quite ladylike on the floor of the library facing the bookshelves, her walking stick leaning against the shelves. She clutched a thin book in one hand with the other hand pressed against the bookshelves.

"Yes?" Philip asked with his haughtiest tone. Let Sorrel see his complete immunity to her.

Her dark eyes flitted to his, an almost nervous expression lurking in them. "I . . . uh . . . seem to have made a . . . miscalculation." She stumbled over the words, her outstretched hand grasping for a moment at a shelf.

"Is that so?" Was she willing to admit the folly of continuing her connection in Ipswich? Finally acknowledge that he had far more in his brainbox than fluff? Philip looked forward to the admission.

"Yes. You see . . . I . . ." She looked deucedly uncomfortable. She'd be better off without her Ipswich beau, he hoped she realized. She'd made a wise decision. "I found the book I was looking for . . ." *Book?* "But, now I . . . I am having difficulty getting up."

Philip's expression soured—he could feel his lips turn down in a frown. She still planned to hold on to her "correspondent"? She hadn't seen the error in her judgment? What was wrong with her!

"I . . . would you . . ." Sorrel stuttered. "Would you help me?"

Now she wanted help? Now! After all the times she'd ripped him up over his attempts to assist her? She'd rebuffed him severely for even the simplest offers in the past. She'd estranged her own brother just that afternoon.

"Sorrel Kendrick?" he scoffed, his frustration taking control of his tongue. "Sorrel Kendrick, who *never* needs or wants help? Sorrel Kendrick, who can do everything on her own?"

"I—" She seemed to squirm.

"I believe I have promised you many times not to offer you assistance of any kind," Philip reminded her, making his way to the library door. The woman infuriated him! Her "correspondent" probably offered her plenty of assistance. She probably readily accepted it. So let *him* help her! "I am a man of my word, Miss Kendrick."

"You would leave me here?" The shock in her tone could not be mistaken.

"A war tactic," Philip replied with a slight bow. "An incapacitated enemy is easier to defeat."

"Touché, *Lord Lampton.*" Sorrel turned her gaze back to the shelves in front of her. "You have finally claimed a victory, it would seem. You employ rather underhanded strategies, I hope you realize."

"Including a belief in strategic retreats," Philip added with a triumphant grin. "Good night, Miss Kendrick."

He saw her cross her arms defiantly in front of her and felt certain she was glowering.

Let her stew, he thought. Perhaps she'd emerge from their latest battle less prideful and less stubborn. Infuriating woman!

Correspondent, indeed! A voice in the back of Philip's brain whispered he had overreacted. Philip ignored it and stomped off to his room, wishing he'd never left London in the first place.

Eighteen

He'd lain on his bed for two hours, cravat, jacket, and boots discarded, shirttails untucked, staring up at the heavy, tapestry bed curtains. Sorrel had conceded defeat. He'd emerged from a confrontation the victor. So why did he feel so dissatisfied?

She had every right to a "correspondent," every right to as many suitors as she chose to have, of whatever class she was willing to consider. The fact that *he* thought she ought not to settle for less than a gentleman did not factor into the equation, though she deserved better.

Philip supposed he felt disappointed that Sorrel hadn't used her obvious intelligence, that she apparently held her own significance so cheaply. She ought to have chosen . . . better.

But none of that was any of Philip's concern. Was it? Logically, no. But no amount of logical arguments had driven the situation from his mind. He *was* concerned.

An almost frantic knock on his door broke his repetitive thoughts.

"Come in," he called.

Fennel Kendrick stepped inside, his eyes wide, his face decidedly pale.

"What is it, Poppy?" Philip swiftly got to his feet.

"We can't find Sorrel." Fennel's words rushed out. "Marjie went to check on her, but she wasn't in her bedchamber. She hasn't been to bed yet. She left the sitting room a couple hours ago. She ought to have been in her room."

With a few long strides, Philip reached his door. "She wasn't in your mother's chambers?"

"No. Nor Marjie's."

Philip tugged Fennel along with him as he made his way down the corridor toward the stairs. "Any idea where she might have gone?" Philip asked, his own heart beating a bit faster. He wasn't usually so easily alarmed, but Fennel's near panic had instantly unnerved him.

"No." Fennel's voice cracked on the word. "She's at the start of more fevers. What if she's ill somewhere?"

"Calm down, Poppy." Philip stopped at the head of the stairs, trying to form a strategy. "Who else knows she's missing?"

"Only Marjie and Mother and I. Mother didn't want to bother the house. I couldn't think of what to do, and Marjie's too overset to undertake it. I needed help!"

"You did the right thing." Philip laid his hand on the lad's shoulder. The poor boy was trembling.

"We have to find her. The fevers can be bad when they are so close together!"

Philip's mind ran frantically. Sorrel was not irresponsible. She wouldn't have simply wandered off, not even in a fit of pique, though she'd obviously been quite put out by their battle earlier. Philip went over that encounter in his mind. Had she been upset enough to stalk off and sulk somewhere? He'd have plenty to say to her if she had. Worrying her family like this!

"Has anyone checked the stables? You've said she's fond of horses."

"She wouldn't go now," Fennel answered, emotion still high in his voice. "Not with your horse in there."

"Devil's Advocate?" Philip furrowed his brow. "Why would he keep her out?"

"He's too much like—" Fennel stopped abruptly. "He reminds her of another horse."

"You're certain that would be enough to keep her away?"

Fennel nodded with conviction. "She was nearly killed by a large black horse," he said quietly, pensively. "Yours is so much like Diablo Negro. Sorrel has avoided the stables ever since she saw him."

"She had a run-in with the Black Devil?" Philip knew the infamous stallion's reputation well enough to understand Sorrel's discomfort at any memory of that horse.

Fennel nodded uncomfortably and pointed briefly at his right leg. Philip tried for a moment to decipher the strange gesture before the message became all too clear. Sorrel's leg. The notoriously dangerous Diablo Negro. The "unfortunate incident." Sorrel had been kicked or, more likely yet, trampled by the great black beast. That probably would be enough to keep her at a distance from Philip's mount. Devil's Advocate had been named, in part, for his sire: Diablo Negro.

"So not the stables," Philip conceded. Fennel watched him with an alarming intensity that spoke volumes of his concern. "When was the last anyone saw her?"

"In the sitting room. She left a couple hours before everyone else, saying she intended to retire." Fennel rubbed his hands in agitation. "Marjie had been making a big fuss over her, and I think Sorrel just wanted to get away. It *was* rather embarrassing," Fennel admitted, "all the ado Marjie made. You'd have thought so too if you'd been there."

"I was in the library," Philip explained offhand. Sudden realization grasped his chest. He'd seen her in the library, probably *after* she'd left the sitting room. "She was in the library when I left," he said aloud.

"She might still be there," Fennel said hopefully. "Sorrel has fallen asleep at home reading in Father's old study."

"I'd bet a monkey that's where she is," Philip said. *Sulking,* he added silently. "Come on."

They made their way down the staircase and toward the closed doors of the Kinnley library. If Sorrel wasn't inside, Philip was going to strangle her. Lud, if she *was* inside, he was going to strangle her. She ought to at least have had the decency not to worry her family. But—his thoughts returned to Ipswich—how much concern could she have for her relations if she meant to foster a relationship with a man decidedly below her station in life?

Philip threw open the library doors and glanced around the dim room. Sorrel's walking stick still leaned against the bookshelves where it had been earlier. The same thin, yellow leather-bound book she'd held in her hand lay discarded beside it. He did not see Sorrel.

"Devil take that woman," Philip muttered, trying to choke down the sudden panic he felt. He'd been entirely sure she'd be in the library still. Now he was beginning to worry.

"Over there." Fennel pointed toward the fireplace.

Sorrel sat on the floor, her arms and head lying haphazardly on the seat of the deep-blue sofa. Her eyes were closed, and she kept perfectly still.

"I think she's asleep," Fennel said as he rushed to her. "Sorrel?" he asked almost pathetically. "Sorrel?"

She opened her eyes a sliver but closed them almost immediately. Fennel placed a hand to her forehead, then breathed a sigh of obvious relief. He turned back to look at Philip. "No fever."

"Go tell Miss Marjie," Philip said. "I'll rouse the prodigal sister and bring her up to her bedchamber."

"Thank you." Fennel jumped to his feet and ran from the room.

Philip moved purposely to the sofa, emotions warring inside: relief that she'd been found and seemed well, mingled with anger that she'd worried her family. Something almost painfully heavy settled in his chest.

He knelt on the floor beside Sorrel. Her eyes opened once more, the lids wearily heavy.

"And what do you have to say for yourself, Miss Kendrick?" Philip asked, trying to rein in his feelings.

She looked up at him, a little paler than he remembered her being. "*Now* will you help me?"

"What?"

"I hate asking for help, Philip." She little more than whispered. "Please don't make me beg."

"I . . ."

"I have admitted defeat. What more do you need me to say?" Sorrel rubbed unabashedly at her right leg, her eyes pinched in what could only be described as agony. "I am certain you would have taken tremendous delight in watching me crawl like an infant across the floor trying to find something to pull myself to my feet with, but I am too weary and too pained to keep trying."

"Crawled . . . ?" Philip's eyes darted back to the abandoned book and walking stick then returned to Sorrel leaning rather helplessly against the sofa. "You mean . . . earlier . . . you truly could not get up?"

"Would I have asked for assistance if I did not absolutely require it?" Her voice broke with barely concealed emotion.

"I didn't realize . . ." Philip's insides twisted with shame. He'd actually left her sprawled helplessly on the floor.

"I have swallowed my pride. Will you please overlook your dislike of me long enough to help me rise off this cold floor?"

The fire had gone out, Philip suddenly realized. The bare floors were probably deucedly cold. She'd been down there for two hours. He did not need to hear the request again. In less than a heartbeat he lifted her up onto the sofa.

"May I have a blanket?" she asked before Philip had a chance to voice the apology quickly forming in his head.

Dash it! The woman was freezing. How could he have been so mutton-headed? Philip crossed immediately to the window box and pulled out a blanket he knew from experience would be there. He'd not managed to utter a single word by the time he'd wrapped it around her shoulders.

Her eyes darted to him, her mouth set in a firm line. Philip saw unshed tears gathering in her eyes.

"Sorrel, I am so sorry." He could not recall being so angry with himself in a very long time. "I should have . . . I know you enough to realize . . . Blast it!" He threw his hands up in self-disgust. "I can't even apologize correctly. What a muddle I am making of everything."

"I would like to go to sleep," Sorrel said quietly. "Will you help me to my room, please?"

Philip took a calming breath. She spoke with so little emotion, despite the obvious pain and disappointment in her eyes. "Of course," Philip replied, realizing with a great deal of frustration that he'd seriously undermined her trust in him. A budding friendship had slowly been forming between them. Perhaps something more than a friendship—he'd very nearly kissed her in the carriage, after all. In one act of utter stupidity, he'd lost that.

"I do not think I can walk," Sorrel warned.

"I would not expect you to endure two flights of stairs, Sorrel. Saving you from that agony is the least I can do considering my role in all of this."

She did not deny his culpability.

Silently deriding himself for being a thoughtless cad, Philip lifted Sorrel from the sofa, one arm under her legs, one supporting her back. She placed her arms rather cautiously around his neck. Sorrel winced as he adjusted his hold. Philip felt his jaw tighten, knowing he'd contributed to that pain.

What kind of a gentleman was he, after all? He'd been defaming an unknown man in Ipswich for not being good enough for Sorrel, and he himself had been far from considerate.

"You won't tell Marjie, will you?" Sorrel asked quite unexpectedly.

"That I left you incapacitated on the floor of the library?"

"That I couldn't get up on my own. If she finds out, I'll have her trailing me around like a nursery maid."

"What would you suggest I tell her instead?" Philip asked, taking the steps as smoothly as he could manage. He noticed Sorrel's expression tighten in pain with every jostle. "She knows you were in the library all this time."

Sorrel let out a breath of frustration. "I don't know. I would like to retain what small amount of dignity I have left. If she thinks I am entirely helpless, she'll—"

"Treat you like a child?" Philip finished for her, slowly beginning to understand Sorrel's family struggles. Miss Marjie did have a tendency to treat her sister like a toddler. Her *older* sister. And Fennel had the unhappy tendency to give her orders as well, and he an Eton lad.

Philip felt Sorrel lean against him a fraction more. For a woman he'd sworn he disliked, he rather appreciated the feel of her in his arms, which only added to the guilt gnawing at him.

"We could tell her you fell asleep," Philip suggested, continuing the conversation in the hope of keeping his mind off her closeness. "The most capable of adults have been known to do that."

"How do you plan to explain our current position?" Sorrel asked, her voice growing quieter, more groggy. Was she falling ill?

"I will tell her I insisted on carrying you," Philip replied, hoping Sorrel was merely sleepy. "She knows enough of my stubbornness to believe I would."

"You won't tell her I couldn't even stand up?"

"May my cravats wither if I breathe a word of it."

He heard the tiniest of laughs from Sorrel. "A strong oath for a dandy," she whispered, her head fully resting against his jaw.

"I fear I am not dressed the part at the moment." Philip took the steps more slowly, though hardly acknowledging his halted pace.

"You look far more handsome when you aren't hiding behind all that pomp," Sorrel said, her words slow and heavy with fast-approaching sleep. "I don't believe you are truly a fop underneath it all."

"You would be correct, my dear." Why he had admitted that, Philip couldn't say. Perhaps he felt safer considering Sorrel's nearly asleep state. Perhaps, for the first time in more than five years, he needed someone to know what he really was. *Who* he really was.

Oh, he was tempted to turn around and carry Sorrel right back to the library, to keep her in his arms a while longer, especially with her peacefully quiet and not attacking or contradicting him at every turn. But that was foolishness and Philip knew it.

Tomorrow would bring back his logical side, and he'd look back on the night and laugh at his own folly, right after he gave himself a firm talking to for being a thoughtless cad in the first place.

Nineteen

Sorrel sunk down on the stairs in defeat. What had possessed her to even attempt such foolery? She could quite easily have rung for Jenny to retrieve her walking stick in the library. Sorrel felt certain she'd left it there the night before. She distinctly remembered Philip haughtily walking out and leaving her on the floor, unable to rise. Only through great effort had she managed to pull herself to the sofa. The rest of the night had dissolved into little more than a blur.

She must have fallen asleep. Her next memories were of Fennel's voice, though she could not recall what he'd said. She vaguely remembered a distinctly masculine scent, something with a hint of cedar and leather. Sorrel thought she'd been carried. In her sketchy memory the arms had been Philip's, but she also recalled a loose-collared shirt, no cravat, no blindingly bright waistcoat. She couldn't imagine Philip ever appearing anything but the flashy dandy.

Sorrel leaned her head against the banister only two steps below the landing and derided herself for being a fool. She'd discovered her walking stick missing with plenty of time to have it fetched. But, for reasons she did not feel ready to examine, she'd struck on this idiotic idea of making her way to the library without it. She had not truly attempted to walk on her own in a long while.

She would be bruised, Sorrel knew. Just the effort of coming down the corridor had sent her reeling into furniture, though she'd

managed to remain upright. With her cane she could reach the landing in less than a minute. Without it she'd needed a quarter-hour. Then she'd reached the stairs. She had not attempted stairs without her cane. A full flight stretched out before her. If she lost her balance, she'd tumble the entire length.

Sorrel had gingerly tried her footing on the first, only to realize she was unequal to the task. Her heart pounding in her throat, Sorrel had slowly, cautiously lowered herself to the step where she sat frustrated at her helplessness and angry at the madness that had convinced her to even attempt a walk of independence.

Footsteps echoed one floor below. Sorrel hoped to see a servant pass the landing beneath her. She could request her walking stick be retrieved, and, before long, she'd be back on her feet and could put this embarrassing episode behind her. She watched rather anxiously for movement, discovering the stairs were extremely uncomfortable.

To her dismay, Philip appeared below. Sorrel suddenly hoped she wouldn't be noticed. Why did he always appear when she looked like a fool? She'd had to practically beg him to help her from the floor in the library only to have him walk away. How much satisfaction would he get out of leaving her stranded on the steps?

"Sorrel?" He'd seen her.

She watched him ascend the stairs and tried to look unaffected, as though being seated on a stairwell were perfectly rational behavior. "Good day." Her voice sounded less desperate than it had the evening before.

"My brothers and I used to sit on the stairs at Lampton Hall when Father was expected home from London," Philip said, quite casually taking a seat beside her. "We made quite a picture, I am certain. Covered in mud, if memory serves, and grinning like the collection of imps that we were."

"I am new at stair sitting," Sorrel said. "Ought I to have rolled in mud first?"

"So what brings you to this inauspicious area of the house?" Philip leaned back, his elbows on the stair behind, his long legs stretched out across the steps below.

He made such a contradictory picture that Sorrel couldn't help staring a moment. His clothes were "all the crack," as Fennel would have said, that same pompous cravat knot Sorrel had come to find almost humorous, coupled with a deep-indigo jacket atop a lemon-yellow waistcoat. Despite being dressed as a fop, Philip reclined on a stairway as easy as anything, something far too undignified for a dandified gentleman.

"Surely you weren't sitting here waiting for me to make my magnificent appearance." Philip raised an eyebrow, which, in any other person, Sorrel might have thought held a hint of self-mockery.

"I am here because I have been acting rather unreasonably," Sorrel admitted with a shrug of her shoulders.

"You are being punished, then?" Philip's lazy smile spread to a mischievous grin. "You realize, of course, that I was one of the official Jonquil Freers of Criminals."

"What?" Sorrel couldn't help a chuckle. His words were almost nonsensical, but the look on his face was positively boyish, unfettered excitement mingled with innocent devilry.

"It started with Layton, the brother just younger than me." Philip's eyes grew wide with animation. "When either he or I would be kept in the nursery as punishment for something I am certain we were wrongfully accused of doing"—he raised an eyebrow as if to say he was certain they'd been absolutely guilty—"we would make a game of freeing the captive brother. Eventually we spread our expertise to extricating the rest of the family from similar punishments."

"Sounds as if you had ample opportunity to hone your skills." Sorrel smiled at the picture of a close-knit, loving family. She'd wished for precisely that all her life.

"Our governesses and tutors were exceptionally cruel." He feigned misery at the fabricated memory.

"So you are going to rescue me from my punishment?" Sorrel asked.

Philip moved nimbly, squatting on the stair directly beneath her, and looked eagerly into her face. She could easily picture him as a lanky seven-year-old planning one madcap scheme or another. Sorrel had the sudden urge to reach out and muss his hair, certain he'd spent most of his childhood in a state of complete disarray.

"It could be dangerous," Philip told her with a raise of his golden eyebrows.

Sorrel nodded quite seriously. "I understand," she said gravely.

"We could tie bedsheets into a rope and climb out the nursery window." Philip rubbed his chin. "But perhaps that is a bit drastic."

"A bit." Sorrel fought back a smile.

"Perhaps, if we move quickly, we can descend the stairs—we will, of course, be terribly stealthy—before your warden notices you have defected."

"My punisher keeps a very close eye on me," Sorrel warned, knowing she had resigned *herself* to her current position.

"Is she watching now?" he whispered conspiratorially.

Sorrel nodded, her gaze locked with his crystal-blue eyes. He looked slyly around them before looking at her again, seemingly scrutinizing her. Philip shifted and sat on the step, continuing to watch her. "Have you endured her chastisement often?" he asked, some of the lightness gone from his tone.

Fighting back a lump in her throat, Sorrel managed a nod. She'd been hard on herself all her life.

"What did you do today that upset her?" He eyed her rather knowingly as he spoke the last word, as if to indicate he knew she referred to herself.

Sorrel let out a humorless chuckle. "I tried to prove something." For some reason, Sorrel couldn't look at him as she made the painful admission. "In the end I mostly just looked foolish."

"What were you trying to prove?" Philip sounded honestly compassionate. Where had the frippery-obsessed dandy gone?

She took a deep breath and found herself confessing despite her determination to do no such thing. "I wanted to see how far I could go without my *affectation*." Sorrel hated the bitterness in her tone.

Beside her Philip fell silent. Sorrel didn't dare look at him. She was not ready to see mockery or disdain. She could not endure further humiliation.

"You came this far without your walking stick?" His voice was quiet, each word spoken slowly and clearly.

Sorrel nodded. "The stairs were too much, though." She bit down on her lip to keep it from quivering. Even a toddler could navigate stairs.

"And for that you are being punished?"

"I suppose my warden is rather harsh."

A warm, strong hand gently caressed her cheek, and Sorrel nearly let a tear slip. Philip softly turned her toward him, his look brimming with compassion. "Why is she that way, Sorrel?"

Sorrel tried to look away, but Philip's hand was deceptively strong. Tears stung the back of her eyes. How had their conversation dissolved into this? She *never* cried. Sorrel could only recall a handful of times in her entire life she'd let a tear escape.

Philip hadn't broken eye contact. His thumb tenderly stroked her cheek as he waited for a reply.

"I don't know," Sorrel managed to mouth soundlessly.

"She doesn't need to be," Philip said, looking directly into her eyes. "You came a significant distance." He pulled his hand from her cheek and chucked her chin. "*I* am impressed."

"You are?" Why did his words make her want to smile?

Philip nodded. "All the way to the stairs without your *affectation*? I couldn't last ten minutes without my quizzing glass."

A laugh escaped before Sorrel could prevent it. "I have not seen your quizzing glass make an appearance in several days."

"Perhaps you are simply learning to overlook it."

"Not likely."

They sat watching each other for a moment. Sorrel wondered if Philip felt the tension in the air between them. Each beat of her heart seemed to come harder, more intensely than the last. Just when she decided Philip could hear the pounding in her chest, he broke eye contact and took friendly hold of her hand.

"Are you ready to escape?" he asked, the boyish grin back in a flash.

Sorrel managed a smile of her own and nodded.

"I believe we've decided the nursery window is out of the question." Philip looked ponderous.

"Absolutely out of the question," Sorrel seconded.

"That leaves us only the stairs." Philip shrugged. "Best get on with it else we'll get caught."

"I cannot negotiate stairs without my cane, Philip."

"If I can give up my affectation for 'several days,' you can give up yours for the length of a stairway."

"Philip," Sorrel protested—she knew for a fact she couldn't make it down without support.

He seemed not to hear but rose and pulled her to her feet as well. The usual moment of precarious balance followed before Sorrel righted herself. Philip's hand on her back proved more unnerving than helpful, though she went to great lengths to hide her discomfort.

"Now, one hand on the banister," Philip instructed.

Sorrel had no choice but obey, lest she tumble top over tail down the stairs.

"And I will take the other," Philip said. He winked at her, and she prayed he didn't see her blush.

She placed her arm through his as lightly as she could manage—the thought of revealing to him the extent of her helplessness nearly undid her. With a white-knuckle grip on the banister and a shaky breath, Sorrel stepped with her right leg, all her weight on the functioning left. That was the easy part, she knew. The next step would require her right leg to bear her weight. She hesitated.

"You can do this, Sorrel," Philip whispered in her ear.

She resisted the urge to look up into his face. She couldn't make heads nor tails of this new compassionate, caring Philip and didn't dare try to solve the puzzle while fumbling down a flight of stairs.

Sorrel lifted her left foot and immediately felt herself reeling off balance. Philip's arm closed more firmly around hers. Pain shot through her shin. Clenching her jaw against the agony, Sorrel brought her left foot to the step beside her right and quickly shifted her weight. Almost immediate relief surged through her leg, and Sorrel breathed an audible sigh.

"Only two flights left to go?" she asked, trying to sound more lighthearted than she felt.

"Try leading with your left," Philip said.

"My—"

"Step down with your left. Let it bear the weight and the balance. Bring the right down to it."

"But wouldn't the right have to hold me up while I stepped down?"

"Use the banister and my massively muscular arm to support you while you step down."

Again that self-mocking tone. Philip usually exerted cocky self-assurance. He confused her more all the time.

"You won't let me fall?" That sounded more like begging than she'd intended—she only wanted to know she wasn't about to break her neck. She braced herself for some glib reply.

"If I can see the steps without my quizzing glass," he answered, squinting quite dramatically.

She gave him an exasperated look that made him laugh. She couldn't help a smile of amusement herself. "You are so absurd sometimes."

"Confess," he said. "You enjoy it."

"Perhaps a little." She would not admit to more than that.

"In that same spirit of honesty I will say that I enjoy your sharp rejoinders *a little.*"

"Only a little?" She had found their battle of wits quite enjoyable at times. Had he not?

"You will not wring further confessions from me," he said. "We have not time. We are in the midst of an escape, you will recall."

"Ah, yes." Sorrel turned her eyes once more to the stairs. What had she gotten herself into? "This must seem terribly pathetic to you." Perhaps if she acknowledged the ridiculous picture she made, he would not find the need to comment on it.

"I know pathetic when I see it," Philip said, "and this is *not* it."

With steely determination, Sorrel muscled back the lump of emotion his words created. She would not add to her embarrassment by growing teary. "Thank you for that," she said.

"Try the left this time," he offered encouragingly.

To her surprise and satisfaction, Philip's suggestion proved sound. The step still was not easy to take, and she still refused to lean on him as heavily as she would have on her cane. He squeezed her hand as if he recognized the relief she felt at even a slight decrease in pain.

"There can't be more than thirty steps left." Philip spoke with all the glee of a seven-year-old with an armful of pilfered biscuits. "At this rate we'll be in the library before your warden has any idea you've escaped."

They took another step. "She always manages to catch up with me," Sorrel said as she eased her way farther down.

"Perhaps *she* is the one you ought to be at war with."

Philip's statement hung in the air between them as they reached the first landing, which marked the halfway point in their descent. Her leg already seared with pain from her difficult walk *to* the stairs. Now, one flight later, she struggled to stay on her feet.

Perhaps she *is the one you ought to be at war with.* With herself?

"Good heavens!" A shrill voice cut through the silence. "What are you doing!"

Sorrel looked to the foot of the stairway to see Marjie's frantic face turned up toward her. She felt her stomach clench. Marjie hurriedly began ascending the steps. Sorrel sighed in frustration—she'd been so close. Now Marjie would fuss and bother for days.

"Stay there, Miss Marjie," Philip called out, his tone offering no opportunity to object. Sorrel watched Marjie freeze.

"But . . . the stairs . . ." Marjie sputtered. "She can't—"

"She can most certainly do this," Philip insisted.

"You won't let her fall?" Marjie asked, her face filled with concern.

"If I had wanted to toss her down the stairs, I could have done so long before now," he answered dryly.

Marjie pinked. "I am not concerned about *your* abilities."

"In other words, *my* abilities concern her," Sorrel muttered.

Philip squeezed her hand. "If you can outrun your warden, you can stand down your little sister," he whispered.

Sorrel took a deep breath and nodded. Not two steps later, both of which were watched by Marjie with wide-eyed terror, Fennel arrived on the scene, stopping abruptly in his tracks at the look on Marjie's face.

"Stairs," was all Marjie could mutter. "Without her walking stick."

Fennel's gaze fell on Sorrel then shifted to Philip before settling on his oldest sister once more. He watched her slow, painstaking progress with obvious concern. Sorrel felt herself grow less steady. She'd not anticipated an audience.

"It will do them good to see this," Philip said to her. "Perhaps they will change the way they think of you."

"You mean they might remember that I am twenty-three and capable of looking after myself?"

"It would be a start, anyway."

They took another step. Then another. A smile spread slowly across Fennel's face. Marjie still looked on the verge of apoplexy.

Sorrel's leg felt like it was on fire. Each movement caused pain to sear through her. "I have the terrible feeling I am going to faint," Sorrel said quietly.

"Six more steps, Sorrel," Philip whispered. "You can make it six more steps."

"I don't know if I can." The admission came far more easily than she would have believed. She never confessed to anyone how very limited she felt at times. "I have never gone this far without my cane. Not since my—"

"—'unfortunate incident?'" he finished for her. "It is time you did. Might I suggest you actually take advantage of the arm I have offered you." He must have seen the guilty expression on her face. "Surely you knew I would notice you were barely touching it. I assure you I am up to the task."

Another excruciating step. Five more to go. Marjie reached out for her.

"No," Philip waved her back. "Let her finish."

"But—"

"Marjie!" Fennel scolded. "Let her finish."

Soon only one step remained but not another inch of banister. Sorrel paused. How would she maintain her balance? With the railing for support she'd managed to negotiate this far. She couldn't bring herself to lean so heavily on Philip. It would be too . . . humiliating. But, after so much effort and such constant pain, she didn't think her leg would support her at all.

She couldn't come that far only to falter at the end. And she would *not* reach out to either of her siblings. She needed to prove to them, to herself, that she was as independent as she'd always claimed to be.

Without a word of warning, Philip shifted her hand from his arm to his other hand and slipped the arm nearest her around her waist.

"One more," he said. She looked up at him, suddenly uncertain of herself. He smiled a little. "I won't let you fall."

The last step was excruciating. Tears stung her eyes, though she did not let them spill over. She closed her eyes as she settled her feet on the floor, standing rooted to the spot. Philip's steadying hand remained on her back, her hand entwined in his.

"You did it, my dear," he whispered in her ear.

A smile slowly spread across her face. Her breath seemed to bubble and jump inside her. Sorrel glanced over her shoulder up the expanse of the grand stairway. She'd taken each step, one at a time, without her cane and without falling. No one would have believed her capable of it, and yet she'd done it. Sorrel instantly corrected the thought. Philip had believed it from the beginning.

"Poppy, would you go get your sister's walking stick? It's in the library."

Sorrel turned her eyes on this enigma of a dandy, who'd just spent the better part of a half-hour helping a deformed woman inch her way down a staircase. He'd so often seemed completely self-consumed, shallow, even. Lately he'd managed to contradict nearly every opinion she'd formed of him. She'd begun to trust him, had even confided in him. Facing the dangers of a staircase and her own uncertain balance, she'd felt safe with him at her side.

He turned his laughing, blue eyes on her, and Sorrel's stomach seemed to knot up inside her. "Another successful Jonquil escape," he said with a lift of his eyebrows.

"The warden didn't catch us, then?"

"I don't believe she did." He looked proud—proud of *her.* Fennel, it seemed, was right. Philip was not at all like Father had been.

"Mother, just see!" Fennel's voice called out, pulling Sorrel's attention back to her surroundings. He rushed back to the base of the stairs, where Mother stood with a look of confusion on her face. "Sorrel came down the stairs, Mother!" Fennel announced, grinning from ear to ear. "Without her walking stick! I saw her!"

Mother looked at each of her children quickly, then her eyes darted to Philip. A deep blush patched her cheeks as she looked away again. With her chin high she began climbing the stairs. Over her shoulder she declared, "Even a halfwit can climb stairs." She waved her hand dismissively and continued her ascent.

Every ounce of triumph drained from Sorrel in an instant. What a simpleton she'd been to feel such pride in so miniscule a thing. As Mother said, even imbeciles could climb stairs, and they managed it unassisted.

"Thank you, Fennel." Sorrel kept her voice as even as she could manage and took hold of her walking stick. She extracted her hand from Philip's and firmly grasped her *affectation.* "Thank you for your assistance," she said, unable to meet his eyes. Mortified beyond bearing, she made her way toward the library, hoping for seclusion and a place to rest.

Rest. She'd done nothing but walk down two flights of stairs, and she needed to rest. She truly was ridiculous.

"She could have hurt herself," Sorrel heard Marjie declare, her voice watery with tears. "And for such a tiny thing. It is horrible!"

Do not fret, Sorrel told her silently. *I will not try again.*

Twenty

Philip barely managed to keep from glaring at Mrs. Kendrick when she entered the west sitting room that afternoon for tea. She straightened her ridiculously ruffled dress as she sat quite at her leisure on a spindle-legged chair as though nothing out of the ordinary had ever occurred in the course of her entire existence.

Even a halfwit can climb stairs.

Could she really be so unfeeling, so callous, to her own daughter's suffering? Sorrel had said her mother didn't believe in being uncomfortable. If he had his way, Philip would like to see Mrs. Kendrick deucedly uncomfortable. Somehow, he'd like to make her see that her daughter was not an inconvenience she could simply brush aside.

Sorrel was remarkable and intelligent. Resilient. Beautiful. *Strikingly* beautiful. And beneath the often chilly façade beat a warm, caring heart. She no doubt kept it so firmly hidden because unfeeling wretches like her mother thought nothing of bruising it at their will.

"Good afternoon, dearest." Mater greeted Philip with a customary peck on the cheek. "I haven't seen you all day, Philip. I hope you haven't been sulking over something."

That look was awfully pointed. Philip set his jaw and looked away.

"You have been sulking. What about, pray?"

"Nothing I would like to discuss at the moment," Philip said, momentarily glancing at the oblivious Mrs. Kendrick.

Mater's gaze followed his. She, too, watched the back of Mrs. Kendrick's neck for a moment before returning her eyes to him. The calculating quality of her stare made Philip decidedly uneasy. "She is not always kind to her eldest daughter," Mater whispered.

"No, she is not." Philip spoke equally as soft.

Another moment of rather obvious scrutiny passed before Mater relinquished the subject with an abrupt dive into a different topic. "Your brothers have arrived. I am not sure you heard."

"Layton and Harold are here?" A grin split Philip's face.

Mater smiled back. "Washing up upstairs, I believe."

Philip bowed his farewell and rushed up the stairs and down the wing of Kinnley they had come to refer to as the Jonquil Ward. The first open door he came to was the room reserved for Harold.

Inside, Harold bent studiously over a writing table, dressed in somber colors and entirely unaware of movement in his own room. Harold was as subdued in his choice of clothing as Philip was flamboyant, and they made an almost comical pair every time Philip visited Harold at Cambridge.

At the moment, Harold was scratching onto a sheet of parchment some, no doubt, deep insight he had gleaned from the book of sermons opened on the table beside him. If past experience were any indication, Harold would be impervious to interruption until he finished his work.

Philip smiled and stepped out of the room. He made his way eagerly down the corridor but stopped just outside the door to Layton's room. He'd missed Layton, and yet he almost dreaded seeing him again. They'd once been the closest of friends, partners in mischief, easy companions, as inseparable as twins, though a year apart in age.

"You might as well come in, Flip," a deep, somewhat disgruntled voice echoed from within the bedchamber. "I heard your fobs clanking all the way down the corridor."

Philip reminded himself to remove his watch, fobs and all, before his next spy hunt and passed the threshold into Layton's room. He easily found his brother in a chair by the empty fireplace, elbows on his knees, head in his hands, fingers rubbing his face wearily. Layton lifted his head enough to look Philip over.

"Still dressing like a peacock?" he asked, his brows creased in disapproval.

Philip made a show of looking himself over then nodded in mock devastation. The slightest of smiles made a brief appearance on Layton's face. He motioned Philip over with his head. Trying to not let his concern show, Philip sauntered over and dropped into a seat opposite his brother.

Layton was the only one of the Jonquils not built like a fence post. Every other brother was tall and lanky. Layton could have been a prizefighter. He stood a little shorter than Philip, who measured a couple of inches above six feet, but Layton had at least two stone on him—two stone of pure muscle. If they hadn't grown up the best of friends, Philip might have resented their physical differences.

"So has Harold been reading you Holy Writ since Cambridge?" Philip asked, opting for a joking tone.

Layton allowed a brief chuckle as he shook his head. "He spoke of nothing but the Archbishop of Canterbury's visit to Cambridge last month. Holy Harry is still in raptures about it."

"'Holy Harry.'" Philip grinned. "How long have we been calling him that?"

"Since he was in leading strings." Layton leaned back in his chair, allowing his head to fall back, his eyes cast upward. "The boy's been sermonizing since birth."

Philip shrugged. "Trying to redeem his wayward family, I suppose."

Layton grunted in response but didn't offer another word. He folded his hands behind his head and kept his eyes staring blankly at the ceiling above. Layton had taken to long, heavy silences of late—*of late* meaning the past four years. The days of light, easy conversations had disappeared without warning. Try as he might,

Philip couldn't seem to get his brother back from wherever he'd gone during that rather bleak time of his life.

"Mater couldn't be happier to have all her boys together again," Philip said, trying for a safe topic. "She's said it is the only Christmas gift she wants."

"It's kind of Crispin to host our reunion." Layton chuckled. "He's enough of a Jonquil that he might as well."

"And I think he wanted to show off his bride," Philip said. "They're pathetically happy, you know."

"I can handle pathetic for a week." Layton smiled unconvincingly. It would be a long week for him, Philip knew that much about his brother.

"It's a shame you can't stay longer." He wanted Layton to know he was welcome and wanted.

But Layton just shook his head. "I promised Caroline I would return for Twelfth Night." He rose abruptly from his chair and walked heavily to the tall window at the far end of the room. Philip recognized brooding when he saw it and knew the time had come to take his leave.

"I'll see you at supper, then," Philip said as he rose. "We make an entertaining group here at Kinnley."

"Wonderful," came the dry reply.

Philip watched his brother for a moment. He hated seeing him that way. Philip had been an expert in their younger days at sneaking his brother out of punishments and getting him to laugh when he'd obviously much rather sulk. Those childhood tricks didn't work anymore.

* * *

"Where did you find a flower on Christmas Day?" Sorrel asked, eyes wide in obvious surprise.

The fever Fennel had predicted reached its peak the morning after her trek down the Kinnley staircase. Layton had found Philip pacing the library later that same day and came as close to smiling as Layton had in four years.

Word had spread that Sorrel was feeling better less than forty-eight hours after the fever had come on. Philip had felt like he was breathing again for the first time in two days. He'd slumped into a chair in the west sitting room and let out a long, strangled breath. Layton had occupied the seat opposite him.

"Flowers," he'd said out of nowhere.

Philip's confusion must have shown.

"Take her flowers," Layton had said with a shrug, not looking up from his copy of *The Times*. "And before you ask 'whom': Miss Kendrick. It would be a convenient excuse to go see her. The flowers just might keep her mind off your ridiculous cravat."

Philip had smiled. "She likes my ridiculous cravat."

"I met your sparring partner my first night here, Flip." Layton had eyed Philip pointedly over the top of his paper. "She didn't strike me as one who would hesitate to tell you when you look preposterous."

"I think *preposterous* is a bit strong," Philip had protested. Sorrel didn't think he was a complete idiot. Did she? The possibility struck Philip with more force than he would have liked.

"Luckily, I think she favors you anyway." Layton had returned to his reading as if he'd made the most commonplace observation. "Just make sure she can see past the strutting peacock," he'd added under his breath.

He'd debated Layton's words for at least ten minutes before jumping to his feet and accosting the Kinnley conservatory. In the end he'd settled on a single rose of palest pink. He'd brought it to the library where Sorrel was sitting near a roaring fire, a woolen blanket draped across her lap.

Sorrel seemed more surprised by his offering than flattered. Was that a good sign?

"I raided the conservatory," Philip said, in effect preempting Sorrel's question about where he would find a flower. "But I am afraid I did so underhandedly. If Catherine comes asking, I plan to deny all involvement."

"You would place the blame on my shoulders?"

He quite suddenly realized that he loved her smile.

"If she banishes you to the nursery, I vow to rescue you." Philip held his hand up as if swearing to the truthfulness of his declaration.

"Bedsheets out the window, right? That would be quite a sight." Her amused laughter filled the library.

Philip could only sit there and stare. She looked a little pale yet, but a lightness had entered her countenance that he hadn't seen before.

"Thank you for the flower," she added almost shyly.

"Even if you are blamed for stealing it?"

"Oh, I plan to tell Catherine it was all your doing." Sorrel waved her hand in a perfect imitation of her mother. "She will easily believe you are the guilty party."

"And do you promise to rescue me if I am incarcerated in the nursery wing?" Philip asked.

"I think a brief imprisonment would do you good." Sorrel raised her brow quite saucily.

Philip felt his chest constrict at her look. He could get used to being eyed that way. He inched closer to her on the sofa. She didn't object. He took her hand in his. "And suppose they torture me?"

"They?"

"The torturers Crispin keeps—"

"—in the nursery wing?" she asked doubtfully.

"Where else would he keep them?" Philip managed to sound completely serious.

"How do you propose I go about rescuing you, Philip? Shall I burst in waving my walking stick and raging with righteous indignation?"

Philip laughed heartily. "I would gladly undergo torture to see that. You would frighten the poor executioners out of their wits."

"So my *affectation* does have its uses, then." Sorrel smiled so brightly, so becomingly, Philip could not have looked away if he'd wanted to.

"I am glad you are feeling better, Sorrel," he managed to say, though his voice sounded strangled.

"Thank you, again, for the rose." Sorrel touched the petals to her nose.

Philip had to look away after that. The temptation to reach out and touch her was far too great. What had happened to their mutual disdain? Had he forgotten so quickly about her beau in Ipswich? Maybe, he thought hopefully, *she'd* forgotten about the man. He realized rather abruptly that he truly hoped she had. He'd come to care a great deal about what happened to Sorrel Kendrick.

"Oh, I have something for you," Philip suddenly remembered aloud. "A Christmas present."

He pulled a package wrapped in brown paper from his pocket and handed it to her, to her obvious surprise. "You really didn't have to—"

"Open it before you offer any gratitude. You will more than likely withdraw any compliments after you see what I've chosen."

She gave him a wary look. He just smiled in reply. He'd stumbled upon the mystery item while in Ipswich and couldn't resist purchasing it for her. When she pulled her hand out of his to unwrap his offering, Philip came to the stark realization that he'd come to feel quite content sitting with her hand in his. That was decidedly unexpected.

Sorrel pulled back the wrapping paper, and Philip felt his grin grow. He barely kept back an overloud guffaw as she pulled out a very ostentatious quizzing glass.

"I couldn't bear the jealousy anymore," Philip explained with a feigned air of pity. "So I found you one of your own. I know how much you admire mine."

She shoved his shoulder and laughed full and deep until tears formed in the corners of her eyes.

"Now, shall we make our way to the sitting room?" Philip suggested. "I believe Mater is reinstating the long-forgotten annual Jonquil Christmas singing festival."

"Singing?" Sorrel eyed him amusedly.

"A painful experience for all involved, I assure you." Philip rose and turned back to her, holding his hand out to help her to her feet. "Luckily I am so devastatingly dapper that inappropriate key changes will most likely go unnoticed."

He'd expected another tingling laugh or heart-pounding smile but received a questioning glance instead.

"Why do you do that?" Sorrel asked, suddenly the soul of solemnity.

"Do what?"

"Say things like that. Act like . . . like a complete imbecile."

Philip shrugged. "Perhaps I am a complete imbecile."

"You're not," she said in a tone that brooked no arguments.

You look far more handsome when you aren't hiding behind all that pomp. Did Sorrel even remember telling him that? Did she have any idea that he hadn't been able to forget it?

She continued to watch him far too closely. Obviously she expected an answer. He could hardly tell her he donned the disguise as part of his efforts at underground intelligence collecting.

"Habit, I suppose," he offered vaguely.

"Why? What convinced you to originally?"

"It was a long time ago, Sorrel." Philip rocked back and forth on his feet, not very comfortable with the direction of the conversation. If he were Hanover Garner, his nose would be running profusely.

He was about to abruptly suggest they be on their way when Sorrel lifted her new quizzing glass to her eye and gave him a stare-down Brummel would have cowered to receive. All his defenses melted, and Philip dropped back onto the sofa.

"I see I have armed you quite dangerously." He smiled in amused resignation.

Sorrel tossed the glass in the air and caught it expertly in her hand, a look of triumph on her face. "You shouldn't hide behind all of this, Philip," she said, gently patting the sleeve of his jacket, the one with buttons twice the size of a guinea. As if sensing her serious tone unnerved him, Sorrel flicked the folds of his cravat with her fingertips. "Especially this monstrosity."

"You suggest I forgo cravats entirely?" Philip tried to look as horrified as a fop ought to have at such an affront to his personal fashion. "I would go straight from dandy to eccentric."

"Just a different knot," she corrected.

"Shall I track down my valet and demand he make another go of it?"

She looked thoughtful for a moment before shaking her head. Sorrel reached up and began tugging at the folds of his neckcloth. Philip certainly hadn't been expecting that!

"You plan to strangle me?" he asked, trying to mask the damage her actions were wreaking on his equilibrium. She smiled a little and continued fussing.

Philip worked hard to swallow and breathe. Her fingers occasionally brushed against him, causing every hair on his neck to stand on end. If she didn't stop soon, he was going to suffocate or collapse or kiss her. Just as Philip became convinced one of those outcomes was inevitable, she pushed away from him, her eyes narrowing as she focused on his cravat.

"That is a vast improvement," she said as though surprised by the outcome. "A little wilted, perhaps, but much better."

"Shall, um—" He cleared his throat and tried to organize his thoughts. "Shall we show off my new look to the others, then?"

"Just don't tell my mother I had anything to do with it." Sorrel allowed him to help her to her feet. Philip kept a reasonable distance between them—he still hadn't entirely recovered from her ministrations. "She would collapse in a dead faint if she knew I'd done anything so unladylike."

"I won't say a word." Philip worked on steadying his breathing.

Lampton War Tactic Number Twelve: The enemy should never be trusted with a neckcloth unless she promises to strangle the wearer.

Twenty-One

"'God Rest Ye Merry, Gentlemen.' I insist." Lady Lampton had been insisting on various carols for more than an hour. Her sons had objected to each, though their reluctance was obviously feigned.

Charlie groaned. "Oh, Mater. Not that one."

"I did not give life to a gaggle of gentlemen only to have them object to such a fitting carol." Lady Lampton gave them all a withering look.

"I refuse to risk Mater spilling my claret and ruining my newly corrected cravat," Philip announced with arrogance Sorrel was beginning to suspect was entirely feigned. The blush she felt steal across her cheeks when he raised that overly expressive eyebrow at her was not feigned in the slightest. "'God Rest Ye Merry, Gentlemen' it is."

A conspiratorial look spread through the group of Jonquils. They'd intended to honor their mother's request, and everyone in the room, except Mater, seemed to realize as much. They made quite an impressive choir, in all honesty. Every male vocal part was accounted for, and they seemed to know the most intricate of harmonies for each carol requested. But, then, Philip had acknowledged caroling was a tradition of sorts.

The entire family came within a few inches of each other in height—even Charlie—who couldn't have been more than seventeen. All the brothers were tall and slender. Only Layton didn't fit the mold. He stood out from the others, and not simply because he was robust.

He also seemed to lack the Jonquil joviality. Even Harold, whom Sorrel had overheard Layton and Philip refer to as "Holy Harry," seemed more lighthearted than his second-eldest brother.

God rest ye merry, gentlemen. Let nothing you dismay . . .

Sorrel found her eyes drifting to Philip as the singing continued. She hardly noticed his ridiculously bright red waistcoat nor the dozen fobs dangling from his watch chain. She found his face far too mesmerizing. The most decidedly happy wrinkles appeared faintly around his eyes as he smiled. He sent looks to his brothers that communicated volumes about their years of connection and camaraderie. What an enigma the man was! At times he epitomized a self-absorbed dandy, and yet there were moments when he proved to be anything but.

The brothers had barely sung the first "tidings of comfort and joy" when a decided change came over Layton. His expression grew pensive, more withdrawn. He rather abruptly stopped singing and stood with his brows furrowed. By the time the group reached the middle of the second verse, Layton's eyes wandered to the windows. A few lines later, his body followed.

The relaxed atmosphere the entire assembly had adopted made his departure easy to overlook. Guests stood about in clusters. The choir itself stood all around the pianoforte. But Philip, Sorrel noted, had taken notice of his brother's defection. Philip's expression grew concerned as soon as Layton's voice dropped out. His eyes followed Layton to the window. But he continued singing with his remaining brothers and even managed a smile and a look of ease.

Sorrel saw his concern beneath the mask. Her eyes darted between the two men through the remainder of the song. Lady Lampton expressed her joy at her sons' indulgence and apologized to the group in general for so monopolizing the evening. Lizzie laughed and dropped down at the pianoforte as the choir dispersed.

Sorrel wasn't at all surprised to see Philip join Layton shortly after the carol ended. The conversation, though Sorrel could not hear a word, seemed tense. Philip appeared determined to be heard. Gone was the nonchalance of the Town Tulip, the fribble-obsessed attitude Philip had exuded the first time they met. He was, at that moment, nothing short of a mature, caring gentleman.

Layton waved off whatever Philip said. Philip laid a hand on his brother's shoulder, obviously attempting to reach him somehow. The gesture was shrugged off. The two men stood in uneasy silence for a moment. Sorrel's heart broke to see it. Though she didn't understand what passed between them, Philip was obviously concerned for his brother but couldn't seem to help.

Philip turned, a look of frustration on his face, and began making his way from the room. Suddenly seized with an almost overwhelming need to do something, Sorrel pulled herself to her feet. Marjie had crossed the room to Stanley's side the minute the Jonquil caroling had concluded. No one objected to nor took note of Sorrel's departure.

She moved more slowly than Philip. He had nearly slipped out of sight by the time she reached the corridor.

"Philip," she called after him, wishing once again she moved as easily as she once had.

Ahead Philip stopped and turned back toward her. The look on his face was almost unrecognizable. Frustration. Agony. Bewilderment. Seeing it made Sorrel want to cry, and she *never* cried.

He seemed to take pity on her and closed the distance between them rather than make her stumble to where he stood. "Is my cravat wilting?" he asked, but the feigned dandified tone fell short.

"Will you walk with me?" Sorrel asked impulsively.

Philip couldn't have looked more surprised. "Walk with you?"

"My limp is acting up."

With a weak smile and a short bow, Philip offered his arm, and they began a slow stroll down the corridor. "Have you been neglecting to walk your limp, then?"

Sorrel nodded. A sadness had entered Philip's eyes, making an answer all but impossible. Obviously he ached at his brother's unhappiness. Sorrel felt her heart constrict with pain at the memory of a few less-than-flattering words she'd uttered about Philip's shallowness. She'd seldom felt so ashamed of herself. She'd apparently severely misjudged him.

Philip interrupted her thoughts. "You seem pensive, Sorrel."

"I might say the same about you," she answered, watching him closely. "You seem concerned about your brother."

"Which one?"

Sorrel really did feel ashamed of herself. The burden of his concerns was more than apparent in his face and tone of voice. She held more tightly to his arm hoping to somehow convey her support.

With a breath of frustration, Philip began a confession of sorts. "Corbin never has outgrown his paralyzing timidity. Jason is working himself to the bone. Stanley cannot seem to heal from the wounds of war—not all of which are physical. Harold retreats behind his studies. Charlie is in constant mischief."

"And Layton?" She noticed he'd left out the brother who seemed to weigh heaviest on his mind.

A look of unsettling emotion flitted across Philip's face. "I can't even reach him anymore." He spoke in little more than a whisper. "He was always my best friend. And now . . ." Philip shifted his jaw awkwardly and kept his eyes diverted. "Every time I see him, it's as if . . . I'm . . ."

"Losing him?" Sorrel finished for him.

He replied with the slightest of nods. His pain-filled eyes focused somewhere down the vast, empty corridor. They'd stopped walking, though Sorrel didn't think Philip realized it.

He let out a long, tense breath. Sorrel closed her arm more tightly around his.

"There. You've reduced the shallow dandy nearly to tears," he said almost bitterly. "I suppose that would be a tactical victory."

"Philip." Sorrel couldn't tear her eyes away from his face. "I shouldn't have said you were shallow."

He still didn't look at her. Where was that easy smile? The carefree dandy had entirely disappeared.

"I hardly even knew you at the time. I was being unkind and judgmental. It has always been one of my faults." Sorrel took a deep breath and steadied herself for confession. "Fennel told me I was doing it again."

Philip looked at her finally, his curiosity obviously piqued. Suddenly she couldn't bring herself to look at him. She studied the marble tile beneath her feet.

"I have made it a habit of mine to . . ." Heavens, she disliked admitting to personal shortcomings. "I have, since childhood, taken to fighting people who . . . who hurt me."

"Have I hurt you, Sorrel?" Philip cupped her face with his hand, his tone soft and tender.

By pointing out what she already knew? By reminding her of her lost hopes and unattainable dreams? By forcing her to realize that more was broken two years earlier than her leg? Yes. It had hurt. It hurt a great deal.

"I have known from the moment I awakened after the incident with the horse that all my . . ." Sorrel fought the sudden flood of emotion her words were creating ". . . expectations, my . . . dreams were shattered. If I lived, which was not entirely certain at the time, my life would be fundamentally different from the one I had always imagined. I knew no one would ever see anything but my injuries." Sorrel felt a warm tear escaping her eyes. She never cried! "I did not particularly enjoy hearing all of that delineated so succinctly by a stranger."

"I was that stranger, then?" Philip brushed the tear from her cheek.

"Reminding me that society could never overlook what had become of me."

"Sorrel—"

"And that a lady with a limp could never be beautiful." Sorrel felt another tear slip, and she hated herself all the more for it. "Yes. That hurt."

"Did I really say such idiotic things?"

Sorrel couldn't bring herself to look at him. She hadn't intended the conversation to become a confessional.

"Then let me say this, Miss Sorrel Kendrick." He gently nudged her face until she had to look at him once more. "Your walking stick is a positively endearing affectation. Your limp is quite easily overshadowed by your wit. And"—he narrowed his gaze as if to emphasize his words—"you are inexplicably beautiful."

No one had ever before called her beautiful. Her father, no doubt, would have chastised her for her vanity if he'd known how much she enjoyed hearing Philip praise her as he had. Sorrel closed her eyes in a futile attempt to steady her emotions. She hadn't cried in years. How had mere words reduced her to tears?

"Sorrel." Philip's voice reached her ears as little more than a husky whisper. She felt his hand slide to the nape of her neck and pull her tenderly toward him. She could feel his breath on her cheek but didn't dare open her eyes. "I don't want to be your enemy. I don't want that at all."

"And what of our war?" she asked as he feathered kisses across her forehead.

"I suggest we negotiate a peace agreement." He kissed her cheek.

"I've told you before—I do not retreat," Sorrel warned, her heart pounding so hard she could hardly speak.

"Then I surrender."

His lips brushed hers, so lightly she wasn't entirely sure she'd been kissed. Philip whispered her name before pressing his lips to hers with more fervor. Sorrel grasped her walking stick as tightly as possible, afraid her aching limb would give way and tear her from a kiss she was only beginning to realize she'd been longing for from almost the moment she'd met her erstwhile enemy.

Philip's arms wrapped around her, holding her so protectively she hardly needed her cane. All her weight seemed to lift off her leg, and relief she hadn't known in years spread through her body. Seemingly on their own, Sorrel's arms wound around Philip's neck as she returned his kisses. Her walking stick slipped from her grasp and hit the floor with an echoing clang.

"A peace offering, my dear?" Philip asked, pulling back far enough to smile at her. "Abandoning the highly disputed affectation?"

Sorrel laughed and laid her head against him.

"This seems a highly efficient way of eliminating one's enemies." Philip chuckled. "Too bad I didn't think of it sooner."

"You mean you don't kiss all of your enemies?" Sorrel attempted to sound surprised.

"Do you?" Philip responded far too seriously. Sorrel only offered a noncommittal laugh.

"Let's walk that limp of yours, dear," Philip said, bending down to pick up her walking stick. "We can discuss your war tactics and every 'enemy' you've ever had."

The man sounded jealous, Sorrel thought with a smile. She laughed again. Philip kissed her hand before tucking it into the crook of his arm. They walked in companionable silence. Sorrel realized that, for the first time in recent years, she was grinning.

Twenty-Two

Philip watched with a heavy heart as Layton's coach disappeared down the winding Kinnley carriageway. He had hoped having his brother nearby for Christmas, amidst his family, would have helped pull him from his lost and wandering state. But Layton had left every inch as impenetrable as he'd arrived. Sorrel had been right. He felt as though he were losing his brother.

Sorrel. The thought of her brought a smile back to Philip's face. He'd spent most of the previous night trying to convince himself that he'd actually kissed her and, even more surprising, that she'd actually kissed him in return. The memory was far too detailed to not be real.

Lampton War Tactic Number Thirteen: Know when to surrender.

Philip made his way from the front doors of Kinnley deep in thought. After the initial disbelief dispelled, he had been left with the rather uncomfortable question of how *she* felt about their rather unexpected kiss the night before.

He'd seen a tear or two slip from her eyes despite having been told by several members of Sorrel's family that she never cried. She'd clearly been upset. They'd touched on rather personal subjects, for both of them. He couldn't help worrying that he'd taken advantage of her during a vulnerable moment. She might not have welcomed his advances if she hadn't already been overset.

He hoped that wasn't the case. Desperately hoped.

The echoing remnants of a female voice spouting a curse gave away Sorrel's location. Philip leaned against the library doorframe

and smiled at her sprawled in a heap on the floor next to a bookshelf. "That is a phrase I did not learn until my days at Eton. Even then it was only whispered."

"Never mind my language and help me up off the floor."

Same Sorrel, Philip thought, wondering if her sharp tone was a good sign or not. "Promise not to beat me with your walking stick?" He crossed the room to her.

"I make no promises."

Philip held his hands out to her, which she accepted without hesitation. *A good sign,* he thought. In a moment she was on her feet.

"Would you grab my book for me?" she asked, leaning against the shelving. "And my cane."

"Where to, my dear?"

"The sofa, please." No reaction to the *my dear*. Hmm.

He assisted her to the sofa as requested. "May I join you?" He couldn't remember the last time he'd sounded so unsure of himself. He was pretty sure his voice even cracked.

The faintest of blushes stole across Sorrel's face. A ray of hope. He sat as close to her as he dared, watching her for any reaction she might offer. None was forthcoming.

Philip found himself almost frantically searching for a conversation topic. He felt deucedly uncomfortable with the silence between them. Did she expect an apology? Or another kiss? Or should he be keeping a wary eye on that walking stick of hers? She most likely knew how to wield it like a true swordsman.

The silence had stretched on far too long. Philip eyed the thin, yellow volume in her hand. Something about it struck him as familiar.

Sorrel seemed to notice his attention. "I didn't have a chance to look at it before," she said. "I couldn't hold on to it and crawl at the same time."

Her words humbled him—she'd pulled herself across the cold floor that evening because he'd left her helpless there.

"Have I apologized enough for that?" he asked, hoping his embarrassment showed sufficiently.

She shrugged. "Probably not."

"I was being an idiot."

"I know."

"You aren't going to make this easy for me, are you?"

Sorrel smiled broadly but offered no words of encouragement.

"I felt rather disgruntled that night." Philip slumped back against the sofa, not feeling the least inclined to play the dandified gentleman. "I was sulking, I suppose. After Ipswich, you know."

"Ipswich?" Sorrel lowered her book to her lap and looked at him with obvious puzzlement.

"I didn't . . . couldn't like the idea of . . . Well, I was bothered by that man in Ipswich you've been writing to." Lud, it was hard to admit that.

"Dr. Darrow?"

"Dr. Darrow?"

"I wrote to a surgeon," Sorrel said, brows knit in confusion. "About my leg."

"Your leg?" The skies began to brighten!

"Oh, heavens!" Sorrel was nearly laughing, he could tell. "You thought I had written *romantic* letters?"

"Uh . . . I . . . um . . ." Philip felt suddenly uncomfortable.

"Philip Jonquil, don't tell me you were jealous!"

"A little . . . I guess."

"And that is why you were so decidedly against my writing to him?"

Did she have to pursue this so acutely?

"Then you don't think I am completely daft?" Sorrel seemed anxious for an answer.

"For writing to a surgeon?"

"For pursuing the surgery?"

Philip sat up straighter and looked her in the eye. "What surgery?"

"Dr. Darrow has a colleague in Edinburgh who he thinks might be able to partially fix my leg." There was an almost begging quality to Sorrel's tone, as though she were extending to him her last ray of hope. "There is no guarantee the operation will even help—simply traveling to Scotland will be an ordeal—but it is a possibility."

"This colleague, he knows what he's doing?" Philip felt concerned already. An operation. A grueling journey.

Sorrel nodded, her eyes boring into his.

"What does Dr. Darrow think can be done?"

Sorrel placed her book on the side table and turned to face Philip full on, an eagerness in her eyes that entirely captivated him. "The bones in my leg were never set after they were broken. My father wouldn't allow it. But if—"

"Wait. Your father wouldn't allow your bones to be set?"

She sighed with obvious exasperation. "Doing so would have been contrary to the judgments of God," Sorrel answered with the same bitterness Philip recalled hearing in her tone when she'd spoken before of her father. "He was rather too convinced of his own authority on all matters: religious and secular."

No wonder Sorrel had taken such a quick dislike to Philip's portrayal of himself as decidedly arrogant. "I think I remember Fennel saying your father had passed away." Philip didn't want to push an already touchy subject, but he needed to know. If that man were still drawing breath, Philip would give him a rather detailed understanding of the judgments of God.

"Yes, and not a soul mourned his passing. The entire family put aside our mourning clothes exactly one year to the day of his death."

Philip had never been more grateful for his own parents than he was in that moment. How he wished Sorrel could have had even a moment of the upbringing he had always taken for granted. Determined to at least not force her to speak of obviously painful memories, Philip took Sorrel's hand in his own and kissed her fingertips. "Tell me about this doctor in Scotland."

Sorrel's smile of reply was thick with gratitude. She obviously had no desire to discuss her father any further. "Dr. MacAslon would break the bones in my leg again"—Philip instinctively closed his fingers tighter around hers—"and then set them straight."

"Break them again? Lud, Sorrel. That sounds awful."

"I know." A look of anticipatory pain crossed her face. "But, Philip, if it works, I might not be dependent on my cane. My limp would improve. Dr. Darrow thinks some of the pain would be alleviated."

"In other words," Philip said, "the outcome would be worth the price."

She nodded.

Philip brought both his hands to hers, his thumbs caressing her palm. "What did your family have to say?"

Sorrel shook her head. "Mother left the room halfway through the explanation and has adamantly refused to discuss it since. Marjie wept from start to finish. Fennel sat and looked at me just as if I'd told him I wanted to drown a litter of puppies."

"They're only worried about you." Philip kissed her fingers again, noticing she hadn't objected before.

"Good morning." Leave it to Hanover Garner to interrupt what could have been a promising moment.

Philip didn't return the greeting but put a little more space between himself and Sorrel then shot a look of venom at Garner's back. Sorrel laughed quietly as she retook her book.

"How much longer are you staying, Garner?" Philip asked.

"At Kinnley?"

"In the room," Philip grumbled

Sorrel quietly laughed. "Stop it, Philip."

"A few more days I suppose." Garner sighed. "Then I really should return to London."

"Hate to see you go," Philip said.

"I doubt that very much, Ph—er, Lampton."

Philip glanced over at Sorrel, wondering if she'd noticed the slip. Two men barely acquainted would certainly not be on a first name basis. She didn't seem to have caught the error.

"Of course if the snow starts up again, we'll all be here a few days longer than planned," Garner said.

Philip found himself truly hoping the prediction came true. He'd really enjoy being snowed in with Sorrel.

"Do either of you speak French?" Sorrel asked quite unexpectedly.

"I do," Garner replied quite confidently. Philip could have throttled the man, boasting the way he was.

"Is there another translation of *pécher* besides 'sin'?" Sorrel's eyes were back in her book, apparently a French–English dictionary.

Garner shook his head. "There is not."

Sorrel seemed to ponder his words, mouthing something silently. "That doesn't sound quite right. Perhaps I heard wrong."

"Heard?" Philip asked, intrigued.

"I overheard a conversation which has bothered me ever since."

"A conversation in French?"

Sorrel nodded. "Partly, anyway. But I am almost positive 'sin' isn't the right verb."

"*Pêcher* is pronounced almost precisely the same," Garner offered. "Perhaps this Frenchman was saying *fish* rather than *sin.*"

"Fish." Sorrel sat silently for a fraction of a moment, mouthing again. She still didn't look satisfied. "Fish does fit better, but it is still bothersome. The man's pronunciation was perfect, but he used a completely incorrect article."

"Are you sure he was incorrect?" Garner sounded doubtful.

"I am certain." Sorrel held up her translator.

"What grievous error has offended your lingual sensibilities?" Philip smiled. There were times when Sorrel's stubbornness was positively endearing.

"Not offended." She rolled her eyes at him. "I'm curious is all. He used *le* instead of *la.* And on a word as common as *fountain.* He ought to have known that, I would think."

Philip's smile faded in an instant, and he felt the color drain from his face. "*Pêcher de Le Fontaine?*"

Sorrel's eyes widened.

"You heard someone say that?" Philip asked. Sorrel nodded. "Where? When?"

"In Ipswich," she answered, watching him with borderline alarm. "Just last week."

"Devil take it," Garner muttered.

"Close the door, Garner." Philip rose to his feet in an instant. The door clicked and locked. Philip ran his fingers through his hair.

"Philip, you're worrying me." Sorrel looked as concerned as she sounded.

"I am sorry, my dear. You just have no idea what you've overheard."

"'Fish from the fountain'? It sounded strange but—"

"How much can we tell her?" Garner asked, his face pulled and drawn.

Philip hesitated. Information could be dangerous. He dare not put Sorrel in peril. But she may have overheard a conversation crucial to the efforts of the Foreign Office.

"Does this have anything to do with why the two of you were in Kent?"

Philip's eyes jumped to Sorrel. He was certain Garner's did, as well.

"Don't bother to deny it," Sorrel warned. "I saw Mr. Garner in the inn that night you attempted to steal my walking stick."

"How long ago did you realize the connection?" Philip asked.

"The night Mr. Garner arrived. I have a very good memory for faces."

"And you never said anything? To anyone?"

Sorrel shrugged. "I thought it curious but assumed you had your reasons."

Philip smiled at her. "And here I thought you didn't trust me."

"Perhaps I don't," she countered. "I may have simply been holding on to the information to use as cannon fodder."

"So how much do we tell her?" Garner asked, his nose running incessantly.

"Everything, Garner. Everything."

Twenty-Three

Sorrel listened with growing shock at the tale Philip weaved. He spoke quickly and directly of the Foreign Office, his role as an agent, the disguise he'd created as a dandy and the information he came across because of it, as well as their nearly three-year mission to catch a dangerous French spy known only as Le Fontaine.

"Then those men weren't referring to a fountain, but to this spy?" Sorrel felt her stomach knot inside.

Philip nodded, his face lined in anxiety. "And that spy is planning to hand over more information to Napoleon's sympathizers. Perhaps he has already." Philip continued pacing a short line in front of the sofa where Sorrel sat watching him with growing agitation.

"What do we tell the Foreign Office, Philip?" Mr. Garner asked, wiping at his perpetually dripping nose—how the man had suddenly come down with a cold Sorrel couldn't say.

Philip released a long, deep breath. "If the exchange hasn't happened yet, we tell them to send reinforcements—that Le Fontaine is within our grasp."

"And if the exchange has already occurred?" Mr. Garner asked after a sniffle. He looked almost hopeful that their chance had slipped by them.

Philip rubbed his face with his hands. "Castlereagh will have our necks," he grumbled.

Mr. Garner tugged nervously at his cravat. Sorrel could tell the moment Philip caught sight of his partner's aggravated movements.

"Calm down, Garner. Not literally. Though I doubt he'll be happy to learn one of Le Fontaine's men was in the Dove and Crow at the same time we were and neither of us managed to uncover as much."

"Maybe we'll be dismissed for dereliction of duty." Again that almost hopeful accent in Garner's words. Did the man find his work so unappealing?

"*Dereliction*?" Philip replied doubtfully. "We hardly missed the conversation purposefully."

"But you could tell Castlereagh we did."

"Confound it, Garner." Philip's patience finally gave out. "Could you not be so scragged lily-livered for the duration of even *one* mission!"

"Your language, Philip," Mr. Garner mumbled, eyeing Sorrel awkwardly.

"Oh, that was mild for Miss Kendrick."

"Thank you for pointing that out, Philip." Sorrel hardly appreciated the reminder of yet another of her unladylike mannerisms.

Philip's eyes turned to her as if suddenly remembering her presence. "Sorry, Sorrel." He resumed his pacing.

"Do sit down before you have a stroke," Sorrel insisted.

With a sigh of frustration, Philip flopped onto the sofa beside her, posture entirely abandoned, looking nothing like the Town Tulip Sorrel had grown accustomed to seeing. Mr. Garner wandered to the nearest window and anxiously stared out into the cold winter.

"You seem rather determined to catch this Le Fontaine." Sorrel knew she sounded like a simpleton but was trying to offer what support she could.

Philip nodded. He leaned over until he could easily whisper in her ear, something she found she rather enjoyed. "Once Le Fontaine is apprehended, I will be released from my duties as an agent."

"And you're anxious to be released?" Sorrel turned slightly to face Philip as she spoke to him, leaving them face-to-face and a mere breath apart.

"Extremely," Philip whispered, his eyes studying her face, seemingly memorizing every inch of it. He leaned closer to her, quite obviously intending to kiss her again.

Though she would have welcomed his attentions under different circumstances, she was not keen on the idea of an audience. Mr. Garner had not left the room. Sorrel put her fingertips to his mouth to stay his attempts.

"What can I do?" she asked.

Philip raised an eyebrow, his message all too clear. Sorrel blushed but shook her head. With a smile of amusement, Philip kissed her fingertips then leaned back against the sofa once more, staring out across the library.

"Do you remember anything else about those men or their conversation?" he asked.

"I saw only one of them."

"Would you recognize him if you saw him again?"

"I would. I have a good memory for faces."

Philip glanced across at Mr. Garner. "True," he conceded. "Did they say anything else?" Then he added with a dismissive wave of his hand precisely like Mother was wont to do, "Besides a secret, coded message?"

Sorrel tried to relive the moment. "Something about north. North of somewhere. And there not being a port."

"North of *where*?" Philip pressed, though he didn't turn his gaze back to her.

"I don't remember." She hated admitting it.

Philip took a deep breath and shut his eyes. "What else?"

"There were several numbers, though no explanation as to what they meant."

"Do you remember the numbers?" Philip lounged with his hands on his torso, fingers entwined, eyes closed as if in deep concentration. He looked positively endearing lounging so undandylike with his hair tousled and his brows knit.

Sorrel leaned silently closer to him.

Mr. Garner's attention remained focused outside.

Hardly believing she was doing such a thing, Sorrel laid one hand on the side of his face and placed a rather chaste, tender kiss on his other cheek. Philip's eyes flew open wide, and Sorrel couldn't help a grin.

"The temptation was just too great," she whispered.

"You, Miss Kendrick," he answered with hardly a sound, "are a distraction."

"Sorry." Sorrel mouthed the apology she hardly felt then settled back to a more distant position.

"Those numbers could be important." Philip returned to his normal voice. "Can you remember any of them?"

"Twelve," she recalled. "Actually, he said 'double twelves.'"

"Which man?"

"The one I couldn't see." Sorrel creased her brow and re-created the scene in her head. "But he spoke as though confirming what the other man had told him at some point."

"They were arranging the meeting, then." Philip nodded as if to himself. "Anything else?"

Sorrel closed her eyes, trying desperately to recall what else she'd heard. Philip had made it sound like a matter of utmost importance. "There were more numbers. But I can't recall them."

"Anything other than numbers?"

She could remember little beyond snippets. "The numbers. And a French name."

"What was the name? The French name?" Suddenly Mr. Garner was intensely interested, though his nose continued dripping with fervor.

"I don't remember. Perhaps if I thought about it."

"That name will be Le Fontaine's contact in France," Mr. Garner said, his eyes threatening to widen. "If we could learn that man's identity . . ." Mr. Garner just shook his head as if overwhelmed by the possibility.

"I don't remember." Sorrel had seldom felt so distraught.

"Devil take it, woman!" Mr. Garner snapped, staring down at her with near mania in his eyes.

Sorrel instinctively shifted closer to Philip, her heart pounding the way it always had when her father launched into one of his tirades.

"We have to have that name!"

"Garner." An edge in Philip's voice belied the calmness of his tone.

Mr. Garner immediately snapped to his senses, his eyes softening. Sorrel took a deep breath. Where had Philip been all those years when Father had yelled and raged and she'd had to defend herself and her siblings on her own? Sorrel reached for Philip's hand. She'd seldom been more grateful for another person's presence.

Philip squeezed her fingers but still looked tense.

"Please forgive me, Miss Kendrick," Garner offered with genuine contrition. "I have been tracking Le Fontaine's French counterpart my entire adult life. To finally have a name would be . . ." He walked away shaking his head, leaving his sentence incomplete and hanging in the air around them.

Sorrel glanced at Philip, feeling the importance of the bit of information she couldn't manage to recall. "I am sorry, Philip. I just can't remember. The name. The numbers. I can't remember any of it."

Philip nodded and smiled. "Tell us if it comes to mind."

"I will. I promise."

"You have a letter to write, Garner," Philip said. "Tell Ol' Rob we aren't certain of the date, but we will tell him as soon as we know. It will be either noon or midnight."

"And if the meeting location is not near here?" Garner asked, dabbing at his nose. "Not knowing the day, we can't know how much time we'll have to gather reinforcements."

"Then you had best start praying again."

Garner sighed and left the room, resigned to his task. Sorrel watched him go, the questions in her mind multiplying by the minute. What kind of agent *hopes* the enemy gets away? And yet he became a man possessed at the thought of uncovering a different spy. How had Philip become involved with such dangerous work in the first place?

"I would offer you a shilling for your thoughts, but I understand the price has gone to a guinea," Philip said.

"I suppose this is all a little hard to take in at once," Sorrel said.

"Perhaps I shouldn't have told you so much." Philip shifted to the edge of the sofa and propped his head on his hands, his elbows on his knees. "You realize, of course, how sensitive this information is."

"Of course. I wish I could offer you more."

"You'll remember it." He sounded so confident.

"Before it's too late?" Sorrel had her doubts.

"Let us hope so." He looked tense. Sorrel reached out to him and laid her hand on his arm.

"How can I help, Philip? Please let me help you."

"You have done a great deal already." He patted her hand. Sorrel knew a dismissive gesture when she saw it.

"I will think over that conversation," she assured him. "I will tell you the moment I recall anything."

He smiled, but his eyes remained strained, his demeanor tense. Watching him dealing with the significant weight on his shoulders, Sorrel almost missed the devil-may-care dandy she'd originally thought him to be.

Twenty-Four

Ol' Rob had come through again. Six well-trained, able-bodied men had arrived in Ipswich that afternoon in response to messages sent out to their nearest contacts. Grimes would be descending from Bow Street in the morning. Would it be enough, though?

Philip had no way of knowing for sure how many men Le Fontaine might have with him, whether or not it was a simple one-on-one exchange or something more involved. He reminded himself, tensing his fists, that they still had no idea where the meeting was to occur, nor at which of the "double twelves" it would take place. A bustling city like Ipswich would be sufficient cover for a midday meeting. An exchange on open land, on the other hand, would almost require the cover of darkness only midnight could provide. Worst of all, they couldn't even guess at a day. The meeting might have already passed for all they knew.

Philip paced to the window of his bedchamber, the floor cold beneath his bare feet, and stared out into the inky black night. Clouds had darkened the sky the past three mornings and had brought a light dusting of snow. If the clouds ever dropped their weight, the snow would decidedly complicate an already desperate attempt at intercepting a dangerous enemy.

When he thought of how close Sorrel had come to someone connected to the infamous informant, his blood chilled. If either man in that taproom had realized she'd overheard their conversation . . . It didn't bear contemplating.

. Lives hung in the balance. Every time Le Fontaine passed information, there inevitably came word of British casualties. Just the morning before, he and Garner had received word from the Foreign Office that the British agent who'd gone missing in Kent weeks before after an apparent confrontation with Le Fontaine had been found. Dead.

The murderous spy had to be caught! If only Sorrel could remember the blasted location!

Philip ran his fingers through his hair and let out a strained breath. The weight of the approaching meeting was getting to him. It seemed to be gnawing at Sorrel as well. Philip had brought up the topic as seldom as he could manage over the past two days, but time was not on their side.

He'd stopped Sorrel just that night on her way up the stairs, pressing her again for anything she could recall, anything at all.

"It is all I think of, Philip," she'd replied plaintively. "I've gone through that conversation in my mind at least a hundred times."

"We have to know where they are going to be and, more importantly, when they'll be there," he'd insisted. On reflection, he knew he'd been too brusque, but he was getting anxious.

"I do remember he said it would be north of somewhere."

"All of England is north of somewhere."

He'd missed it at the time, but recalling the moment, Philip could clearly see that Sorrel had flinched at his curt response.

"This could be happening any day. It could be tonight. Tomorrow."

"I know," she'd whispered. "I will let you know if . . ." But her words had trailed off.

Philip had trudged away, lost in his own concerns. Looking back after hours of quiet reflection, he wished he could relive those few moments. He'd have been more understanding, more comforting. The burden of attempting to recall what had seemed at the time an insignificant conversation was obviously taking its toll on her. He couldn't remember seeing Sorrel smile even once in the past twenty-four hours.

A faint scratching at his bedchamber door caught Philip's attention. "Probably Charlie," he muttered.

With Layton gone, the bedchamber on one side of his sat empty. Corbin had actually once slept through a small tornado, so Philip wasn't worried about waking anyone.

"Come in."

Philip rubbed his eyebrows and let out a long breath as he listened to the door open, not bothering to watch Charlie bound in. He could only imagine what coil his youngest brother had gotten himself into this time.

"Be quick about it, Charlie." Philip leaned his head against the window frame. "I am in no mood to preach like Holy Harry."

"I'd rather not be preached to, and I will be quick."

"Sorrel!" Philip turned and faced her before she'd uttered the last word. He'd expected a story of youthful mischief, not a ravishing beauty, glossy black hair falling around her shoulders. "What the devil are you doing in here?"

"Blast it, Philip, keep your voice down," she whispered harshly, pushing the door closed behind her. "Do you want all sixty-seven of your brothers in here?"

"Not a one of them will hear a thing," he answered. "Which is all the more reason why you shouldn't be in here."

"I had to come before I forgot."

"Forgot what?" Philip asked anxiously. He wouldn't muddy Sorrel's reputation for the world but was, at that moment, finding her far too attractive for either of their well-being.

"Brownlow," she said in a slurred rush. "Brownlow."

"You are making absolutely no sense, I'm afraid."

"I thought—you said—you seemed so insistent." Her expression clouded with obvious doubt and disappointment. "I didn't want to risk . . . forgetting . . . again."

She seemed to lean more heavily against the door.

"Where is your walking stick?" He crossed closer on impulse before stopping himself at a safe distance. The fact that she was still dressed precisely as she'd been at supper did not detract from the inappropriate intimacy of their situation. He himself was hardly dressed to receive female company, being only in his shirttails and breeches.

"I was afraid it would make too much noise," Sorrel said.

"You came down a flight of stairs without your cane?" Lud, she was lucky she didn't break her neck.

Sorrel nodded. Strain showed in her eyes. "It took an hour on the stairs alone. I'm not certain the banister will ever recover."

The tiniest of smiles escaped and flitted across her face. How he wanted to reach out for her, hold her close to him, tell her what a wonder she was.

"As impressive as that is"—he couldn't help a chuckle of amazement—"what could possibly have been important enough to endure all of that?"

She suddenly looked exasperated. "I have been trying to tell you. I remembered it. Where they are meeting."

She had his whole attention.

"Brownlow." Sorrel had said that a few times since coming in, he realized. "'North of Brownlow,' the man said. Then the second man complained that there was nowhere to make port. So the first man told him to make port somewhere else and row down to the meeting place."

"All he said was north of Brownlow?"

Sorrel nodded.

A beach meeting if Philip didn't miss his mark. That most assuredly meant midnight. But "north of Brownlow." That could easily refer to miles of coast. He'd have to consult a map, perhaps ask Crispin about local inlets and small ports.

"I am sorry I didn't remember sooner. And I'm sorry you still don't know the date." Sorrel watched him with a pained expression. "I hope I'm not too late."

"Actually, you are here far too late," Philip said. "Which is precisely why I am going to insist you return to your own room."

"Telling you seemed important."

"Crucial," Philip reassured her. "I am not sending you away for lack of appreciation, but because I am a gentleman and you are a lady." He picked up his own walking stick and crossed closer to her. "And it is quite late, and we are alone *together.* In my bedchamber." He eyed her as pointedly as possible. A slight blush spread across her face. "Despite your doubts when we first met, I am not a rake."

"Obviously I didn't think this through very well," Sorrel muttered. "I am sorry."

She looked so forlorn. So adorable. So . . .

"You need to go," Philip insisted, placing his walking stick in her hand and opening the door behind her. "Now, in fact."

She took one step, and Philip instantly realized her hour-long descent of the stairs had taken a heavy toll. Her right leg, even with his walking stick, refused to hold any of her weight. She all but dropped to the floor with the next step she took.

Philip snaked an arm around her waist and pulled her upright once more.

"I will have you know, Sorrel," Philip said, helping her out his door and closing it silently behind them, "I do not approve of torturing prisoners of war."

"Tor—"

He swept her into his arms in as businesslike a manner as humanly possible. "Yes, torture," he said gruffly, ignoring the tantalizing scent she exuded and the warmth of her in his arms. If he hadn't been entirely convinced she'd tumble down the stairs on her own, he'd have locked himself in his room until his heart rate slowed significantly.

The woman was torturing him. He only maintained a hold on his thoughts and reactions by remaining silent until the moment he deposited her outside the door to her room.

"I am sorry, Philip." Sorrel looked decidedly uncomfortable and a touch guilty.

He just shook his head. "If you think of anything else from that conversation, let me know." He hastily added, "In the morning. Somewhere other than my private chambers."

If he'd thought carrying her, flowing hair and all, back to her room had been torture, he dismissed the task as easy the moment he discovered the difficulty of walking away from her when she smiled at him the way she did just then.

Twenty-Five

"BROWNLOW?" CRISPIN REPEATED. "It's not a town at all."

"But you've heard of it?" Philip had cornered Crispin in the library late the next morning, having searched the atlas to no avail.

"I grew up here, Philip. Of course I've heard of Brownlow. It is one of the Hartley holdings."

"Is the Duke in residence?" Philip asked, quickly registering the manifold complications His Grace would add to the operation if it occurred on his land.

Much to Philip's relief, Crispin shook his head. "The property stands empty most of the year. The family occasionally descends in the summer months."

"Good. Good."

"What is this all about, Philip?" Crispin eyed him with obvious curiosity. "And don't say you are looking to share fashion advice with the Duke of Hartley. Your dandy mask has slipped lately. As glad as I am to see it, I'd like to know what you're about."

A twisting of the locked knob halted their conversation. "Philip?" He recognized Sorrel's voice immediately and felt himself smile.

"For a couple of sworn enemies you two have become rather friendly." A smile tugged at Crispin's mouth.

Philip ignored the implied question and unlocked the door. A pair of midnight eyes greeted him as they'd done every time he'd closed his eyes the night before. She smiled uncertainly, almost

timidly. She was ridiculously lovely. How had he ever thought of this woman as the enemy?

"I wanted to apologize," she said, little louder than a whisper. "Looking back, I realize I should have come to . . . shouldn't have been in your . . ." She shifted awkwardly.

"No harm done, my dear," Philip whispered as he motioned her inside. In reality, her presence in his room the night before had done considerable damage to his peace of mind, bringing an awareness of his growing attraction to her.

"I feared you would think me a complete hoyden. I didn't—" Sorrel stopped short as her eyes fell on Crispin. "Oh."

"If *she* starts asking about Brownlow, I am going to get suspicious." Crispin eyed Philip with a lighthearted look of warning.

Sorrel turned her questioning eyes on Philip, seemingly unsure what could be revealed in front of their host. So Philip locked the door once more and sat in a chair across from his oldest friend and beside Sorrel. He looked Crispin in the eye. "I have a story you might be interested in hearing."

How he'd thought Crispin would respond to his confession, Philip couldn't say. But when he admitted to inventing his guise as a Town Tulip in order to glean more information for the Foreign Office, Crispin unexpectedly grinned.

"All these years, Philip, I wondered if you'd been thrown from your horse or something drastic like that. You were so completely changed and so suddenly, too."

"I appreciate that you never cut me," Philip said quite seriously. "There were many who did."

"So what does all this have to do with Brownlow?" Crispin never had been comfortable with overly sober discussions.

Philip took a deep breath and explained their suspicions that a meeting of a French spy and his contacts would occur on an undisclosed night around midnight somewhere along the coast north of Brownlow. Crispin's eyes grew wider with each revelation.

"Kinnley is north of Brownlow, Philip." Crispin was on his feet pacing the room. "Is there danger? I did not extricate my wife from the grasp of one madman only to have her endangered by—"

"Covertness is key to Le Fontaine's operations," Philip said. "He'll not come two miles inland to a house where he would be outnumbered by footmen alone. Keep the guests inside and lock the doors, and everyone will be fine."

"I don't like this happening so close."

"Neither do I, Crispin. Nearly every person I care about is here at Kinnley. I would be far more at ease over this if it were occurring in some remote corner of the kingdom."

"At ease?" Crispin eyed him with exasperation. "You *have* been at this a while. I couldn't imagine being at ease with this sort of thing *ever*."

"Like it or not, assuming the meeting has not already occurred, 'this sort of thing' has dropped into your lap."

"And you've no way of knowing the day?"

Philip shook his head. "The men were speaking in code. The first number would have been the date. The second, 'double twelves,' indicates the time. Without that first number, we simply don't know."

"So you are operating under the assumption that it has not yet taken place."

"Precisely. I need to know the nearest inlets or coves north of Brownlow."

"There are quite a few." Crispin continued pacing.

Sorrel joined the conversation. "They would need to be within rowing distance of a port of some sort."

"Unless the ship simply dropped anchor offshore," Philip said.

Sorrel shook her head. "The moon is full tonight. The next few nights will be quite light. A ship of any significant size would hardly go unnoticed."

"She has a point," Crispin said. "Felixstowe could certainly dock a ship, but it is considerably far to the south of Brownlow."

"Something more remote." Philip rubbed his face with his hands. "Abandoned, even."

Crispin's face grew immediately grave. "The north end of Brownlow has something of a dock. Ancient almost but probably sufficient for something like this."

"But with a docking point so close," Sorrel said, "that would most likely put their meeting place—"

"—at Kinnley," Philip finished the unsettling thought. "Probably the tiny inlet at the southern tip of the property."

"That's quite a distance from the house," Crispin said as if reassuring himself.

"Five miles, at least." Philip did not want Crispin's panic added to his current load. "There is another more secluded cove up the beach. Several good rowers could get that far. So we can't rule that out."

"How will you know which one?" Crispin asked.

"We won't. Both locations will have to be watched."

"For how long?" Crispin looked more uneasy by the moment. "Are the grounds of my home to be under constant watch for weeks on end?"

Philip heard Sorrel's sudden sharp intake of breath. "Twenty-nine, Philip."

He couldn't say what she meant by the remark.

"Those were the other numbers. I'm certain of it. 'Twenty-nine. Double twelves.' That's what the man in the inn said."

A mere moment passed before the weight of that struck him. "Today is the twenty-ninth. That means their meeting is tonight. Tonight."

No one spoke. Philip's mind spun with the implications.

"I need to send word to a contact in Ipswich," he said. "I'll need your swiftest horse and most trustworthy servant, Crispin, one who can be counted on not to read the letter I send with him nor fail in his assignment."

"There's a lad in the stables who can be counted on. You're sending for the others, then?"

Philip nodded. "They'll need to take positions tonight and watch for Le Fontaine's men."

"A word of warning, Philip." Crispin stopped his pacing. "I have tenants who have been known to walk the coast on nights with a full moon. The cloud cover we've been under the past two days has finally broken. I'd hate to have any of those good people scared out of their wits by a gathering of Bow Street."

"And I would hate to have them come to an even worse end at the hands of Le Fontaine and his seedy associates," Philip said.

Tonight. The realization repeated endlessly in his mind. He had mere hours to prepare for what could prove to be a violent encounter.

"How do you plan to tell the difference between simple people and these spies?" Crispin resumed his circuits.

A very good question, but one to which he had no answer. "I don't know. No one has ever seen any of the men involved."

"But you will approach cautiously?"

"Actually, I planned to run screaming and waving my arms up the coast. In my lemon-yellow waistcoat, of course. I would hate to look ridiculous."

Crispin smiled and shook his head. "I will have Hancock double-check all the locks tonight, though how I am going to explain my absence to Catherine, I can't say."

"Your absence?" What was Crispin talking about?

"You don't think I am going to suck my thumb in my bedchamber while the beaches of Kinnley are inundated with spies and agents, do you?"

"You were not trained for this, Crispin." Philip hadn't anticipated unwanted assistance.

"Bl—" He abruptly stopped as he seemed to suddenly remember the presence of a lady. "I know Kinnley lands better than anyone, Philip. If you are going to locate anything out there in the dark, you are going to need someone who knows where he's going."

"You forget how much of my life I have spent here, Crispin." Philip had spent many a school holiday at Kinnley. "I think I know the south end as well as you."

"But you have to watch two different locations."

"Grimes will take one."

"If he can find it." Crispin gave him a look of pure stubbornness. "I am not backing down, so you might as well accept."

"A guide, then." Philip knew Crispin's willfulness well enough to not fight. "You can get Grimes's men to the southern inlet, but let them handle the confrontation if there is one."

"Agreed."

A tense silence hung over the room. Philip practically held his breath, planning out the uncertain night ahead of him. Crispin would be out in the middle of it all.

"If nothing else," Crispin said out of the blue, "I can let Grimes know if anyone we encounter is a local. I can recognize them. *You* won't have that."

"Will the beach be so inundated, do you think?" Philip doubted it. Surely the Kinnley tenants didn't make a festival of late-night beach combing.

"The possibility alone will make identifying your criminals more chancy."

"If only I knew what they looked like. Even just one of them." Philip knew all too well what was generally said about wishes and beggars.

"I do," Sorrel said.

Philip had almost forgotten she was in the library. "I'm sorry, what?"

"I know what one of them looks like," she said. "I saw him at the Dove and Crow. I would recognize his face anywhere. And his voice. I could pick it out, as well."

"That would be helpful if you were going to be with us." Philip rued the lost information.

"Then let me come."

"No." He spun around to face her, his heart lodged in his throat by her unexpected request.

"Philip." She rose awkwardly to her feet. "Crispin can let the other group know if he sees someone he doesn't know. I can let you know if I see the man from the inn."

"No." It was all Philip could do to keep from yelling. "You will stay here where you will be safe and leave this to Bow Street and the Foreign Office."

"You are allowing Crispin to go."

"That is different."

"How is it different?" The belligerent Sorrel he remembered from their first few encounters reemerged with a vengeance. "I am not asking that I be permitted to march onto the beach and challenge the lot of them to fisticuffs. Nor do I plan to run up and down the beach waving my arms like a lunatic—I leave that entirely in your capable, trained hands. I could hide in the bushes, like Crispin."

"The picture you paint is not very flattering," Crispin said dryly.

"Recognizing them would be invaluable." Sorrel sounded too calm. If she fully understood the danger, she'd be far less determined. Or would she? This was *General Sorrel,* after all.

"They might not be at the location you would be watching." How on earth was he going to steer her from this disastrous course of action?

"Then I would hardly be in any danger, would I?" She looked almost menacing with her walking stick in a death grip and her mouth set in a stubborn line.

"You want to back me up here, Crispin?" Philip said.

"Who me? The chicken-hearted man hiding in the bushes?"

No help from that quarter. "Sorrel—"

"I will ride out there on my own, Philip," Sorrel cut in. "It would be far simpler if you let me come."

"Suppose things turn violent?" Philip said. "You want to be in the midst of that with little but foliage to hide you?"

"My land agent's cottage is a little more than five hundred yards from that cove, Philip," Crispin said. "It would be a safe place for her to stay once she's offered what help she can."

"I did not ask for your opinion."

"Actually, you did."

Philip rounded on Sorrel, physically shaking. "I will lock you in your bedchamber if I have to."

"I understand bedsheets can be tied into a rope," she said. "There are ways to escape."

"From two floors above ground level?"

"Quite a few bedsheets, then."

"I will let you two work this out." Crispin unlocked the door. "Once you've written that letter, let me know and I'll send Jimmy from the stables with it to Ipswich." He stepped out, closing the door once more behind him.

Sorrel didn't waste a minute. "Hear me out on this."

She got no further. Philip stepped to her the moment the door closed and, taking her face in his hands, kissed her almost desperately. How could she even think of putting herself in danger? How could she expect him to do so? He could not. She'd become too important to him. Somehow he felt as long as she was there, at that moment, as long as he could touch her, hold her in his arms, that she would be safe.

"Philip," she whispered as he pulled back from her. "Let me help."

"I will not risk your life," he countered. "I will not."

Twenty-Six

A DISTANT SPLASH GAVE THEM AWAY.

Philip turned his spyglass out to sea. Sorrel watched, holding her breath. They'd waited in the dark shadows of the small cliff top above a remote cove along the Kinnley coastline for what must have been an hour. Sorrel had long ago begun to feel the cold, though she didn't remark on it. She'd barely managed to convince Philip to allow her to come, in hopes of identifying the man she'd seen in the inn two weeks earlier. She didn't dare show any signs of weakening to her task.

"Small rowboat," Philip whispered, his voice hardly loud enough to be heard.

"How many men?" the man Philip called Rob queried with the same expert quietness.

A moment passed as Philip peered through his small retractable telescope. "Three," he finally said.

"But are they the ones we're looking for?" Rob asked almost soundlessly.

Philip pulled Sorrel to him and motioned her to look through the spyglass that he'd kept astoundingly still during their shift of positions. She followed his unspoken instructions and searched the magnified boat just off center in the telescope's line of sight.

"Can you see them?" His breath tingled her ear.

Sorrel nodded, not trusting her voice to be as perfectly quiet as the men's around her.

"Hold this." He brought her hand around the spyglass. She joined it with her other. "Tell me if any of them look familiar." Sorrel felt his arm settle around her waist, a gesture so comforting she involuntarily leaned back against him as she searched each face in the boat, one by one. Then she lowered the spyglass to her lap.

"I'm sorry, Philip." Sorrel whispered as quietly as she possibly could. "He is not in that boat."

"I didn't expect him to be," Philip answered, so close she felt his jaw move beside her own. "The man you saw should be waiting for that boat."

"On the beach?"

Philip's gaze scanned the crescent-shaped beach brightened by the full moon and cloudless night. Sorrel shifted the spyglass to one hand and slipped her other one into Philip's warm grip. He squeezed her hand gently but with a strength she needed.

She sat there, hand in his, her head resting against his shoulder, eyes shut to the night around her. If she didn't think too hard on the reason for their unusual circumstances, the situation was almost peaceful. If she weren't so blasted cold, she might have simply drifted off to sleep.

She felt Philip suddenly tense.

"Just down there, Sorrel." He motioned slightly with his head to their right, down on the sand. "Something moved in the shadows."

Sorrel scanned the beach with the spyglass for a moment before finding a pair of silhouettes crouched at the base of the cliff in an indentation where the moonlight barely illuminated their solid figures.

"Two men," she whispered as she studied them closely.

Philip didn't speak nor move. She knew he was waiting for her to identify one of them. Sorrel almost hoped they would be unfamiliar. She hoped Crispin's tenants were not only drawn to the beach on moonlit nights but tended to row about in the ocean, as well. The first man was rotund and almost entirely bald.

Her view of the second man was not terribly revealing. He had the right physical build, and his hair appeared the appropriate shade of brown, though the shadowy quality of the light made that debatable. The man shifted slightly, and a beam of moonlight passed momentarily across his face.

Sorrel jerked back, clasping the spyglass to her chest. Philip's arms closed tightly around her.

"You recognized him." It was a statement, and a grave one at that. "The man from the Dove and Crow?"

Sorrel nodded mutely.

"Should we ride for team two?" Rob asked.

Sorrel jumped again. She'd forgotten about the three others lurking in the trees around them.

Philip took the spyglass from her and began searching the horizon. Apparently settling on what he sought, Philip kept the glass steady and remained quiet as the moments dragged on.

"No time," Philip said. He motioned over his shoulder with his head, and the group slowly, silently rose to their feet. Philip kept an arm possessively around Sorrel as he helped her join the others a few feet further from the low cliff edge, safely hidden behind a thick hedge.

"Check your arms," Philip instructed the men. A heavy silence descended over the group. He turned his attention to Sorrel. "You remember where the land agent's cottage is?"

She nodded. He'd pointed it out as they'd ridden past it what seemed like an eternity earlier.

"And you're sure you can dismount on your own?"

Another mute nod.

"Do not come out," he instructed, cupping her face in his hands. "No matter what you hear."

"But, what—"

"No matter what," he repeated sternly.

"Philip." Her whisper cracked with emotion.

"Do not turn missish on me, Sorrel." Philip walked her back toward a waiting Kinnley mount. They moved slowly, lest her walking stick slip on the snow-covered ground.

"You have to promise me you will be careful," she said. His warnings to her about the dangers of this mission came flooding back into her mind.

"I am always careful." All hints of emotion had left Philip's voice. "Up you go."

Philip's hands encircled Sorrel's waist as he lifted her into the saddle. It was not a sidesaddle, but they'd planned on that, having found a gown in the Kinnley attics with the very full skirt of decades earlier, dark enough to help hide her in the darkness of midnight. More of her dark-stockinged legs showed than was strictly acceptable, but, considering the peril of their current situation, Sorrel hardly noted it.

Philip slipped the cottage key into Sorrel's palm then closed his fingers around her hand. He kissed her fingers softly, caressingly. Sorrel had to bite her lip to keep them steady. He'd asked her to remain in control, and she vowed she would. For a moment he stood silently holding her hand to his cheek. One more brief kiss on the back of her hand and he stepped back, though he did not yet let go.

"Lock the door," Philip instructed.

Sorrel nodded.

He squeezed her hand then released it and stepped away. She slipped the key into the pocket of her coat.

Sorrel took a deep breath before heeling her mount to a slow, quiet walk just as Philip had instructed as they'd ridden out. It was vital, he'd explained, that they not make any more noise than absolutely necessary.

She didn't look back as the horse walked away, knowing her heart would sink if she turned around to find he'd slipped out of sight already. Not a single sound other than the distant waves broke the night as she slowly made her way from the coast. She'd thought she'd come to understand helplessness in the two years since her unfortunate incident. She'd been wrong. Never had she felt as helpless as she did then, leaving Philip moments from storming a group that outnumbered his own, a group probably every bit as heavily armed, perhaps more so.

Dismounting was more difficult than she'd anticipated, having no experience with anything but a sidesaddle. Her skirts snagged as she slid her stiff right leg over and tore as she tugged to free herself. Battered from the jarring ride and aching from the bitter cold, her leg simply gave out as she alighted, and she landed on the ground with a thud.

The horse startled at the sound but did not run. Sprawled on the wet snow, Sorrel managed to shift enough to avoid the horse's hooves. With tremendous effort and more than a little pain, Sorrel pulled herself to her feet, grateful she'd managed to keep her walking stick in her hand.

"Come on, then," she cooed to the horse, hoping to keep it calm. One of them needed to be. "To the trees." They moved slowly, snow crunching beneath her, toward the back of the cottage. Just as Philip had promised, a heavy woolen blanket sat waiting on a small bench beneath an ancient tree. Sorrel pulled the horse closer to a low, sturdy branch and wrapped the reins around it.

Her leg protested every step and threatened to drop her again. She stumbled toward the bench and picked up the blanket. Sorrel rested against the tree trunk for a moment. Then, with a deep breath of determination, she moved to the side of the horse with which she'd been entrusted and draped the heavy blanket over its back.

Sorrel left the horse with a rub on the nose and struggled toward the cottage, praying she'd find a heavy blanket inside for herself. She reached the back door, her leg on fire with pain. Her boots were caked in mud. Philip had emphasized the importance of leaving the cottage with no trace of having been there. Muddy footprints would be a giveaway. Sorrel struggled a moment, but managed to get her shoes off. She set them beside the door then fumbled through her pocket for the key. As she did so, Sorrel leaned her forehead against the door, exhausted. She pulled the key to the lock.

Somewhere in the distance, a gunshot split the air. Sorrel's heart raced in her chest, her breath suddenly lodged deep in her lungs.

She slid the key into the lock and turned. A tear ran unbidden down her cheek. This was what Philip meant by "no matter what." She stepped inside the dark cottage.

Another shot reverberated. Sorrel closed the door, turned the lock, and collapsed to the floor. In the next moment a third shot sounded, dulled somewhat by the thick walls around her. She refused to allow her mind to dwell on the scene playing out on the beach. Instead, she focused her thoughts on navigating through the darkened house, finding a candle, at least.

Unsure of her limbs and completely unfamiliar with her surroundings, Sorrel slowly lowered herself to her knees. Knowing from experience that crawling with a cane in hand could be remarkably difficult, Sorrel abandoned her *affectation* not far from the back door and crawled, her bare palms against the frigid floor, extending her arm now and then to feel for furniture nearby. She felt certain the Kinnley land agent would have a lamp in his home. A little light would dispel some of her nerves.

How she wished she could light a fire. The air inside the cottage felt nearly as cold as that outside. Sorrel shivered despite her heavy coat.

She reached a wall first. She felt along it—perhaps she'd find a sideboard or wall table. Her hand slid along a doorframe, then a door. She stretched for the knob then turned it. The door opened easily, though the hinges protested with a high-pitched squeal. Inside the room the windows were uncovered and the bright moon illuminated a sparsely furnished bedroom.

She might very well find a candle inside. But she might do well to stick to the outer room if she could pull back a drapery or two.

A scratching at the front of the house froze her midthought. Philip? Had he come for her already?

She heard the sound of the doorknob being twisted anxiously. Then the door violently shook.

Philip had a key. Someone else was trying to get inside. The French spy and his counterparts immediately crossed her mind.

Panic gave way to stark determination. Sorrel pulled herself to her feet, despite the agony such movement caused, and stumbled inside the bedroom. She needed a place to hide.

Too late.

The sound of splintering wood signaled the arrival of her unwanted guests.

Twenty-Seven

Sorrel held her breath and kept as still as she could manage.

"You will be lucky to not have woken the household," an unfamiliar voice loudly whispered. The man could not possibly be anything other than French, though he spoke English.

"The household will be lucky if they haven't awoken." That voice turned Sorrel's blood to ice. He was the man from the inn. His voice was stamped in her memory, so often had she relived his conversation.

If they haven't awoken. A tiny seed of an idea sprouted in her mind. She moved slowly, cautiously, willing herself to stay upright, commanding her leg to get her to the bed. She vowed never to ask another thing of her broken limb if it simply didn't fail her.

The room was quite small. Only a few steps saw her to the low bed. She took slow, calming breaths then pulled back the coverlet. The bed creaked quietly as Sorrel slid on it. She carefully, slowly pulled her feet up.

"Find some bandages," the Frenchman said. "And see if they keep any horses."

He groaned as he spoke, the sound one of a man in a good deal of pain. Had he been injured in the gunfire Sorrel had heard? Her thoughts turned immediately to Philip. How had he fared? Was he injured as well? She refused to ponder a far worse possibility.

She heard footsteps. The men were searching the house. Would they check the room she was in? Had they heard the bed creak?

Sorrel pulled the blanket to her chin, hoping she was a good enough actress to convince them she was sleeping despite her pounding heart and strained breathing. She reached up and pulled the pins from her hair and ran her hand frantically through the knot, letting her tresses fall messily around her. She laid her head on the pillow and closed her eyes just as the footsteps halted outside her room.

She'd left the door open, too afraid it would squeak to risk closing it. If either of the men stood in the doorway, they would be looking directly at her in that moment. The idea sent a wave of dread over her.

"A woman back here," the man from the inn called out in a hoarse whisper. "Asleep."

Sorrel held as still as possible, offering up a desperate prayer. If only the men let her be, chose to let her sleep, she might yet escape.

"A woman? Is she alone?"

"She appears to be," the man at the door answered.

Sorrel's pulse pounded in her neck, fear setting it racing hard. She was, in that moment, completely alone. Alone. Unarmed. Crippled.

"Wake her," the Frenchman ordered.

With those two words, Sorrel's fears escalated. She hadn't the security of pretending to be oblivious. She couldn't attempt an escape undetected.

"Do you really want a witness, Bélanger?"

Bélanger. That was the name she'd been trying to remember from the conversation in Ipswich. Bélanger was the French contact Mr. Garner had been trying to apprehend for years and the man Philip believed to be at least as dangerous as Le Fontaine.

"Wake her." Bélanger repeated his orders with a growl.

Footfall immediately sounded, drawing closer to the bed.

"Help me," Sorrel silently pleaded with the heavens. She could hear the man breathing, he stood so close. She'd never been so frightened in all her life.

"Wake up, woman!" the man barked.

She pretended to be startled awake. If she kept her movements slow and groggy perhaps the man would believe she'd been asleep. In the moment before she opened her mouth to speak, she realized the ruse had to go beyond appearing tired. They'd found her in the cottage of an employer of the estate. If the men realized she hailed from the upper classes, they'd grow instantly suspicious. Far better that they think her of little importance.

"Who are you?" She did her best to imitate a lower-class accent. "What are you doing in m' house?"

"Get up."

Slow and groggy, she reminded herself. Sorrel sat up and made a show of being a bit disoriented. She set back the blanket and moved to slip her legs off the side of the bed.

"You're wearing a coat." Suspicion touched the man's tone.

Sorrel thought fast. "The night's cold. A coat's cheaper 'n burning coal."

The man eyed her closely as she sat frozen on the edge of the bed. She knew some of her fear showed in her eyes—she couldn't prevent it. But, she reasoned, any woman would be afraid to wake and find a stranger in her house.

"You're fully dressed under that coat," the man said. "Why aren't you in night clothes?"

"It's warmer." She hoped he'd accept the same reasoning a second time. Thank heavens she didn't still have her boots on.

Bélanger called out from the sitting room again. "What is taking so long?"

Though the Frenchman's voice sent a chill down her spine, Sorrel felt the slightest hint of relief that his orders took some of his partner's scrutiny off her attire.

"Come along." The Englishman jerked his head in the direction of the corridor.

The idea of leaving the room felt far more dangerous than remaining. "I can't walk," she said. "I've a broken leg. M'father went for the apothecary."

He seemed to debate with himself a moment.

Please let me stay. Please let me stay.

Without a word of warning or explanation, the man grabbed her arm and pulled her to her feet. Sorrel hadn't a chance to correct her balance. Her leg simply gave out and she stumbled to the ground.

Her assailant muttered a curse, one even her father's stable hands had only whispered when she was present. He yanked her upright once more. None too gently, he pulled her arm around his neck and wrapped his arm around her waist. The pungent smell of him threatened to turn her stomach.

She couldn't match the breadth of his strides as he dragged her from the room and down the corridor. A lamp had been lit in the sitting room, illuminating the face of Bélanger. Fear wrapped its icy fingers around her heart. Even from a distance his eyes were hard and unfeeling.

"What is this?" Bélanger had clearly run out of patience.

"Says she broke her leg."

The Englishman dropped her onto a hard-backed chair. She didn't need to pretend his rough treatment caused her pain. Though her wince was entirely genuine, Bélanger looked unconvinced.

"Are you hoping to gain our compassion, *ma fille*? You are out of luck. We possess not a drop of compassion."

He grabbed the edge of her skirt and flung it back enough to reveal her legs from the knee down. Sorrel understood, though she experienced the briefest moment of real panic. He intended to check her story.

"Show me," Bélanger commanded.

Sorrel slowly tugged on the toe of the dark stocking covering her deformed leg. She made certain the men saw that doing so caused her very real discomfort. The stocking pulled free. She let it fall to the ground in a heap. The Englishman drew near with the lamp, its light spilling on her legs. Both men's faces turned in surprise and disgust. Sorrel knew exactly what they saw. The break in her leg, though two years old, remained obvious. One could easily see where each of the bones had snapped.

"The girl said her father went for the gallipot."

Bélanger stepped back. He spoke to his partner in French. "Then we'd best be gone before he returns."

"And what of the girl?" The Englishman not only appeared to understand but answered in flawless French as well.

Sorrel listened, all the while pretending to have no idea what they said to one another. A young woman of the lower classes would not understand French.

"We will get what we need out of her, then we'll take care of it."

The Englishman nodded.

"Watch the window." Bélanger still spoke in his native tongue. "The last thing we need is company."

"And if the girl's father returns?"

"Shoot him."

Sorrel hoped, prayed, she kept her reaction to those instructions hidden.

"Now," Bélanger addressed her in English once more. "Where do you keep your physicking supplies?"

Unsure if an uneducated woman would be familiar with that term, Sorrel pretended to be confused.

"Bandages. Medical powders." Bélanger spat the words, frustration clear in his tense stance and unwavering glare.

Sorrel hadn't the slightest idea where such things were in this house. Fumbling around through drawers and cupboards would give away her ruse in an instant.

"M'father works for the great house," she said. "When we need those things, we go up there for them."

"Then we'll have to be creative, it seems." Bélanger pulled off his mud-stained jacket inch by inch. His tightened lips and pulled expression indicated doing so caused him pain. "Tear a long strip from your skirt."

"From my—"

"I need a bandage," he snapped.

Sorrel pulled at the hem of her long, full skirts. Two decades or more in the attics had rotted the fabric enough to make tearing it possible. She took three inches off the entire bottom of her dark dress, her white petticoat showing underneath. Never had she been more grateful for her very practical taste in underclothing. Had her underskirt been trimmed with all the lace and ribbons Mother and Marjie favored, Bélanger would have seen in an instant she was not the poor woman she pretended to be.

She held the strip of dark fabric wadded in her hands. Bélanger pulled another chair near hers and sat with his left side to her. He'd removed his jacket, and Sorrel could see for the first time why he needed bandaging. Blood stained the back and side of his left sleeve from just below his shoulder nearly to his wrist. He'd been shot.

"Wrap it tight," he said.

For just a moment, she considered refusing. He'd eventually grow weak from lack of blood. But the strategy was foolish. Disobedience would likely get her killed faster than he would bleed out.

Without a word, she began to work. She made the bandage as tight as possible. Though Bélanger winced, he did not object.

"Have you seen anyone?" he asked his comrade at the window, speaking once again in French.

"There is movement, but at a distance. No one seems to be coming in this direction."

Sorrel didn't know whether she ought to be disappointed or relieved to hear that. No one was coming to her rescue. But the men might just as soon shoot her if it meant a faster, less complicated escape. As she worked on the man's arm, her eyes scanned the room, looking for anything she might use as a weapon. She didn't doubt the men were fully armed.

Her thoughts turned to the fire poker. But what good would that do against two men? Even if she managed to subdue one, the other would not give her the opportunity to do the same to him. No hunting rifle hung above the mantel. She did not see an ax anywhere near the small pile of firewood. Perhaps a knife could be found in the kitchen, but she would never be fast enough to get there before they stopped her.

"It is only a matter of time before they find us here," the man at the window said, still not speaking in English. "They'll not give up their search."

Bélanger looked over at him, bringing his gaze closer to Sorrel as well. She made certain to keep her focus on the bandaging, lest he catch her searching the room.

"The English will scour this countryside at the mere thought of catching both Bélanger and Le Fontaine in a single night's effort. But I did not come here to die like a dog at their hands. I will return to my homeland."

Her shock pulled a gasp from her lungs. When Bélanger shot her a questioning look, she scrambled for an explanation. "M'leg pains me, sir."

His attention returned to his partner, though Sorrel felt little relief. *Le Fontaine.* The Englishman, the one she'd somehow come to think of as less threatening than Bélanger, was Le Fontaine himself. Sorrel knew without a doubt in that moment that her chances of survival were exceptionally slim.

Bélanger watched her tie off the bandage. She tried not to let his scrutiny unnerve her.

"I'm not a doctor," she said. "I can't say if I did this correctly."

"You've made a valiant effort," he said.

Just as she pulled her hands back, his right hand snaked out and snatched her by the wrist. Bélanger pulled her hand closer to him and flipped it palm-side up. Sorrel tried to wriggle free, but his grasp was firm.

He slid one finger down the palm of her hand, sending shivers of revulsion through her.

"Isn't this interesting," he said, his tone oily. "So very, very soft." His cold eyes bored into hers. "*These* are not the hands of a servant."

Sorrel pulled hard, trying to free herself, but his grip only grew surer.

He tsked and shook his head. "Someone's been telling lies." His grasp tightened painfully. He spoke through his teeth. "I despise liars."

Sorrel made no response. What could she say? He'd seen through her disguise, there was no point denying it.

He did not release her, but with his bandaged arm he pulled from a well-hidden sheath a short dagger. "Perhaps, *ma fille*, you'd like to tell me who you really are." He set the menacing tip of his knife beneath her chin with just enough pressure for her to feel it there without it drawing blood.

The man meant to kill her either way. She'd maintain some control of her final moments, even if in no other way than deciding what he would be permitted to know about her. "I'd rather not."

His expression remained impassive, calm. "Very well. I shall call you Jeanne." His small smile proved utterly terrifying. "Adieu, Jeanne."

Thoughts of Fennel and Marjie and the pain of never seeing them again passed swiftly through her mind. It was Philip's teasing smile, however, that settled there. She hadn't stopped in their last moments together to say she'd come to care for him, more than care for him. She hadn't even bid him farewell. Now she'd never have that chance.

She felt a sting as the tip of his dagger pricked into her skin.

"Someone is coming," Le Fontaine said, his voice a harried whisper.

Bélanger froze, the tip of his blade still pressed to the top of Sorrel's throat. His gaze shifted away to his partner. "How many?"

"Two. And they are definitely coming this way."

Had Philip come for her? What relief she felt quickly subsided. What if he drew near only to be shot?

Bélanger's lips thinned. His forehead creased deeply in thought. "The rest of those English rats will be watching the roads."

"And will likely send for others," Le Fontaine said.

Bélanger let forth a string of French curses. His knife hand lowered ever so slightly. Sorrel still could not be at ease. He was distracted for the moment, but she doubted it would last. She hadn't the swiftness nor agility to make an escape and had absolutely no weapon to wield in her defense.

Le Fontaine's footsteps drew nearer from behind. "Dispatch her quickly," he said. "We haven't time to waste." He walked past them toward the corridor leading to the back of the house.

Bélanger kept still. Though his blade no longer touched her flesh, she felt far from safe.

"She may be of use to us yet," he said. "Suppose we run into one of those rats. They're less likely to fire on us when we're holding a hostage."

"They care nothing for the lower classes." Le Fontaine spat on the ground. "Pigs," he said in disgust.

"Ah, but she is a highborn lady." Bélanger's sinister smile returned. "I understand that is still worth something in England."

Le Fontaine stood at the far end of the room, watching them. He seemed to contemplate the idea of using Sorrel as insurance against capture. Though she hated the idea of going with them, doing so would keep her alive. She'd have a chance to find a way of escaping.

"What about her leg?" Le Fontaine asked. "She couldn't have feigned that injury. If she can't even walk, she'll slow us down."

Bélanger lightly tapped her nose with his knife in a mockingly playful manner. She could see a small dot of red on its tip. "Then, for her sake, I hope *la petite fille* knows where we can find a couple of horses." He eyed her expectantly.

Honesty seemed the best approach at the moment. "There is one just outside the back door. But only one."

Something changed in his face. His gaze grew more intent, his expression less indifferent. "You have a very fine voice when you are not trying to sound unrefined, *ma chère.* I like it very much indeed."

Sorrel shuddered. His was not the tone of one offering an honorable compliment.

"Time to go." He sheathed his knife at his side once more. Sorrel dabbed at the spot where his blade had pricked her and came away with a swath of red on her fingers. She wiped her fingers on her skirts, the arm of the chair she sat on, anything to relieve herself of the sight of her own blood.

"Come," he said to Le Fontaine. "You must carry her. I cannot with this bullet lodged in my arm."

Le Fontaine did not argue with that. Bélanger took up the lantern while his partner scooped Sorrel up off the chair. She held herself stiffly, trying to keep her mind off the fact that this vile murderer had his arms around her.

They moved swiftly down the corridor and out the back door into the cold. Sorrel was grateful she'd not taken off her coat. She tried to make out shapes in the darkness of night but had little success. Philip had intended to come for her through the back. If he'd been one of the two they saw, he might come into view any moment.

How she prayed he'd do so carefully. If he were hurt or worse because of her, she'd never forgive herself.

Le Fontaine set her on the back of the same horse she'd ridden to the cottage not more than thirty minutes earlier. This time, however, Bélanger held the reins, walking in front of the animal. Sorrel grasped the saddle, adjusting her balance with each sway of its back.

She resisted the urge to look back as they moved quietly into the cover of trees a few yards distant from the cottage. Her captives watched her too closely for the movement to go unnoticed. They'd know she was expecting someone and might stay around just long enough to dispose of her would-be rescuer.

Philip would look for her. She knew he would. And she had every intention of being alive when he found her. That meant devising a means of escape, or at the very least ensuring her own survival.

The task felt monumental, the odds insurmountable. But, then, had she not lived through an injury the doctors all had declared fatal? Had she not refused to succumb to countless fevers and infections? She'd spent her entire life proving her mettle, first to her father then, after her accident, to the doctors, her family, and everyone else who refused to believe her capable of anything.

Except Philip. He believed in her.

Sorrel set her mind to it. She'd find a way to escape. She swore she would.

Twenty-Eight

PHILIP DIDN'T EVEN STOP TO catch his breath. They'd stormed the spies' meeting without warning and managed to apprehend all but two. Rob's men had their captives well in hand. Philip traded out his expended pistol for a freshly loaded one. He sheathed the knife he kept in his boot during these altercations.

"Goin' after them two on yer own?" Rob asked.

Philip paused only long enough to say a simple no before beginning his trek.

Rob kept pace with him. "Yer off to the cottage. Those two rogues are loose out there, and yer sweetheart's alone."

Without Sorrel identifying the man she'd seen in Ipswich, they couldn't have acted as quickly as they had. Still, Philip had second-guessed his decision to allow her to come along ever since watching her ride off into the darkness. Now with two of the criminals unaccounted for, he could not be easy. He'd not join the manhunt until he saw Sorrel safely inside Kinnley.

"Slow and cautious, there, Daffodil." Rob only knew Philip by the false name given him by the Foreign Office. "Ye'll not do yer lady friend a bit o' good making a heap o' noise and getting yerself shot."

The man had a point. Philip checked his pace. They moved carefully in the direction of the land agent's cottage. Philip kept a wary eye out but saw no movement in the bushes nearby.

Far in the distance he saw a twinkle of light precisely where he knew the cottage to be. Had Sorrel lit a lantern? He'd cautioned

her not to do so near a window. If *he* could see the light, so could anyone else.

It wasn't like Sorrel to be reckless. She was stubborn, yes, but not stupid.

A few more times he spotted a brief flicker of light. He moved more swiftly, still keeping watch over his surroundings.

Put out the light, Sorrel.

"I'm sure them two are well past here by now. They'll not've seen that light." Rob's tone was not at all convincing. The fact that he'd had the same thought as Philip only made Philip more concerned.

As he closed the distance to the cabin, Philip didn't see the light again. Perhaps she'd settled in and extinguished the flame for good. Even that didn't dispel his sense of urgency.

He reached the back of the house and stopped short. The horse was not tied up under the tree as it was supposed to be. Perhaps she'd forgotten to tie it up and the beast had wandered off. Or maybe she hadn't been able to find the cottage and simply kept going the rest of the way to the house.

"Them's women's boots," Rob whispered from near the back door.

Philip turned to look. Sure enough, boots that could easily be Sorrel's sat beside the door. "I have a key," he said, fishing through his pocket for it.

"'Taint necessary. Door's unlocked."

Unlocked? The knot in his stomach tightened. She had to have come. Crispin checked the cottage earlier that day, and all the doors were bolted. Had she been so careless as to leave the door unlocked? Lud, he was going to throttle her!

Philip stepped inside, Rob at his back. He could barely make out the dim interior. A small swath of moonlight spilled in through the door they left open behind them.

He motioned with his head in the direction of the first door off the corridor. Rob understood and cautiously looked inside. Philip checked the next door, which hung slightly ajar. The window let in enough light for him to make out a bed. The coverlet was thrown haphazardly back as though someone had only just gotten out from under it.

The land agent was a full county away. But, Philip reasoned, the man was a bachelor. He had no one about to insist he straighten his bedcovers.

Rob joined him in the doorway. "She weren't in the kitchen," he said. "But I found this by the back door."

He held up an ivory-tipped ebony walking stick. Philip pushed down a sudden surge of panic. Sorrel was there, she had to be. So why hadn't they found her yet? The cottage was extremely small. Only the sitting room remained.

He moved immediately toward it. She had to be in that room. He stepped inside, telling himself all the while that he'd find her there.

The room sat empty. Empty and cold, as if a window had been left open. It wasn't a window, but the door. It didn't close properly. The wood was splintered violently around the lock. The hinges were bent. Someone had forced it open.

He knew, then, without a doubt, that Sorrel was in danger.

"Sorrel!"

No answer.

"Sorrel!"

"Found a lantern out back," Rob said, bringing the light with him.

Philip could see more of the room. A man's jacket, one arm soaked in blood, sat discarded near two chairs arranged next to each other. Someone had forced his way inside—a man who'd been bleeding. It was not at all outside the realm of possibility that one of the spies who'd escaped had been shot in the exchange of fire.

Philip crossed closer to the chairs. Something dark lay on the ground.

"Bring the lantern over here."

As Rob complied, Philip bent down and picked up the heap. A single black stocking. Philip's insides clenched in growing fear. Sorrel had been wearing black stockings. Her shoes were there. Her walking stick was there. But Sorrel was not.

"On the chair." Rob motioned with his chin.

Philip's heart stopped at what he saw. Streaks of red in the shape of four slender fingers marred the arm of the chair. Small fingers from a small hand, though too large for a child's. He knew, somehow, it was Sorrel's blood.

In the five years he'd worked for the Foreign Office, Philip had never once lost his head during a mission. But standing there looking at the bloodied handprint of the woman he loved almost desperately, he couldn't form a single coherent thought. He could not formulate a plan, a course of action. No one associated with Le Fontaine would bat an eye at killing a woman. Sorrel was in the hands of a murderer.

Think, man. Think.

"Obviously the men we're looking for came here," he reasoned out loud. "And they've taken her with them." Hearing those words spoken drove new fear into his heart. "But why?"

"Hostages can be useful, Daff."

"Only until they aren't needed any longer." Lud, he had to find her quickly. "Where would they have gone?"

"A couple of foreigners? They'll make for a port first thing." Rob nodded decisively.

Of course. "They have a ship waiting at an abandoned dock south of here. We'd best head in that direction."

Rob seemed hesitant. "If they've a horse and we're on foot . . ."

"Three adults can't ride the same horse," Philip said. "At least one of them has to be on foot. They won't be any faster than we are."

"But they've a head start."

Philip touched his fingertips to the red streaks Sorrel left behind. The stain proved wet to the touch. His fear gave way to anger and an iron-clad determination. The blood hadn't even had time to dry.

"They haven't been gone long."

As he clenched his fists, the blood on his fingertips felt wet against his palm, a reminder of the danger Sorrel faced. He refused to waste another moment.

Philip strode from the room down the corridor. Rob came as well.

"Send any available men southward," he instructed. "But with all possible caution. A lady's life is on the line."

"Understood."

"Make certain the gentleman serving as guide to the other group returns and secures his home." Philip would not have Crispin in mortal peril as well.

"Will do."

They stepped out into the night once more. The air had grown colder in the few short minutes they'd been inside. Sorrel hadn't any shoes. At least one of her feet was completely bare. Her captors weren't likely to have allowed her to bring a blanket. She was somewhere in the dark of night, cold and bleeding. And it was his fault.

"Daff?"

Philip turned toward Rob's voice. The man offered him his firearm.

"I'm not taking your weapon."

"I'm returning to our men," Rob said. "Ye're chasing after two murderers. I'd say ye need it more than I do."

So Philip took it. The more shots he had, the better.

Rob moved swiftly in the direction of the coast. Philip set himself to studying the muddle of foot- and hoofprints in the thin layer of snow. He'd never make sense of the human tracks but wanted to know which direction the horse had gone.

He'd never been more grateful for a full moon. Leaving the lantern lit posed too great a risk. But there was enough natural light to make out the horse's prints through the snow.

The animal had gone around the back of the house, toward the south. Philip would wager they'd not walk too near the beach. The men would assume they were being hunted and would keep as hidden as possible. Philip knew well how to keep out of sight.

With a combination of speed and stealth he'd honed over years of covert undertakings, Philip made his way in the direction he knew they'd gone. He'd never be able to guess their exact route, but he knew he was on the right track.

Through the underbrush and around trees Philip moved. His eyes constantly scanned the area, picking out the occasional broken tree limb or light print in the snow, though he didn't see his quarry. He only hoped he was shortening their lead.

The wind picked up, nipping at his face and ungloved hands. Onward he pushed, thoughts of Sorrel pressing heavy on his mind and heart. He had every reason to believe she was injured already, perhaps badly so. Once they reached their waiting ship, the men would no longer need her as collateral against capture. They'd kill her without hesitation.

How could I have been such a fool? I should never have allowed her to come.

Sorrel, of course, would have insisted. Still, he could have locked her up somewhere safe. She'd have chewed him up for weeks on end over it, but he'd have gladly endured that rather than the torture of chasing after her, praying she'd be alive when he found her.

He heard a horse neigh in the distance, though how far ahead he couldn't say. Philip wasn't terribly familiar with the area. He did not think he was still on Crispin's land. Yet, if memory served, the coastline was more or less devoid of dwellings. The sound likely hadn't come from a stable.

If only the horse would neigh again. Philip listened but heard nothing.

Get the animal to make a sound, dear. Philip needed to know just which way to go. He wanted some idea of how far ahead of him they were. *Anything, Sorrel. A simple sound.*

The night hung in frustrating silence.

He moved ever more cautiously. He had no intention of being caught off guard by them, and he knew better than to startle them into rash action. Every noise jumped out at him, unnaturally loud in the still of night. Each of his footsteps seemed to echo, though his rational mind knew he hardly made a sound. He would not even be heard over the wind rustling the bare tree branches.

A rumbling of voices stopped him. Philip listened more intently. The voices were low, decidedly male, though he couldn't make out their words. He took careful steps in the direction of the sound. Each movement was intentional, smooth. He did everything in his power not to draw attention to himself.

The voices grew more distinct.

"We're almost to the boat. We don't need her now—she's only slowing us down."

"Imbécile!"

Two men, one a Frenchman, speaking of a woman in their company and a boat. He'd found them. Philip fought the urge to rush to Sorrel's side. Foolishness could cost them both their lives. He moved slower than ever. While carefully choosing each step, he pulled his pistol, holding it at the ready.

"You think because we have come this far that the English rats have given up their chase? *Crétin!* They knew of our meeting, the where and the when. They likely guard our dock as well."

Philip knew otherwise. There hadn't been sufficient time to gather the men needed to guard both possible meeting places as well as the abandoned port. Still, these men didn't know that, and their ignorance meant Sorrel had more time.

"She can't even stay seated," the first man said. "We cannot keep stopping so she can regain her balance."

Stopping? Philip had ridden with Sorrel not many days past. Though she'd not been ready for a gallop, she hadn't halted their ride repeatedly. Was she purposely slowing them down, then?

Well done, Sorrel.

Now. How to approach? Philip kept to a small stand of trees, not more than three, but growing close enough together to provide some concealment. From behind their trunks, he glanced into the very small clearing ahead.

His heart lurched at what he saw. Two men stood near the very horse Philip had sent Sorrel off on. One of the men held the reins. Seated atop it was Sorrel. Her hair whipped about in the bitingly cold wind. The moon illuminated her pale features. He saw no signs of panic in her face, only sheer determination. Her eyes darted between the men and her immediate vicinity.

She'd told Philip in no uncertain terms that she did not surrender. He was infinitely grateful for that. So long as she didn't give up, they had a chance.

"You planned everything about this night," the Frenchman spat at his partner, "and everything has gone wrong."

The men were distracted. But how to get Sorrel away? Philip knew she couldn't dismount with any degree of speed or subtlety. If he moved closer, he might have a clear shot at her captors. But even if he felled one of the men, the other would have ample time to retaliate.

Philip had never been one for giving the Almighty ultimatums, but he manufactured a few in that moment. If only he could get his Sorrel back, whole and safe, he'd never ask another thing. He'd attend services every Sunday. He'd do any number of things—the heavens had only to make a list. He would gladly accept a trade, his life for hers, if that was what fate demanded.

The thought gave him pause. His life for hers. He'd worried about making a move lest the men turn on Sorrel. What if he could draw their fire? Surely she would know enough to make good her escape. It might very well be the only possible approach.

For the first time since setting out to find Sorrel, Philip felt no uncertainty about his chosen course of action. He'd second-guessed nearly every step, wondered again and again if he'd taken a wrong turn. That feeling, however, had vanished. He knew exactly what he had to do.

Twenty-Nine

Sorrel could only hope she hadn't pushed the men beyond bearing. She needed more time, and acting as though she might tumble off her horse at any moment seemed to be working. Though she hurt from hip to ankle, Sorrel found her balance steadier than she'd expected. The men, however, didn't need to know that.

While they argued over what to do with her, Sorrel thought frantically. From her position, she'd never get hold of their weapons. She didn't know how to fire a pistol anyway. Bélanger's knife sat sheathed directly against his side. She couldn't get that without being stopped.

There had to be something else she could use to defend herself. She thought briefly of the iron stirrups but quickly dismissed the thought. Since they were tied to the saddle, the possible ways to wield them were extremely limited.

Several colorful expressions ran through her mind. She had no other strategies but knew her opportunities were quickly running out. She hadn't a weapon nor the skills to use one. The only true talent she'd ever really possessed was that of being a bruising-good rider. That ability had long since been taken from her.

And yet her mind wouldn't let go of the thought. She had once been the best rider in all of Kent, perhaps beyond. She, conveniently enough, sat on a horse. If she could somehow gain control of the reins—

Don't be daft. You aren't the rider you once were.

But what other course of action could she take? During her ride with Philip she'd kept her seat until fever rendered her too weak. But she wasn't ill any longer, and she'd learned a great deal during that ride about how to adjust to the change her injuries required. She would never be able to take a fence, nor ride at a full gallop, but she might manage to maneuver the animal quickly and agilely enough to get away. Provided, of course, Bélanger and Le Fontaine did not simply shoot her as she rode off.

Better to make the attempt than simply wait to be executed. She hadn't lived her life as a coward, and she would not die that way.

Now, how to get the reins?

A soft rustling immediately caught her attention. An animal maybe? The sound had come from just beyond the small stand of trees not far off. For a moment she entertained the idea of someone having come to assist in her escape, but the thought quickly followed that it might just as easily be one of the men's comrades come looking for them.

She had no time to waste. The dilemma of taking control of her mount needed to be paramount in her thoughts.

Another noise stopped her short. Bélanger and Le Fontaine took note of it, too. In unison their heads snapped in that direction. Conversation halted between them immediately. Neither seemed relieved nor expecting company. Sorrel took that as a sign their possible new arrival was not in league with her captors.

If only she could get the reins from Bélanger while the men were even a little distracted. She slid her hand slowly forward, careful not to draw attention.

"Do you see anything?" Bélanger asked his companion.

Le Fontaine shook his head, taking a step closer to the trees.

Sorrel inched her fingers gently along the horse's neck toward the bridle. She shifted her weight forward, glancing at Bélanger to see if he noticed. Farther she stretched, but the truth became quickly obvious. She couldn't grab for the reins without drawing attention to herself.

Think, Sorrel.

Bélanger's eyes darted in her direction. "What are you doing?"

"I am attempting to find some relief from the pain this ride has caused me. Shifting position is the only recourse you have given me."

He glanced briefly at Le Fontaine before returning his unsettling gaze to her face. "Your ride will be over soon, *ma chère*. Play nice and I may let you sail with me rather than see you dumped in the ocean once we reach our ship." He ran his free hand down her leg. She kicked back, throwing off his touch.

"I'd far prefer the second option," she spat.

He only smiled before facing away once more. "Did you find anything?"

Le Fontaine turned back toward them. "No. It was likely only an animal."

"Come, *ma fille*. We've some distance to cover. I have a feeling you'll see things my way soon enough."

Sorrel leaned low over the horse's neck, one hand grasping hard at the front of her saddle. Her balance was not at all what it had once been. She'd grab the reins at the first opportunity.

"Let us be on our way," Bélanger called out.

"And no more stops," Le Fontaine added. "I don't care how much pain she—"

The loud report of a gun shattered the night. Sorrel barely managed to stay mounted as she and the horse both jumped, startled by the sudden sound. What was happening? Who had fired?

She saw Le Fontaine crumple to the ground without so much as a moan.

Sorrel didn't waste a single second. She grabbed for the reins, but Bélanger took tighter hold of them. In an instant, he brandished his pistol and aimed for her. They stood at too close a distance for him to possibly miss.

"Show yourself!" Bélanger shouted into the eerily still night.

"Show yourself, or I'll shoot her dead!"

"I am afraid those terms are entirely unacceptable."

Sorrel nearly gasped aloud. Philip! That was Philip's voice!

Bélanger seemed thrown off by the response. He inched closer to the horse, aim still more than true.

"If you shoot her," Philip continued, still entirely concealed, "I'll have no choice but to kill you. Now you don't want that, do you?"

Bélanger followed the sound of Philip's voice as easily as Sorrel did. He was somewhere very near the trees Le Fontaine had searched but a moment ago.

Sorrel's heart pounded hard in her chest. How could she get away? More important still, how could she be certain Philip escaped as well? They were both in very real danger.

"What terms do you prefer, then, *Monsieur*?" Bélanger's eyes scanned the darkness as he spoke. "Shall we mark off ten paces and fire on each other like gentlemen? Or have you a prisoner to swap for mine?"

"I do not take prisoners, as your friend there has so clearly demonstrated."

Sorrel could not pin down Philip's exact location—his voice echoed off the trees scattered about. How she prayed Bélanger could not find him either.

"What terms, then, do you suggest?"

While Philip kept Bélanger occupied, Sorrel searched for the slightest opportunity to assist in her own escape. Bélanger held his weapon a bit away from himself, elevated enough to point up at her. Surely she could find a means of knocking it away, especially considering his current distraction.

"My terms are thus," Philip answered. "You lower your weapon and I won't shoot you in the head."

Just enough of his dandified mannerisms touched Philip's tone to do Sorrel's heart good. The familiarity of it settled her nerves a tiny bit.

"You must think me a fool. If I lower my weapon, there will be nothing to stop you from firing on me." If anything, Bélanger looked more determined than before.

"Yours is a one-shot pistol," Philip called out. "I suggest you use that bullet wisely."

Sorrel's heart lurched as Philip stepped from the protective cover of darkness provided by the nearby trees out into the moonlight. He held his pistol aimed at Bélanger.

The Frenchman shifted his focus firmly on Philip. Good heavens! Bélanger meant to shoot him.

She'd not have another opportunity. Sorrel shifted her weight and kicked at his hand with all the strength she had. His hand and weapon wavered as he stepped back to keep his balance. Philip would not have a clear shot so long as she remained close. Bélanger's grip on the reins had slackened. Sorrel grabbed at them, heart racing as she took control of the horse for the first time.

Maneuvering on horseback came as naturally in that moment as ever it had, though the movement proved painful and tricky. A quick flick and pull of the reins turned the horse about in a swift movement. Out of the corner of her eye, she saw Bélanger regain his position.

She leaned low over her horse's neck even as her enemy aimed his pistol directly at her. She pressed her feet hard into the horse's flank, setting him swiftly into motion.

In French, Philip shouted, "Shoot her and you're dead where you stand!"

A gun went off. Sorrel pulled her horse to a stop as she realized *she* hadn't been shot. Her eyes fell on Philip. Had he shot Bélanger? Had the danger passed?

Philip didn't look in her direction. He stumbled backward, before falling to his knees.

No!

Bélanger had his knife in hand once more, having apparently tossed aside his now-useless firearm. He moved menacingly toward Philip's bent frame.

Sorrel nudged her mount into motion again, swiftly changing its direction. The sudden shift nearly unseated her. She wrapped the rein around one hand and firmly gripped the front of her saddle with the other as she rushed in Bélanger's direction. So help her, she'd run him down if necessary.

The Frenchman heard her coming and turned to face her, knife wielded. She didn't know the horse's temperament well enough to guess how it would react. It might kick out, might suddenly halt. She'd be thrown. But if she didn't do something, Philip might very well be killed, if the shot hadn't killed him already.

Sorrel urged the horse on. She could feel herself slipping. Her joints were not equal to the severe jarring they were enduring.

They drew nearer. Sorrel braced herself for whatever reaction the horse might have.

It bucked, kicking its legs out at the livid man who stood too near their path. Sorrel grasped the saddle, grabbed at the horse's neck—anything to keep from being thrown.

It wasn't enough. She felt herself slip, though without the force she'd feared. She fell, landing hard on the ground. Disoriented, she crawled, despite the pain searing through her leg, trying to move clear of the horse's hooves. Flashes of memory clouded her vision. She'd be trampled again. She knew she would.

Sorrel scrambled, desperate. She put some distance between herself and the angry animal, but the relief was short-lived. The horse shot off like a bolt of lightning, leaving her the only barrier between Bélanger and Philip, who still hadn't moved. She had no weapon, no means of escape.

But she would not back down.

Sorrel watched the Frenchman approach, his breathing heavy, either with rage or the effort of avoiding a rampaging horse. She glanced back only briefly to make certain she blocked Bélanger's path to Philip.

"You are a foolish woman, *ma fille.*" The words crackled in the air. "Now you will die here alone in the cold like the imbecile behind you."

He still had his knife. Sorrel had nothing.

"I do believe I should like to hear you beg first. Beg for your life, *ma chére*."

She spoke not a word, refusing to cower before him.

Moonlight glinted off the wide blade of his dagger. Each step brought him closer. Sorrel shifted from her crawling position to her knees. If she could manage it, she'd face him standing, not kneeling as though pleading with him. She grabbed hold of a low branch on one of the trees that had concealed Philip but a moment earlier. Straining with the effort, Sorrel pulled herself to her feet. She swayed but managed to remain upright.

"A brave show," Bélanger acknowledged. "But too late."

Sorrel took in a deep breath and told herself to face death calmly. He stepped closer yet, no doubt moving purposely slowly to prolong her suffering. She simply watched his approach in silence.

"You ought to have accepted my offer while you had the chance. I would have made—"

An explosion sounded from behind. Bélanger's face froze in shock, and he dropped his knife. He swayed.

"I told you I don't take prisoners."

Philip! She turned toward him. Where he'd been little more than a motionless heap but a moment earlier, he sat back on his feet, pistol yet pointed at Bélanger. The Frenchman fell to his knees then dropped silently. No sounds, no movement.

Sorrel lowered herself once more to the ground, pain and exhaustion taking a sudden toll. She'd been so afraid Philip was dead. She'd fully expected to be killed herself. She couldn't form a single coherent thought.

Philip seemed to have no such difficulty. "Well, that was an adventure."

The fear she'd been feeling turned swiftly into an odd mixture of relief and anger and heavy emotion. "If you were only pretending to be shot, I'll never speak to you again," she said, forcing down a fresh wave of tears.

He slowly moved, sitting himself on the ground, his back against a tree. "And if I wasn't pretending?"

She heard strain in his voice. He was hurt, after all? Or was he merely teasing her? "So help me, Philip Jonquil, if you're making a joke in a moment like this I'll . . . I'll kill you."

Enough light broke through the trees for her to see the smile spread across his face. "That's my Sorrel."

She pulled herself along the ground to where he sat. Philip's eyes never left her face. As she reached his side, he gently touched her cheek with his hand. She leaned into his caress, pressing her hand against his.

"Did they hurt you, my dear?" he whispered.

Sorrel shook her head.

Philip studied her doubtfully. His eyes settled on her neck, and he tipped her chin up. So much of her ached that she'd not thought of the wound Bélanger had given her with his knife.

"They did this," Philip said.

"It isn't bad," she told him.

His expression didn't lighten. "I should never have let you come along tonight. I should have locked you in the attics or something. Anything."

She would not allow him to blame himself for what had happened. "Philip—"

He cut across her. "You might have been killed. I was terrified I wouldn't find you in time."

"But we're safe now." She took his hand in both of hers. "We're—" His hand was wet to the touch.

Sorrel looked down at it. Good heavens! His entire hand was covered in blood.

"Philip, you're bleeding!"

He leaned more heavily against the tree trunk. "I've been shot. What do you expect?"

Her heart dropped. "You said you were pretending."

"No. I said I *wasn't* pretending."

She ran her hand up his sleeve only to find it damp as well. He was bleeding enough to soak layers of clothing. Sorrel tugged at the buttons of his jacket.

He groaned in obvious pain. "Lud, woman, are you trying to kill me?"

Sorrel peeled back his jacket and froze in panicked horror. He was covered in blood—his *own* blood. Even Bélanger had not been bleeding so much when she'd tended his wound in the cottage.

"You need a doctor. We have to get you to the house."

"Can't. Your horse ran away." His voice had grown quieter, more halting.

She watched as color drained from his face. "We have to get you help."

"The men are searching for you. They will have heard the shots."

Please find us! Quickly!

"I believe that is . . . another success for the . . . Jonquil Freer of Prisoners." His eyes were alarmingly unfocused.

"Philip?" She took his face in her hands, willing him to look at her.

His eyes slowly began to shut.

"Talk to me, Philip. Please."

He made no sound beyond his labored breathing.

"Philip?" Still no response. "Philip, please." She couldn't hold back the tears any longer. "Philip. Please. Don't leave me."

His eyes closed. She watched the slow rise and fall of his chest and told herself she'd not lost him yet.

"Stay with me," she instructed on a whisper. "Help is on the way. Only stay with me."

Thirty

LIMES. PHILIP SMELLED LIMES.

After a moment's concentration he could hear a sound, muffled and at first unrecognizable. He focused on it, willing the voice—he realized it was a voice—to become clear. The words were still jumbled, but he could at least tell now that the speaker was a woman. The first word he made any sense of was one his father had once blushed to hear him utter.

"Sorrel."

When the voice stopped, Philip realized he'd spoken out loud.

"Philip?" She sounded frightened! Was she in danger? Hurt?

Philip tried to move, but a firm yet gentle hand pushed him back down onto something remarkably soft. "Where am I?" His voice sounded gruff and hoarse.

"At Kinnley," came the tentative response. "In your bedchamber."

How had he gotten there?

"I'll fetch the doctor." That wasn't Sorrel's voice. It sounded far more like . . . Mater? Blast it, he felt confused!

"Oh, Philip! You have to at least open your eyes. You have to look at me so I know you are alive. Please."

How could he not oblige Sorrel when she sounded so horribly afraid? But doing and wanting were two different things. The effort required to simply pry open his own eyelids was tantamount to swimming the Channel. With weights tied to one's ankles, he added, after further effort.

He somehow managed it. The sight that greeted him was well worth the effort. Sorrel. Beautiful Sorrel seated like a guardian angel beside his bed. Relief crossed her face, and Philip would have smiled if he thought he could have managed it.

"You've been unconscious for hours." Sorrel's forehead was creased with worry. "We hoped it was only the laudanum. That you weren't—" She stopped midsentence and bit her bottom lip.

Philip wanted to smooth the lines of worry on her face, but his arm hurt like mad and his body felt like lead. Somewhere in the recesses of his mind he recalled gunfire and pain. "I've been shot!" he remembered aloud.

Sorrel's mouth set in a grim line, and something flashed in her eyes. "You smushing well have, you blasted fishmonger! Making yourself a target like a deuced knight off to save his blasted damsel in distress. Didn't stop to think about how getting yourself killed wouldn't have done anyone any good!"

He hadn't expected her criticism. Where had the sympathy he'd heard in her voice gone?

"Bleeding like you'd been run through! Collapsing like you were a wilting debutante."

Philip opened his mouth to protest—perhaps she hadn't noticed the part where he'd helped save her life—but then he noticed her chin quivering.

"Then you just lay there, pale and . . . lifeless . . . and . . ." She tried to disguise a sniffle. "You wouldn't talk to me or move or . . . I thought you were going to die, you blasted idiot!"

"Dying is not nearly as easy as you seem to think it is." Hadn't she told him as much shortly after they'd first met?

"Oh, Philip." His stoic Sorrel dissolved in front of him, tears flowing unchecked, her head dropped into her hands. "I was so afraid."

"Nonsense." He reached out and stroked her arm with the hand not currently hiding in a sling. "You were far braver than anyone could have hoped. You kept yourself alive when faced with two murderers, and I vaguely recall you coming at one of them like an avenging angel on horseback. That is nothing to—"

"Not the deuced spies," she snapped, even as emotion splintered her voice.

What could possibly have been more frightening than that?

"You wouldn't wake up." He could hear the tears in her voice. "You wouldn't answer me. I thought you would die right there in my arms."

In her arms? Lud, he was sorry to have no recollection of *that.*

"I thought you'd left me," she whispered.

Philip raised his hand to stroke her hair. "Never, my love."

She looked directly into his eyes, her own red-rimmed and overflowing with falling tears. "Don't ever do that again."

From her position seated in the chair pulled directly beside his bed, Sorrel laid her head on his chest, her warm tears seeping through his nightshirt. He stroked her hair and enjoyed the smell of limes and the sound of her breathing, halting at first but growing calmer. A man could get used to having a woman at his side, tears and all. But how to keep her there?

"You realize, of course, you will never go on another mission with me," Philip said, savoring her nearness. "I don't think I would survive another night like I've just had."

"Getting shot?"

"Seeing you with a gun pointed at your heart, Sorrel." He pushed himself toward an extremely personal confession. What's the worst that could happen? He'd already been shot. "No man should have to see the woman he loves in that kind of danger."

"You love me?" She sounded shocked. How could she possibly be surprised?

"Enough to rush in like—how did you put that? It was so eloquent. Ah, yes! Like a 'deuced knight off to save his blasted damsel in distress.' You make me sound so heroic."

"Do you really love me?" She watched him earnestly.

"I really do," he answered. He tried for a characteristic shrug, but his shoulder refused to cooperate. "Lud, I feel like I've been shot."

"Even though I limp?" Sorrel pressed.

"I adore your limp."

"And swear?"

Philip laughed. "Endearing." He stroked her hair once more.

"And am stubborn?"

"As an old mule," Philip confirmed, recalling Fennel's declaration.

"Father said no one would ever—"

"Your Father was—" Philip cut himself off before going on. He had a definite opinion of the man he'd heard so much about, but now was not the time for an evaluation.

A hint of a smile stole across her face. "You're nothing like him, you know," she said quietly.

"I should hope not."

"So we're not at war?" Sorrel asked, leaning her cheek into Philip's outstretched hand.

Words seemed entirely unnecessary. He leaned forward ignoring the pain in his shoulder and kissed her, gently and slowly. She responded precisely as he hoped she would.

No. This was not a war at all!

Someone cleared his throat. With a low chuckle, Philip pulled himself away and glanced at the door. Crispin watched the two of them, a look of amusement playing on his features.

"You owe my land agent a new front door, Philip." Typical Crispin. Plunge in and avoid the obvious topic. "Though he'll most likely be so pleased to hear his blessedly boring abode was the scene of such a fracas, he'll probably refuse to part with the splintered remains of it."

"If only he realized the damage was done by a cohort of one of the world's most dangerous spies," Philip said.

"*Cohort?* You haven't heard?" Crispin looked quite pleased to know something Philip didn't. "He wasn't one of Le Fontaine's men, Philip. He *was* Le Fontaine."

Philip felt the blood drain from his face. The man himself. The spy he'd tracked all over England for years. Dead.

Sorrel grabbed his hand. "Philip?"

"And the other man?" Philip managed to ask. "The Englishman?"

"Le Fontaine was the Englishman," Sorrel answered. "The Frenchman was his contact, Bélanger."

"We were so certain Le Fontaine was French," Philip mumbled. "Spying for his own homeland."

"He was nothing but a—" Crispin bit off his words.

"—a traitor," Sorrel finished for him. "Spying *against* his homeland."

"Has Garner been told about Bélanger?" Philip asked.

Crispin and Sorrel nodded.

"Bélanger murdered Garner's brother and a cousin," Philip told them, leaning against the headboard of his four-poster bed, beginning to feel the strain of the day. He was grateful for the feel of Sorrel's hand in his.

"He'd have killed you, too," Crispin said. "Both of you."

"He certainly tried."

"So you're not going to die, after all?" Crispin asked.

"Sorrel won't let me." Philip feigned disappointment.

Crispin's gaze fell on Sorrel. He smiled. "I hope you've thanked her properly."

"I plan to." Philip laid a kiss on her fingers.

Sorrel blushed a deep scarlet, deeper than he'd ever seen her color rise. Philip grinned at the sight of it.

"You see." Mater's voice reached him from the doorway. "He is awake."

"A good sign." An unfamiliar man stepped into the room and watched him with an obviously keen eye.

"Dr. Darrow says there shouldn't be any permanent damage to your shoulder." Mater dabbed at a tear.

Dr. Darrow? The doctor from Ipswich?

"I am very pleased to meet you, Dr. Darrow." The doctor looked a little confused at Philip's declaration. He explained, "Miss Kendrick has spoken of you before."

"Ah, yes." Dr. Darrow nodded his understanding. "*She* suffered few ill effects from the night's adventure. Minor bruises and a cut that did not even require stitching."

"You have no idea how relieved I am to hear that." Philip smiled at Sorrel and pressed their clasped hands to his chest.

"Oh, I have an inkling." Dr. Darrow smiled.

Mater did, as well, Philip noticed. Crispin seemed on the verge of laughter. Was there a single person in this house that *didn't* know his and Sorrel's war had come to an end?

"Will he recover, then? Fully?" Sorrel asked, still more concern in her voice than Philip wanted to hear, though the sound of it did his heart good.

"A few days' rest and he'll be up and about."

"How long before I can travel?" Philip asked.

"End of the week, I'd say."

"And how will I be in a month or two?" Philip pressed. "In, say, March?" The eyes of every person in the room were on him now. *Think they know exactly what is going on, do they?* Philip thought with a smirk. They'd be surprised, he'd guess.

"Fine, I'd say," Dr. Darrow replied with obvious confusion.

"What could possibly be so pressing about March?" Mater looked as though she suspected he was in the grip of a fever. He barely managed to keep from laughing.

"I am thinking of getting married," Philip answered, offhand. He felt Sorrel's hand grip his tighter. He probably shouldn't have surprised her like this. Oh, well. In for a pound, as they said. "Spring wedding and what."

The room stood in shocked silence.

"Of course, I haven't asked my prospective bride yet." He glanced at Sorrel out of the corner of his eye. She looked surprised but not upset. Definitely a good sign.

"Afraid she'll turn you down?" The corner of Crispin's mouth twitched the way it had since their days at Eton whenever he tried to hide his amusement.

"As a matter of fact," Philip answered.

"Why on earth would she do that?" Mater's forehead creased in concern, obviously afraid her eldest son had taken complete leave of his senses.

"She doesn't care for me much." Philip sighed rather dramatically. He turned to look at Sorrel, who watched him with marked intensity. "She doesn't care for dandies. Can't bear the sight of my quizzing glass. And she thinks I despise her walking stick."

A smile slowly spread across Sorrel's face. "Those are difficult things to overcome," she said, looking thoughtful. "You don't despise it, though, do you?"

"No," Philip whispered. The rest of the room seemed to have caught on and were making rather discreet exits. "That's not the worst of it, I am afraid."

"It isn't?"

"I love her." Philip reached up and touched her face. "But to her I'm the enemy. We're at war, you see."

"No, Philip," she said softly, laying her hand over his as he caressed her cheek. "She loves you more than you can possibly know."

He let her words sink in as he stroked her eyebrow and then slid his hand to her jaw. She smiled at him, the same adoring, loving smile he'd so envied when he'd seen Catherine send the exact look Crispin's way.

"I'm going to kiss you, you know." Philip thought it only fair that he warn her.

"I wish you would."

So he did. He kissed her like he meant it, which he did. He kissed her until Mater's joyous exclamations from the corridor grew too loud to be ignored. Philip had the satisfaction of having Sorrel next to him as his brothers wished them joy. Lizzie claimed credit for the match. Catherine smiled approvingly, and Crispin smiled knowingly.

Once the line of unwanted visitors had finally left and before Sorrel could take her leave as well, Philip kissed her once more. *March can't come soon enough,* he thought.

"I think you really do love me, Sorrel," he murmured, fighting the temptation to kiss her again. "Unless this is one of your underhanded battle strategies. I remember hearing that you do not retreat."

"And I seem to remember that you had surrendered."

"Completely," he admitted with a whisper.

"So do I."

"Both sides surrendering?" Philip pretended to truly ponder the situation. "Unorthodox, to be sure. I cannot even imagine how the treaty talks will go on."

"Can you not?" An amused smile spread across her face. "It is a rather simple ceremony, I believe."

Philip laughed lightly. "Both sides promise to love and honor to the death, right?"

"*Until* death, you widgeon," she answered with a chuckle.

"We agreed to a cessation of hostilities," Philip reminded his betrothed. "Calling your prisoner a widgeon is rather cruel."

"Torture, you'll undoubtedly claim." Sorrel shook her head. "Do you plan to present a list of grievances at the altar? Negotiate for reparations?"

Philip took her hand in his and kissed her fingers. "No reparations, my dear."

"You are a fierce negotiator, then?"

"No." He shook his head. "All I want from you is love."

She closed her eyes and smiled. "You have that already, Philip."

"Then this may be the easiest peace ever brokered." He watched her smile, completely contented.

"Or the longest war ever fought." She laughed, looking at him once again.

"No," he answered firmly. "I take surrender very seriously."

"I love you, Philip Jonquil." Her words, coming out of the blue like that, momentarily emptied his mind of all thoughts.

In a moment such as that there could be but one course of action. He kissed her until he no longer minded that he couldn't produce a rational thought. Kissed her in a way that promised theirs would be an enjoyable peace, even more enjoyable than their war had been. A kiss that promised this would truly be a complete surrender. And it would be sweet, indeed.

About the Author

Sarah M. Eden read her first Jane Austen novel in elementary school and has been an Austen Addict ever since. Fascinated by the Regency era in English history, Eden became a regular in the Regency section of the reference department at her local library, painstakingly researching this extraordinary chapter in history. Eden is an award-winning author of short stories and has been a Whitney Award Finalist for her novels *Seeking Persephone* (2008) and *Courting Miss Lancaster* (2010). You can visit her at www.sarahmeden.com.

DISCARD